LOVE FANG

BY SUSAN BLEXRUD

DCL Publications, LLC
www.dclpublications.biz

DCL Publications, LLC

First Edition January 2010

DCL Publications
1033 Plymouth Dr.
Grafton, OH 44044
United Stated of America

Cover art and photography Annie Marshall, Beyond the Book Productions

This is a work of fiction. Names, characters, places and incidents are the product of the author's imagination, and any resemblance to any actual persons, living or dead, events, or locales, is entirely coincidental.

PUBLISHED IN THE UNITED STATES OF AMERICA

TABLE OF CONTENTS

DCL Publications, LLC

Writing is hard work, that's for sure, but there are many people without whom the hard work would still be languishing in my computer.

First and foremost, thanks to my Heavenly Father for getting me through the tough times and making me believe in the power of prayer. Without His grace, I am nothing.

Next, hugs forever and much love to my supportive husband, John, and my terrific kids, Christopher and Allison. They're proud of me, but not nearly as proud as I am of them.

Thanks to the great crew at DCL Publications for having faith in this book from the beginning.

My critique group, the Pink Fire Writers, has been an incredible resource, and the three gals who slug it out with me every week on the written page have become my close friends. Thank you from the bottom of my heart, Jeanne, Tara, and Beth.

And to the wonderful blogs and review sites that have supported *Love Fang*, from its inception as an e-book to its debut in print, big, sloppy Chihuahua kisses. In particular, heartfelt appreciation goes to Fang-tastic Books, Bitten by Books, Patricia's Vampire Notes, Embrace the Shadows, Pen & Muse, Blazing Trailers, and SciFiGuy.

Finally, nothing pleases this writer more than hearing from readers, so please keep those cards, letters, and e-mails coming.

All my best...always,
Susan

DCL Publications, LLC

LOVE FANG

DCL Publications, LLC

CHAPTER ONE

John Wright's infected left fang put a real damper on his puncturing prowess.

As his personal assistant Doreen opened his coffin at sunset for his nightly rounds, his eyes flew open, and he sat up straight as the board he'd been lying on. He groaned and cradled his throbbing jaw with his hand. He hadn't slept well for days.

"You need to see a dentist," Doreen said for the umpteenth time.

"I'd almost rather have a stake in the heart, but this tooth is killing me."

Doreen lugged the huge Orlando Yellow Pages from the sideboard to the dining room table and plopped it down next to his coffin, creating a cloud of dust and eliciting a huge sneeze from John. She was good at keeping him on schedule, but a housekeeper she wasn't.

"I'll need a dentist who works nights." John reminded Doreen.

"Think I don't know that?" Five years had passed since

Doreen answered the employment advertisement: "Busy executive seeks personal assistant." It should have read: "Vampire with severe allergies seeks director of hazardous materials."

John and Doreen had clicked. Something about her Hell's Angels' tattoo and pierced eyebrow let him know she wasn't the squeamish type. For her first interview with John, she'd zoomed into the circular driveway of his Victorian manor house on her Harley. Dismounting like a bull rider who just cleared the buzzer, she sauntered to his front door with her licensed practical nurse certificate in hand. When John told her he was a vampire, she'd said "Cool."

John sneezed again, and Doreen rolled her eyes. "Honestly, your allergies are worse than ever."

Blowing his nose with a monogrammed handkerchief, John motioned for her to get on with finding a dentist.

"Let's see." She flipped the pages. "Here we are. Dentists. Dr. Bennett, Dr. Harper, ah yes, Dr. Lauren Marsh has evening hours on Mondays and Wednesdays to accommodate her working clients. Now, isn't that nice of her?"

John's rich baritone voice lowered a few notches. "She's probably a sadist who likes nothing more than torturing people after dark."

"You should be able to identify with that. It's not like you're passing out lollypops after the sun goes down."

"Now Doreen, be fair. You know I only prey on criminals. I'm the exterminator of the city's lowlife."

"Truth is, you're a nice guy. With that inhumanly handsome face of yours, aren't you ever tempted to take a chance on love?"

"I avoid that kind of temptation like the Bubonic Plague."

The plague had nothing on Orlando. Violent crime had skyrocketed, and John was getting more work now than in the 1500s. The Orlando newspaper made him an urban legend with headlines like "Vampire Vigilante Strikes Again."

"So, do I call the dentist or not?" Doreen slammed the Yellow Pages back down on the table. "Jeez, it's not like you to be so indecisive."

"If you'd had the experience I had two hundred years ago with a dentist, and I use that term loosely, you wouldn't be so anxious to open your mouth, either."

"Times have changed, John. I'm sure she won't shoe horses with the same instruments she uses on your mouth."

"All right, give her a call. The sooner I get this over with, the better," he said, peeling all six feet, two inches of his muscular frame out of his oversized coffin. "And put the phone on speaker. I can tell a lot about a person from her voice."

"I doubt I'll talk directly with the dentist," Doreen said. It was after hours, so she got the answering machine. With a punch of the pound key, it rang through to the emergency line.

"This is Dr. Marsh."

"Oh, Dr. Marsh, I wasn't expecting to get you."

"I answer all my emergency calls."

John gave a thumbs-up to Doreen.

"This is Doreen Adkins, and I'm calling for my employer, John Wright."

"What's the nature of his emergency?" Dr. Marsh asked as John listened to her multi-tasking in the background. It sounded like she was retrieving something from a microwave, while a blender whirred and a dog whined.

"He has a fa--, I mean a tooth, that I think is abscessed," Doreen said. "He's in great pain."

John could hear Dr. Marsh flipping pages.

"I can come in early and see him at seven a.m. In the meantime, have him take Ibuprofen for pain, and if you have any frozen peas, they work great as a compress."

"Of course. But Doctor, he can't be there at seven o'clock in the morning. He has, uh, uh, a deposition to take tomorrow, so he'd have to come in the evening."

"Well, if he's okay to go through the day in such pain, I could see him at seven o'clock tomorrow night. Please tell him only the back door is open after five p.m."

"Perfect. He'll be there." Doreen hung up the phone and turned to her employer. "She sounds pretty. I hope you haven't bitten off more than you can chew. Hardy-har-har."

"Believe me, I'm in no frame of mind or body to be attracted to anyone, no matter how beautiful they may be," he said, favoring the left side of his mouth. "Besides, I don't like the lilt of her voice, sexy with a tinge of southern accent. With my luck, she's Scarlet O'Hara. And that's all I need...another brunette with green eyes."

"I've always thought that gazebo out back would be a great place to get laid," Doreen said.

"Oh, please."

"I worry about you. It's not natural for a man who looks like you not to have hot sex," Doreen said.

"I can't have sex without a blood exchange, and I won't doom another woman to my fate. Need I remind you of what happened the last time I fell in love?" He thought about how much he'd loved his first wife and how inconsolable he was when she began preying on children.

"You just haven't met the right woman," Doreen said. "When you do, she won't go to the dark side like your former bride."

"Don't get mushy on me, Doreen. True love is to be avoided at all cost."

"All I know is, the women of this world are missing out. And don't tell me you don't notice women salivating over you."

"I don't know what women you're talking about."

"Oh, let's see. First there's the gal who owns the gardening service. She takes every opportunity to come round to check the night-blooming jasmine. Then there's the woman who delivers the dry cleaning. And there's the..."

"Enough," John said. "I'll stick to my convictions. And in the meantime, I suppose I should bone up on the law since I haven't been a barrister for a few hundred years."

"Wrong century. Wrong country. They're called attorneys in the U.S.," she answered. "You should thank me for covering for you."

"I'm forever in your debt." With a flourish, John bowed to Doreen, and then he grimaced as the blood rushed to his head and his gum began to throb, again.

* * *

Back at Dr. Lauren Marsh's house, she was assembling her specialty salad, loaded with almonds and artichoke hearts, and topped with her homemade raspberry vinaigrette. She could splurge on the salad with Lean Cuisine as the main course. Just ten pounds to go before she'd squeeze back into her favorite jeans and possibly get up the courage to join Match.com.

She'd been a runner in college, but once she hit dental school, the books took precedence. Now that she had her own practice, work accounted for her lack of exercise, as well as for her messy house. And getting home to her little Chihuahua was more important than stopping at the gym. Smokey would be waiting patiently for her, legs crossed in rapt anticipation.

After dinner and their nightly walk, Lauren soaked in her tub, brushed and flossed her teeth, and then spent more time than she should have searching for her retainer. She found it in the middle of Smokey's stash of dog biscuits on the bathroom floor. She really did need to get organized.

As she crawled under the covers of her queen-sized bed, she bent over to turn off the bedside lamp and kiss Smokey on the head. She had high hopes for sharing her big bed with someone besides her dog. "I'm making this promise, here and now," she said to Smokey. "The next guy I date is going to be sexy and exciting. I want to experience that 'weak in the knees' feeling, whatever that is."

Night person that she was, she tossed and turned for an

hour before getting up to pop some microwave popcorn, settle into her living room couch, and dig between the overstuffed cushions for the romance novel hidden there. Even farther under the cushions lurked her state-of-the-art vibrator, capable of thrusting, spinning, and tickling with one flick of the switch. Lauren pulled it out and stared at it for a few minutes.

"Hello, friend. I guess it's just you and me."

* * *

John had morphed into bat form for his nightly rounds. He liked to wait until the real bats ended their initial feeding frenzy because he'd gotten pummeled one night by a particularly large female who wanted more than her share of mosquitoes.

With his gum throbbing, he knew it wouldn't be a long night, but he needed a decent pint of blood to endure the dental procedure tomorrow. He wouldn't kill his victim, so any respectable drunk would do. He chose a vagrant who was curled up in a gutter, sleeping it off, empty bottle at his side. Swooping in silently, he targeted the jugular, and the guy never knew what bit him, even when John issued a loud "Ouch!" Unfortunately, feeding on a drunk meant the blood alcohol level was high, and when John fluttered off, he crashed into a wall.

Morning was a welcome relief as he eased himself into his coffin. Before Doreen closed the lid, he asked, "What does one wear to a dental appointment?"

"Well, definitely not your cape. I'll go to the mall today and pick up something casual. Everything in black, of course." She rubbed her hands together. "One more thing." She looked at his very long, razor-sharp fingernails. "You'll need to cut your nails before your appointment, so I'd better wake you just a bit early."

"Any other traits I should disguise?"

"Hmm," she said, tapping her finger to her lips. "Well, you could use a good dousing with Old Spice because that musky odor you exude is a real sex magnet. You need your dentist to be concentrating on the work at hand, not thinking about how much she'd like to mate with you. So please be liberal with the after shave."

"Anything else?"

"You have a tendency to slip into the King's English. Remember this is the 21st Century. And please be careful with your eyes. She's bound to be suspicious if they start glowing red."

"That only happens when I'm aroused," John said. "And I'm in too much pain for that."

"Okay, one last question before nighty-night," Doreen said. "Why is it that you have the strength of a locomotive and are near impossible to kill, yet you can't fix your own tooth?"

"I have no idea. It's my only weakness, unless you count my allergies and a stake in the heart," he said, hands crossing chest in his sleep position.

"Right. And beautiful women," Doreen said as she lowered the lid to his coffin. Speaking to the closed lid, she added, "I have a feeling temptation is just a dental chair away."

CHAPTER TWO

Lauren's Wednesday began with a howling eight-year-old whose ten o'clock appointment for two fillings lasted until noon, and progressed through a difficult root canal for 85-year-old Mrs. Brady.   She worked through lunch, adding a splitting headache to her tense shoulders.

Luckily, her five o'clock appointment cancelled, so she nuked an individual pizza, took two Ibuprofens and curled up for a nap in one of her comfortable dental chairs.

She woke to the buzzer that signaled her back door opening. Her pregnant hygienist, Rosetta, wobbled down the hall to meet the new patient and escorted him into the reception area.

Still groggy, Lauren peeled herself out of the chair and checked her appearance in the medicine cabinet mirror. She scooted to the bathroom, brushed her teeth, splashed water on her face, and combed her shoulder-length hair until it semi-behaved.   She still looked tired, but at least she was respectable.

As she walked down the hall from the bathroom to the

reception area, she sniffed the air, which was heavy with Old Spice. She wondered why some men had to bathe in that stuff. When she laid eyes on John, she did an obvious double-take.

"You were expecting someone else?" He looked up from the *People* magazine he was paging through.

"Are you Mr. Wright?" Lauren asked.

"Yes, that's me, Mr. Wright the lawyer."

"Well, Mr. Wright the lawyer, come on back." She considered the kind of ego someone must have to immediately identify themselves with their work.

"Have a seat in that big chair," she said. "How long has your tooth been bothering you?" She washed her hands at the sink, put on her rubber gloves, adjusted the overhead mirror and picked up her sickle probe. "Open wide." What Lauren saw next was one for the dental books.

"Whoa," she said, and then quickly added, "I am so sorry. That was unprofessional of me. I just haven't seen incisors quite like that in awhile."

"They run in my family."

"I detect a slight British accent. Are you from England?"

"Yes, originally, though I've been in this country since the American Civil War."

Lauren laughed. "When was the last time you saw a dentist?"

"It's been many years. I believe he doubled as a blacksmith."

Lauren laughed again, and then she looked up to ask Rosetta to prepare a shot of Novocain. Her dutiful assistant was plastered against the examining room wall.

"Rosetta, sit down," Lauren said. "You're as white as your lab coat. You'll have Mr. Wright thinking you've seen a ghost."

"Jesus, Mary and Joseph," Rosetta said, crossing herself. "I'd welcome a ghost."

Lauren took two steps toward her assistant, turned her

by her shoulders toward the door and gently pushed her from the examining room, following her into the hall.

"Excuse me a moment, Mr. Wright." She pulled the examining room door closed.

"Are you feeling faint?" Lauren turned to face Rosetta. "Please tell me you didn't skip dinner tonight."

"I had my usual double cheeseburger with extra pickles," Rosetta said.

Lauren was a good head taller than tiny Rosetta, who resembled a beach ball in her pregnant state. Bending down to examine her face, Lauren noticed Rosetta's upper lip had bloomed with tiny beads of sweat. "So, what's the problem?"

"You know what that guy is?" Rosetta whispered huskily. "He's a *vampiro*, and those incisors are FANGS."

"There are no such things as vampires," Lauren said. "Mr. Wright is a lawyer with long incisors. It's not uncommon in his profession." She registered the look of panic on her hygienist's face. "Lighten up, Rosetta. That was a joke."

"Didn't you notice his eyes? They're glowing as red as a traffic light."

"All I saw was a beautiful violet color and thick black eyelashes."

"Holy frijoles, he's got you under his spell."

"Rosetta, that's ridiculous. Now, get hold of yourself and get me a syringe of Novocain." Lauren shook her head at her assistant as she returned to her patient.

"You'll feel a little pinch, and then the area around your tooth will become numb," Lauren said.

Rosetta's hand was shaking as she handed her boss the syringe. Lauren gave her a stern look and motioned with her head for Rosetta to have a seat in the chair that was usually reserved for parents of young patients.

"Wait just a minute. What do you mean by numb?" John asked.

"Well, you probably won't be able to chew anything for several hours. I'd suggest just a little soup tonight."

The look of distress on his face touched Lauren. She patted his arm, letting her hand linger on his bicep for a moment before she picked up the syringe. She waited for the Novocain to take effect and then thoroughly examined the infected tooth and surrounding gum. "I'm an endodontist, so I could perform a root canal, but this tooth really should come out."

"No, absolutely not," he said. "I can't be without this tooth."

"I can have a porcelain tooth made to replace it within a week," Lauren said, "but I really can't save this tooth. It's too far gone, and the antibiotics won't be effective unless I eliminate the cause of the problem."

"One week?" John asked.

"I may even be able to get it sooner, but I promise, no longer than a week."

"All right," he said, "disfigure me."

"Would you like to listen to some music? I've got a full repertoire here; jazz, rock, pop, classical?"

"Any funeral dirges?"

She laughed. "I think I have some Mahler. Will that do?"

With the Novocain numbing the pain, Lauren could see her patient relax into the dental chair. As she leaned over him to adjust the headphones on his ears, her breast, though well-hidden behind her white lab coat, brushed his shoulder.

His eyes began to glow red, but Lauren was concentrating on the job at hand, and she didn't notice. She also didn't notice the bulge that was pushing against his new black jeans.

Lauren had to exert considerable pressure to wrench the tooth from its socket, though it had been loosened somewhat by the infection. John held onto the arms of the chair as Lauren tugged with the dental pliers.

Luckily, the tooth came out whole, so Lauren could easily obtain a good mold. She finished the procedure with a couple of small stitches and packed the incision site with gauze.

Turning to the wastebasket to dispose of her rubber gloves, she said, "Bite down on that gauze to keep any bleeding at bay, and try not to open your mouth too wide. You don't want to traumatize the site with too much activity."

"I can't thank you enough," John said. "And I appreciate your seeing me in the evening and on such short notice."

"Not a problem," she said. "I'm a night person, anyway. If I could see all my patients after the sun went down, that would be great for me."

"Really?" John asked. "I'm a creature of the night, myself."

Rosetta nudged Lauren in the ribs and opened her eyes wide.

Lauren ignored Rosetta's nudge. She was concerned that he might be a bit woozy after the procedure. Rosetta reluctantly took one of his arms, and as he swung his long legs to the side of the chair, the two women helped him stand.

Lauren put her arm around his waist, noting his taut frame and full height. The top of her head brushed his chin as she steadied herself, and her breast pushed against his ribs.

"You should walk around a bit before you try to drive," Lauren suggested.

"I don't drive. My assistant is waiting for me," he said, as the two women led him down the hall to the rear door.

Doreen was parked just outside the door, and when she saw John emerge, flanked by the two women, she rolled her eyes.

She jumped from the driver's seat to run around to the passenger's side. "You poor dear. What an ordeal you've had! Oh, doctor, whatever shall I do to keep him comfortable?"

"Tone down the melodrama," John whispered to his assistant.

As John settled into the front seat, she whispered back,

"Tone down the eyes," which could have illuminated the parking lot.

Lauren handed Doreen prescriptions for pain and an antibiotic. "He may or may not need the pain medication, but he should start taking the antibiotics this evening." She noted a smile the size of Cleveland on Doreen's face and wondered what that meant.

"What are you doing tomorrow night?" John asked Lauren.

"Nothing," Lauren answered abruptly.

"You are now," he said. "Doreen will get in touch with Rosetta to figure out the logistics. I'll pick you up at eight o'clock."

As Doreen wheeled out of the parking lot, Lauren tipped up Rosetta's jaw to close her gaping mouth. "Don't want you swallowing any mosquitoes."

"Are you nuts?" Rosetta asked. "That guy will take a bite out of you."

"Puh-leez. I've lived my whole life playing it safe, and that includes everyone I've dated. This guy is a great combination of funny and drop dead gorgeous, and just having my arm around him was the biggest turn-on I've had in a long time. No, can I be honest here? It was the biggest turn-on EVER. He's a bit arrogant for my taste, but he's intriguing in a dangerous sort of way, and I'm overdue for some excitement."

"You've had a rough day. You should think this over carefully before you commit to something you'll regret."

"Rosetta, I'll admit it was a long day, and my thought processes may be a bit jumbled, but my body knows something about this guy. I'm going on my gut here."

"I don't like it one bit." Rosetta tapped her clunky white lab shoe on the asphalt. "But since you're determined, is there anything I can do to help?"

"Do you know someone who could work a miracle on my house by tomorrow night?" She made a mental note to

Love Fang   Susan Blexrud

remove the romance novels and vibrator from between the couch cushions.

"Are you kidding? You'll need an army in hazmat suits, but I'll see what I can come up with."

"Thanks, Rosetta. And please don't worry about me. If worse comes to worse, I'll outrun him."

"Just answer me this...what kind of guy doesn't drive?"

"A rich lawyer?" Lauren suggested.

"I guess it's true that the rich get richer. We forgot to bill him."

"No problem," Lauren said. "Elaine will send him an invoice."

"At least rich is good," Rosetta said. "He won't be looking at you like a meal ticket. Wait, I take that back. It would be a different kind of meal."

* * *

Doreen couldn't wait to get out of the parking lot to give her employer a high five. "I can't believe you asked her out. Congratulations!"

"I don't know what came over me," John said. "I was so interested in watching her sensuous lips move that I had a weak moment. You're going to need to cancel."

"Nothin' doin'," Doreen said. "You got yourself into this, and you're going through with it."

"She really is beautiful, isn't she?"

"And nice and smart and obviously attracted to you," Doreen said.

John buried his face in his hands. "Her scent really did me in."

"I'm amazed you could smell anything over that Old Spice. Did it hurt when the tooth came out?"

"No, I liked it. I held on to the chair, and she tugged. It was highly physical. The last time I had a bad tooth, a blacksmith wrenched it out, though I did have the consolation

23

of his beautiful daughter holding my hand."

"Don't tell me...she was a brunette with green eyes, just like our fair dentist."

"What else? And it's 'our dentist' now?"

* * *

Doreen called Lauren's office bright and early Thursday morning. She asked Elaine, the receptionist, if she could speak to Rosetta.

"Good morning," Rosetta said cheerfully.

"Hi!" Doreen said. "I'm calling to find out where Dr. Marsh lives for her date with Mr. Wright tonight."

"About that..." Rosetta started. "Dr. Marsh actually had something come up and won't be able to..."

Lauren grabbed the phone out of Rosetta's hand. "He can pick me up at 1100 Wayside Drive," she said into the receiver.

"Great," said Doreen. "And Mr. Wright asked me to ask you what you like to eat?"

"Well, steak's my favorite," Lauren said, "since you asked."

"That's Mr. Wright's favorite, too, though you probably don't like yours raw like he does," Doreen said.

* * *

Date night arrived in a flurry of activity. It was hard to say whether Lauren or John was more nervous, but John's allergies were blooming in spite of the fact that no flowers were.

Doreen meandered through the large house, and finally tracked him down by following the sound of sneezing. She found him in his study, upside down on his inversion machine. He wore a black "Phantom of the Opera" t-shirt and black running shorts, though gravity had pulled them down to expose an eyeful of toned muscle.

"It must be difficult sneezing in that position," she said as she cracked her knuckles and looked away from more skin than she'd seen on any man except her husband, Bill.

"You know that cracking sound drives me crazy," he said, righting himself with a quick flex of his tight stomach muscles. He freed his feet from the inversion boots and swung from the bar to a standing position.

"I can't help it," she said. "I crack my knuckles when I'm nervous, and all I can think about is your date."

"What do you have to be nervous about?" John asked. "I'm the one who has to use every fiber of my being not to become aroused. What was I thinking?"

"You need a mental image to stay focused," Doreen said. "Just think about me cracking my knuckles when your pants start to get tight. And speaking of pants, your Armani suit will be perfect. You can wear it with the blue shirt and your Peter Max tie."

"Dressing was easier in the 16th Century," John said. "We had far fewer choices."

"I'm trying to imagine you in tights and bloomers," Doreen said, crossing her arms, "like those portraits of Henry VIII."

"He was very jealous of anyone who had calves as shapely as his."

"You must have had to hide," Doreen said.

CHAPTER THREE

"*Magnifique*," John said, as Lauren opened her front door.

She wore a black shift with a woven silver bolero top that met in a large pearl button just at the juncture of her collarbones. Her only jewelry was pearl earrings. Her neck was bare.

"Thanks," Lauren said, averting her eyes as she blushed. She'd bought the outfit specifically for the evening at a new little boutique her friend Meredith had just opened. Her dress was strapless, which was a bold move for her, but Meredith had talked her into it, as well as pointing her to two-inch strappy sandals that matched her bolero.

Smokey was barking his Chihuahua head off as Lauren picked him up and clamped her hand over his little muzzle. "How are you feeling?" she asked John. "Any pain?"

"No, thank you, you're a miracle worker," John said. "And don't worry about your dog. He'll calm down in a minute."

Lauren continued to hold Smokey's teeth together

while her dog whined out of the side of his mouth. She invited John into her house, which was sparkling clean for the occasion. As soon as Smokey got a good whiff of John, the little dog was completely enamored. His tail pumped so fast, Lauren thought he might levitate.

"Wow, he's never taken to anyone so quickly," she remarked.

"Except for wolves, all animals like me." John picked up Smokey and stroked his head.

"Amazing," Lauren said.

Looking around her living room, John said, "Your house is nice and very orderly." The pillows on her peach and green floral sofa were freshly fluffed, and the two matching wing chairs were upholstered in a plaid fabric that coordinated with the sofa's floral. A large ottoman in solid green was adorned with a silver tea service.

"I have a confession to make," Lauren said. "Until yesterday, I couldn't even see the ottoman for all the old magazines on top of it. My house had been overdue for a good cleaning, and you were the perfect excuse to get it done." As soon as she said it, Lauren's hand went to her mouth. "I guess I shouldn't have admitted that."

"No, I'm flattered, but I have a confession to make, too," John said. "I'm completely disorganized. If it weren't for Doreen making sense of things, I'd never be on schedule."

"Does she clean your house, too?" Lauren asked.

John laughed. "I'm not sure you'd call it cleaning, but she does keep things relatively neat."

An awkward moment of silence, in which Lauren allowed herself to briefly look in his eyes, was followed by her question, "Would you like a glass of wine?"

"Yes, red if you have it," he said. "Doreen's waiting in the car, but she brought a copy of *Motorcycle Times*, and she won't mind if we tarry a bit."

"Tarry? Now there's a word I haven't heard in awhile."

She led John into her now immaculate kitchen,

catching a whiff of his Old Spice, which wasn't nearly as strong as when he was in her office. Underneath the after shave, there was another intoxicating scent that was making her legs shake.

Lauren looked down at her legs to see if the shaking was visible. When she looked up, she saw John staring at her blood-red toenails.

Suddenly, her microwave oven started up on its own.

"Sorry," John said. "I have that effect on appliances."

Nervously, Lauren uncorked a bottle of Cabernet Sauvignon and tried to steady her hands as she poured two glasses. He took the glass she offered him and clinked it to hers. She avoided looking him in the eye.

"Are you afraid of me?" He turned her chin with his hand until she had to look up at him.

"I'm terrified," she said, looking away to grab a dishtowel to wipe her sweating palms.

"Then that makes two of us," he said.

"Well, that's somewhat of a relief," she said. "How about we take our wine out to the back patio?"

Walking through her living room to the French doors that led to the patio, John stopped in front of a large bookcase. There were two shelves full of books on Tudor England, including all of Philippa Gregory's historical novels and Antonia Fraser's biographies.

"You have an interest in 16th Century England?" John traced his long fingers across the spines of the books on the top shelf.

"Yes, I always have," Lauren said. "If I could meet anyone in history, I'd choose Anne Boleyn."

"She was a remarkable woman," John said, "and quite misunderstood."

"You say that as though you knew her," Lauren said.

"I did," John said.

Just as Lauren opened her mouth to ask what he meant, the front doorbell rang.

She almost tripped over the ottoman in the living room, which she looked at as though she'd never seen it. She opened the door to find Rosetta and her husband, Manuel. Rosetta was straining to look around Lauren for a glimpse at John.

"This really wasn't necessary," Lauren said.

"Uh-huh," Rosetta said. "Where is he?"

"He's out back on the patio, sipping a glass of wine," Lauren said. "Everything's perfectly fine, and as you can see, Smokey is humping his leg. Whoa, that's weird. And his assistant is waiting in the car to take us to dinner." Lauren pointed toward Doreen, who waved back, and then looked back to John, who was gently pushing Smokey off his leg.

Lauren turned Rosetta by the shoulders and headed her back to her car with Manuel following.

"I promise you'll be the first person I call if I need help," she told Rosetta as she opened her car door and gently pushed her into the passenger seat.

"Call 911 first," Rosetta said, "and then call me."

When Lauren came back into the house, she walked toward John. "Sorry. She's like the big sister I never had."

"That's commendable," John said, "and she's not wrong about me."

"Bet I can outrun you." Lauren teased.

John looked at Lauren underneath his eyelashes. "You have no idea how quick I am."

For the first time that evening, Lauren looked directly at John, but before she could speak, he swept her into his arms and bent his head to kiss her. She met his mouth with her lips parted, and he traced her mouth gently with his tongue before finding her tongue and exploring her welcoming mouth. He ended the deep kiss and briefly nibbled her ear.

By this time, Smokey had completely lost it. He was bouncing up and down like a ping-pong ball, trying to get in on the action.

"We should go," John said.

Scooping up Smokey, Lauren closed him in her

bedroom and grabbed her keys and evening purse, but not before checking herself in the mirror above her dresser. Her face was flushed with passion, and she smiled at her reflection.

* * *

Doreen hopped out of the car as John and Lauren approached. She opened the back door for her passengers.

"Doreen, I appreciate your efficiency, but you don't need to play the chauffeur," John said.

"Oh, let me have my fun," she whispered to him. "He doesn't drive, you know," she said to Lauren. "He thinks it's plebian."

John rolled his eyes and slid in the back seat next to Lauren.

"Delmonico's, right?" Doreen asked.

John took Lauren's hand and held it during the ten-minute ride to Delmonico's. They didn't speak. They couldn't. Doreen was talking a mile a minute about the Orlando Magic season opener, which was to begin on the radio in a few minutes.

"I just hope this new coach is good," she said, looking at her passengers in the rear view mirror. "We need a good start to the season. We've got two rookies who are getting great press. I hope they live up to expectations."

Knowing Doreen as well as he did, John realized she was almost as nervous as he was about his date.

"Do you like basketball?" John asked Lauren.

"Yes, very much," she said.

"I knew I liked her," Doreen said. "John is a basketball nut. He has his own skybox."

"I actually bought it for Doreen," John said, "but I use it on occasion. Would you like to go with me sometime?"

"I'd love it," Lauren said.

Doreen winked at her boss in the rear view mirror.

31

* * *

Once they arrived at the restaurant, the maitre d' escorted John and Lauren to a candlelit table in a small room reserved exclusively for them. John ordered a Bloody Mary for himself and a Cosmopolitan for Lauren, both with Ketel One Vodka.

"I don't date much," Lauren blurted out, and then wondered what made her make such a pitiful confession.

"Me, neither," John said.

"Practicing law doesn't allow time for romance?"

"It's more complicated than that. I was in love...once...but it didn't end well."

"Well, you're one up on me. I've never been in love, but for some weird reason, I think you already knew that."

"I have a sixth sense about people. I'm usually right."

Lauren gave John a sideways glance. "You seem to have wisdom far beyond your years."

John laughed. "Let's save that for another night." He reached for her hand across the table. "Tell me about Lauren."

"I have a feeling my life has been boring compared to yours, but I'm in a pretty good place right now. I love my job, and I'm just getting ready to go on an annual mission trip to South America with a group of dentists. For the past three years, we've spent a month in Venezuela providing free dental care for children there."

"That's wonderful. I've done some mission work in Venezuela myself, though I had to compete with the vampire bats."

"Excuse me," the waiter interrupted. "Are you ready to order, sir?"

"The lady will have the petite sirloin, medium rare, with a baked potato, butter on the side, and a buffalo mozzarella and tomato salad. And I would like two, 24-ounce T-bones, raw."

"No salad or potato for you, sir?" The waiter asked. "And did you say raw?"

"Steak only, and yes, raw."

"How did you know what I wanted to eat?" Lauren asked John as the waiter walked away, shaking his head.

"Well, I hope this doesn't freak you out, but I can often tell what people are thinking."

"Do you know what I'm thinking now?" The candlelight made her peachy complexion shine, and the apples of her cheeks sparkled as she smiled.

"Yes, I do, but I don't think you're ready to admit it."

Lauren blushed and looked down at the tablecloth.

"My God, you're beautiful," John said, and then he added, "And that is something Anne Boleyn would never have done."

"What?" Lauren asked, looking up.

"She wasn't as beautiful as you, but she knew how to seduce a man with her eyes."

"I'm not beautiful, and I border on what the fashion industry would call 'plus size.'"

"I think you're perfect." John's voice was husky. "Anne was ruled by her pride and ego, and it was her downfall in the end. You have a humility that for me is much more seductive, and your scent is intoxicating."

"Rosetta's Christmas present to me...Chanel No. 5."

"No, it's underneath that."

Again, Lauren looked down, and John realized he was coming on a bit strong.

"This is all very foreign to me," Lauren said. "I'm not experienced at seduction, and I don't know what happens next."

"What happens is that we have dinner," John said as the waiter arrived with Lauren's salad. He ordered another round of drinks. "And could you make that Bloody Mary a little bloodier the next time?"

"More vodka, sir?"

"No," John said, "more tomato juice."

Lauren sipped on her second Cosmopolitan. "There's something about you," she started. "I can't quite put my finger on it, but I have a feeling that people either trust you completely or find you dangerous. Like Rosetta. You know which side she falls on."

"And you?" John asked. "Which side does Lauren fall on?"

She shook her head and took a moment to respond. "For some reason, I trust you. I don't know why. Can you tell me?"

"It's a characteristic of my kind. We have few relationships, but when we love, we love intensely and passionately. And trust is essential."

"What do you mean by your 'kind'"?

John wouldn't lie to Lauren, but he wasn't ready to reveal his identity, either. To skirt the issue diplomatically, he said, "I trace my family back to William the Conqueror, and we are a stalwart lot of royalists and warriors." *Stalwart?* "We kept secrets for our monarchs that changed the course of history, and through the centuries of our bloodline, we never betrayed our sovereigns or our spouses. No Wright has ever divorced."

"Impressive," Lauren said. "You've never been married then?"

"I was married...once. She died."

"I'm so sorry. Was her death recent?"

"In some ways, it seems like yesterday."

A chill came over the small private room. Lauren rubbed her arms, and John got up to wrap his jacket around her.

"I have a better idea," she said. "Let's go out to the terrace for a minute."

The restaurant was on a small lake, with a dock that ended in a broad rectangular platform with a wrought iron railing. The warm October air was heavy with moisture, and the western sky blinked heat lightning as Lauren stood at the railing. John wrapped his arms around her from behind, and she leaned into him. He tucked a strand of her wavy hair behind her ear and pressed his lips to her temple, feeling her pulse there and inhaling her scent. The thought of her blood coursing through her veins and the prospect of them exchanging that life force almost made him swoon. He longed to scratch his wrist and offer his fresh blood to her. He imagined her sensuous lips dripping with his blood, and he shivered from the thought of making love to her.

"Now, you're the one who's cold," she said.

"I'm not cold, but I'm damn hungry." The intensity of his longing was like a gale wind stirring his emotions. "I've been hungry for five hundred years."

Lauren laughed. "No more Bloody Marys for you," she said, touching his cheek. "Combined with those antibiotics you're on, I can see you need to get some food in your stomach."

"Is that the dentist's order?"

"Absolutely, with one caveat," she said.

"I've lived my life on caveats. Please tell me this one is a kiss."

"How ever did you know?" She stood on tiptoe to raise her face to his. Parting her lips, she traced his lips with her tongue, and then met his tongue with an explosion of heat that shot an ache directly to his groin.

When he reluctantly disengaged to look into her eyes, she opened her eyes slowly.

"Don't go there," he said.

"I'm not going anywhere," she said.

"I know what you're feeling, and you need to stop."

Lauren took one step back and put her hands on her hips. "What are you, clairvoyant?"

"I've been on this earth a long time, but it's been centuries since anyone moved me like you do. You're heading into dangerous territory."

35

"You're talking centuries? I'm talking NEVER. No one has EVER moved me like you do, and I'm ready for it."

"I'm not sure you are," he said. Sniffing the air and wanting to change the subject, he added, "Our dinner is on the table."

"You can smell it from here?"

"I have extraordinary senses. It goes with my lineage."

"So, you come from a long line of bloodhounds?"

"Yes, and snakes, eagles, and my favorite, bats."

"I'm more of a Koala Bear, myself."

"I thought I detected a scent of eucalyptus." John sniffed the air around Lauren's head, and then put his arm around her to walk back to their table.

John had to confine his chewing to the right side of his mouth, but he was able to get enough blood from the huge steak to keep up his energy level.

Lauren glanced at her watch. "Darn, my watch stopped. I just got a new battery, too."

"Sorry," John said. "My mistake."

"Don't tell me...you can stop time."

"No, I wish I could," he said. "But watches are another of those objects that tend to malfunction around me."

"Do you have your own electrical field?" Lauren asked.

"It's not electricity; it's energy. But I can redirect it. Check your watch now."

The second hand on Lauren's Seiko began moving again.

"This is all a bit scary.'

"I won't hurt you, Lauren. I won't let that happen."

The waiter cleared their plates and brought the dessert menu. John glanced briefly at his, and then asked Lauren, "What chocolate concoction speaks to you this evening?"

"How did you...never mind...I won't ask how you knew I was a chocoholic. Ordinarily, I'd love a piece of the Red Velvet cake, but I'll only order it if you'll share."

"I don't do sweet. Besides, I'm saving myself for

36

another taste of your lips."

Lauren motioned quickly for the waiter. "No dessert, thanks."

As the waiter took John's credit card, Lauren fidgeted in her chair. John knew her discomfort was the result of her heightened libido, and he suspected the feeling was foreign to her. He had just the cure.

"Let's get out of here," he said.

When Doreen pulled the car around the circular drive at the restaurant to pick them up, John put his finger to his lips to let her know that he wasn't up for a basketball play-by-play on the way back to Lauren's house.

Doreen gave him a thumbs-up while Lauren got into the backseat. John put his arm around her and when they reached her house, he helped her out of the car, and then turned to Doreen, "Come back in forty-five minutes. Any longer than that, and she'll be in trouble."

They walked arm in arm into Lauren's house and headed straight for the couch, where he turned her to face him. He gently pushed her hair away from her face and gathered it behind her head with one hand. He kissed her temple and traced her ear with his tongue. He blew his intoxicating breath across her eyes before finding her mouth. He kissed her deeply, and then slid his other hand under her dress to find her core. She drew back briefly to look into his eyes, which burned with desire. She closed her eyes as he slipped his fingers under her panties.

"I...I...," she whispered, and then she pushed his hand away. "I don't know what to do with these feelings," she said, breathing heavily.

"Shhh," he said. "Let me pleasure you." He unbuttoned the pearl closure of her bolero and slipped it off her shoulders. He reached around to the zipper of her dress and unzipped it to her waist, freeing her breasts from the dress's self-contained bra. "Beautiful," he said, lowering his head to take a nipple in his mouth. He circled the pink, erect nipple with his tongue, and then took it full in his mouth. She closed her eyes, tossed her head back, and ran her fingers through his dark, curly hair as he suckled her.

He again slid his hand up her thigh, but this time, she relaxed into his body. When he found her wet center, he circled his fingers against her feminine bud, and then plunged two fingers inside her sheath as he continued to rub her sensitive and aroused bud with his thumb. He felt her relinquish control as she opened herself to his exploration. Her legs began to tremble, and he whispered to her, "Let go, Lauren. You've waited so long for this. Take it. Take all of it. Trust me."

Her chest flushed from her arousal, and her full breasts pressed against John's shirt, creating friction on her erect nipples. She parted her lips, and John closed his mouth on hers, finding her tongue as she wrapped her arms around his neck. Her breath was deep and audible, and John knew she was close to ecstasy. He wanted his mouth on her feminine core when she came, and he pushed her gently back on the couch and lowered his head. She moaned as he parted her with his fingers. He licked her inner thighs before closing his mouth on the source of her pleasure. He slipped two fingers inside her and began circling her bud with his tongue. She arched her back and grasped the cushions underneath her tightly with her fists as the waves of her climax almost lifted her off the couch. He felt the undulating motion of her sheath as it grasped his fingers, and he longed to be inside her, plunging into her depths while he simultaneously tasted the blood of her blue, pulsing jugular. He licked her bud once for good measure and sat up to take her hand and kiss her fingers. Tears streamed down her face, and he brushed them from her cheeks. He wasn't prepared for her reaction.

"I was hoping for a smile or a 'thank you.'" He gently pinched her cheek.

"It's just...I don't know...so emotional." She squeezed the last tears from her eyes. "You're so...I'm so...I don't really know you, and yet..."

"I'm not a normal man, Lauren, and I don't approach love lightly."

"But you...you did that for me. I've never...I want to know how to pleasure you."

"That's a bit more involved." He touched her cheek gently. "Here, let me help you back into your dress, and we'll rescue that little canine who's been scratching frantically from behind your bedroom door."

"Oh my gosh, I didn't even hear him. But I suppose your hearing is more acute than the average person?"

"Bingo." He opened the bedroom door to admit a crazed Smokey, who vented his frustration by running around the ottoman.

Through the bay window of Lauren's living room, the lights of Doreen's car illuminated the driveway.

"I must go," John said. "You'll sleep well tonight. I've willed it."

He kissed her on the nose, and she watched him practically glide out to the car.

She turned to her little dog and said, "Wow!"

* * *

As John approached the car, he could tell by Doreen's posture, leaning forward and wide-eyed, that she was dying to know how the evening went.

"Don't ask," he said as he opened the passenger door and slid his large frame inside.

"Ah, come on, boss. At least give me an overview."

John covered his eyes with one hand. "Okay, here it is. I love her," he paused, "and I can never see her again."

"And in between deciding that, what the heck happened?"

"I'm not going to reveal details. We had a lovely time. She's absolutely fabulous. I want to marry her. I have to let her go. That's all I'm going to say. If you want to have a conversation, you're going to have to ask me innocuous questions."

"So, how was dinner?"

"Dinner was delightful, though I'm still hungry."

"What's her house like?"

"It's lovely. She had it cleaned to impress me."

"What do you like best about her?"

"Now you're getting personal." John smiled. "I guess it's her wonderful sense of humor, though she has a tendency to think I'm funny when I'm being serious. When she smiles, her face lights up, and she has one gorgeous dimple in her left cheek."

"That would be the cheek on her face?"

"Very funny."

Looking out the car window, John idly stared into the dark night while contemplating his future, an unusual thought process for him.

"If I took the Florida Bar Exam, I could practice law here," John said.

Doreen pulled the car to the curb, and turned off the engine. "What does that have to do with anything?"

"I was just thinking about what it would take to become a regular citizen."

"You've got it bad," Doreen said. They drove the last two miles to his house in silence.

* * *

Lauren floated into her office on Friday morning to face a stern Rosetta.

"Come out with it," Rosetta said. "I want to hear everything."

"He's incredible. What more can I say?"

"I was afraid of that." Rosetta sighed. "Frankly, I was worried he might be a *chupacabra*."

"What's that?"

"It's a vampire that drinks the blood of domesticated animals. Poor little Smokey wouldn't have a chance."

Lauren laughed. "Rosetta, your already active imagination kicks up a notch when you're pregnant."

Rosetta had to laugh, too. "Considering this is my sixth baby, do you think it gets worse every time?"

"I don't know, but please don't worry about me. I'll admit that John is a bit quirky, but he's kind and smart, not as arrogant as I first thought, and unbelievably sexy." Lauren fanned herself with the closest *Dental World* magazine. "Besides, he and Smokey are already fast friends."

"Okay, I'll back off. You know it's just because I care about you," Rosetta said.

"Yes, I do," Lauren said, touching Rosetta's cheek. "But I've never been happier. He's awakened feelings in me that I didn't know existed."

Looking over the appointment book for the following week, Rosetta said, "Looks like his new tooth should be in on Thursday. I'll call his assistant today to book an appointment."

Lauren's pleasant manner was even more so today. Two of her regular patients commented that she seemed to glow. She accepted their compliments and shot a look to Rosetta who couldn't help but smile with her.

When Rosetta called Doreen to schedule John for his return visit, they went back and forth on a time for the appointment.

"He can't come in first thing Friday morning?" Rosetta asked.

"Well, I suppose if he absolutely has to come at that time, he can wear sunglasses," Doreen said.

Rosetta held the phone away from her ear and looked at it as if it were an alien. Replacing the receiver to her ear, she said, "Whatever he needs to do, but that's the only time Dr. Marsh has until the following Monday, and I know he's anxious to get his new tooth."

"We'll make it work," Doreen said.

Never shy, Rosetta had to squeeze in a comment about their employers' date before she hung up. "Things are certainly happy over here. How's it going on your end?"

She'd met her match in Doreen. "Jeez, I hardly know him. He's on Cloud Nine."

"Whew, I'm glad to hear that. I was Dr. Marsh's first hire. She took a chance on me. My advisor at hygienist school told her I was a spitfire." Rosetta laughed, and then became serious. "So, we're very close, and I sure wouldn't want to see her get hurt."

"I feel the same way about Mr. Wright," Doreen said.

"I don't have to be concerned about him calling her back?" Rosetta asked.

"Not unless he thinks she needs some space," Doreen answered. "In the five years I've worked for him, this is the first time he's really liked a woman. He may want to take it slow."

"She don't need no space." Rosetta said. "She's been rolling around in too much space for too long."

"Well, thanks for the advice," Doreen said. As they said their goodbyes and Doreen pushed the button to end the call, she smiled to herself.

* * *

When Doreen lifted the lid of John's casket on Sunday evening, she didn't wait for his eyes to open to ask, "When are you going to call Dr. Marsh, again? It's been three days since your date. She'll be thinking you don't like her."

"Great Scot, Doreen, do you think I've thought of anything else since Thursday night?" John yawned, displaying his lopsided tooth alignment.

"Okay, so when?" Doreen cracked her knuckles. "You've got an appointment to have your new tooth put in next Friday, but you're certainly not going to wait until then to talk with her."

"It seems like only yesterday that I was talking about how true love was to be avoided at all cost."

"Too late now, Buster."

"Thanks for your vote of confidence, but it's not that easy. I have the capacity to bend her to my will, but I won't do that. She'd have to want to join my kind, fangs and all. And then there's the issue of how compelling her scent is to me. At some point, I'd have to take her."

"So, what's your next move?"

"As much as I want her, I have to stay away."

"Wrong. Lay your cards on the table. You've told me that vampires can live pretty conventional lives, right? Just because you've chosen to sleep all day and carouse all night doesn't mean you couldn't change your ways."

"With sunscreen and dark glasses, I could function on a cloudy day." John tapped a finger to his temple as he considered the prospects of living a more human existence.

"The most pressing issue is not whether you could be more human," Doreen said, pulling copies of <u>Law for Dummies</u> and the <u>LSAT Study Guide</u> out of a book bag. She'd stopped by Border's on Saturday. "It's whether the good dentist could be happy as a vampire."

Doreen handed the book bag to John, who began extracting books and carefully examining each title: <u>Don't Sweat the Small Stuff in Love</u>, <u>One Year to an Organized Life</u>, <u>The Seven Principles for Making Marriage Work</u>, <u>Emily Post's Etiquette, 17th Edition</u>, and <u>The Rules of Parenting</u>.

"I'd say you've covered the bases," John said. "I'll just need a few copies of <u>Popular Mechanics</u> to round out this bunch."

"I was tempted to get <u>Naptime is the New Happy Hour</u>, too," Doreen said. "I know I've gone out on a limb, but I also picked up some clothes for you that aren't black. They're in your closet."

43

"Thanks, but you're getting ahead of yourself, Doreen."
"Level with her, John."

* * *

John wasted no time on his Sunday feed. He intercepted a big heroin transaction, and then called the police to alert them to the location. Tomorrow's headlines would be big, and he decided the best way to let Lauren know about him was for her to read about it. If he told her in person, he'd be tempted to persuade her. It had to be her decision if she wanted to see him again.

He swooped back into his house at around ten p.m., in plenty of time to call Lauren.

She'd been moping around all weekend, talking to Smokey about John. "Why hasn't he called?" she asked her little dog. "I trusted him. Was I a complete idiot?"

She wasn't getting any answers from Smokey.

Her heart skipped a beat when her cell phone rang. "Hello?"

"Hi, Lauren. I'm sorry I haven't called before now, but I needed to tell you something, and I didn't know how to begin. If you still want to see me after you read tomorrow's headlines--"

"You're in tomorrow's headlines?"

"I should be front page, above the fold, so it'll be hard to miss."

He said goodnight, and then willed her to get a good night's sleep. He wasn't going to persuade her, but at least she should be well-rested when she read the news.

* * *

Smokey performed his morning duty of dragging the newspaper from the driveway to the front door, where Lauren patted him on the head and traded the paper for a dog biscuit.

She flung the paper on her kitchen table and stared at it for a minute before mustering the courage to slide it out of its plastic wrapper. John had been correct about the location of the story. There on the front page, above the fold, was the headline, "Vampire Vigilante Thwarts Mega Drug Deal."

"Oh....My....God." Lauren dropped the newspaper like it was contaminated. She began pacing the small kitchen, and then she slammed her fist down on the counter, causing the toaster to bounce and spew bits of dried toast. "Damn him!" She plopped down on her kitchen floor, buried her face in her hands, and sobbed.

CHAPTER FOUR

"You seem to be feeding more than usual," Doreen remarked to John on Friday morning as she opened his coffin. "Things are getting a bit tight in there."

"You know I eat more when I'm upset. By mid-morning, my expanding girth will dissipate."

"Just in time for your appointment."

"It's all I can think about."

"Once you get through today, you can put all this behind you. And did I apologize for encouraging you to find love?"

"Yes, you've apologized, and I'm not angry with you." John eased himself out of his coffin, shook his head, and said, "I'm going to hang upside down for awhile. Let me know when we need to go."

John headed for his study where his inversion machine's gleaming steel seemed to have lost its luster. In truth, all color and gleam had disappeared from John's life in the past week. He was going through the motions, nothing more.

* * *

The atmosphere wasn't any cheerier at Lauren's house or office. She spent her evenings with Smokey, teaching him to roll over for a treat. During the day, she maintained her positive chair side manner with her patients, but Rosetta knew she ached inside.

"Is there anything I can do to make you feel better?" Rosetta asked.

"No, nothing, but thanks. I considered trying to comfort myself with a chocolate binge, but it wouldn't help."

"Time is the great healer," Rosetta said. "See him today, and then go on with your life."

Tears welled in Lauren's eyes. "I'm angry at him and angry at myself. All those years of being cautious, and the one time I let myself be vulnerable, the guy turns out to be a vampire. It would be funny, if it weren't so pitiful."

"Don't be so hard on yourself. We've all fallen for the wrong guy at some point. And I can't believe I'm saying this, but he was just being what he is."

"I don't know what you think, but it wasn't weird or anything. He was extremely tender and loving, more so than any guy I've ever known."

Rosetta patted Lauren's hand. "Put on your lab coat. He'll be here in a few minutes."

* * *

Doreen wished John luck and stayed in the parking lot to wait for him. He was Lauren's first patient for the day. Rosetta led him to Suite One and draped him with a small cape for the procedure. He kept his Versace sunglasses on.

"Good morning, Mr. Wright," Lauren said as she entered the examining room and walked straight to the small sink to wash her shaking hands.

"Good morning, Dr. Marsh," he said.

Rosetta had already prepared the Novocain for the procedure, and as Lauren put on her thin rubber gloves, her hands stopped shaking. She knew he'd willed her hands still. "Thanks," she said.

"I'd rather have the tooth in its socket than up my nose," he said.

She couldn't help but smile. "That would be a first. The dental board would revoke my license."

"I'd still let you work on me," he said.

The procedure took more than an hour, and when it was done, Lauren held up a mirror for John to inspect her handiwork.

"Vampires don't have reflections, so I'll have to rely on your expert opinion." John took off his sunglasses and looked straight at Lauren.

His gaze melted her resolve, and she looked away. Holding on to the arm of the dental chair to steady herself, she said, "I believe you'll be pleased with the result."

Her voice quavered, and she knew he recognized the dip in her composure. She hoped he wouldn't make this any more difficult for her.

"Then I shall take my leave, Dr. Marsh. It has been a pleasure."

Without looking at her again, he snapped his fingers and vaporized, leaving a faint musky scent in his wake.

"Wow," Rosetta said, "I didn't know he could do that."

"He has many talents," Lauren said, remembering the night at her house.

* * *

He materialized in the passenger seat of Doreen's car.

She almost jumped out the door. "No matter how many times you do that, I never get used to it."

"It uses a lot of energy. I save it for special occasions, like when I need to get away from the woman I love."

Doreen tried to cheer him up. "Let me see that new smile of yours."

John displayed a toothy grin, belying the sinking feeling that was making his bones ache.

"Lovely. So what now?"

"The Vampire Vigilante resumes his quest for justice," he said, though his heart wasn't in it.

* * *

Lauren told herself she needed to get on with her life, but after four depressing days, she decided some vampire research would be just the ticket to scare her out of her sad state.

She was surprised at the wealth of information about vampires on the Internet, but what was even more surprising was the relative normality of their lifestyles. She had no idea vampires were everywhere, and looking back over her life, she suspected her French teacher in high school and her college running coach were of that ilk.

"I'll be darned," she said to an illustration of a pregnant vampiress in Victorian England. But then, the Addams Family had children. Wait a minute, they weren't real. Or were they?

It seemed that vampires could be good or bad, just like regular people. They lived in every corner of the planet, and they typically blended in seamlessly with their surroundings.

She pored over page after page of information. Vampires were loyal and trustworthy to the people they chose to love. Their immortality provided them with great insights into human nature. They recognized insincerity and deceit much easier than normal people. On the flip side, as John had told her, people generally either trusted vampires immediately or found them dangerous. She had trusted him, and her research confirmed that she hadn't been an idiot in that regard.

The more she read, the more she knew she wasn't crazy, and John, though a vampire, was a good guy. Her research provided many answers, but it also raised a lot of questions. She'd told herself a relationship with John could never work, but shouldn't she ask him the burning questions her research had raised?

She found his telephone number on the "Incoming Calls" list on her cell phone. She wrote the number down on a hot pink sticky note and stuck it to her refrigerator. For the next three days, as she continued her research, she avoided the kitchen. It was one of the most effective weight control methods she'd ever used, knowing the hot pink note would be glaring at her from its stainless steel backdrop. She lost two pounds.

When she'd assembled a long list of questions, she got up the courage to face the sticky note and make the call.

Doreen answered the phone and passed it to John, who was watching old reruns of "Buffy, the Vampire Slayer" on his plasma television. Doreen gave no indication that the call was from Lauren.

"Hello?"

"How soon can you get over here?"

"That's a silly question."

"Don't make it instantaneous. I need a few minutes." She hung up the phone.

Doreen, who'd been standing behind John, said, "That was quick."

John decided to build the suspense. "I don't know why I watch this show. There are no good vampires in it. And I can't get used to this plasma TV. Why would anyone use a synonym for blood to name a television set?"

"Stop! You're driving me crazy!" Doreen shook her hands as if she had an itch she couldn't scratch.

"Wish me luck. I'm going to Lauren's house."

"Wear something sexy, like that new stuff I bought."

John looked at Doreen from under his eyelashes.

"Okay, now you're making me nervous," Doreen said.

"What I wear is hardly the issue."

"Just don't wear black."

* * *

John materialized at Lauren's front door wearing a sage green linen shirt, open at the collar, tucked into dark khaki slacks.

The magnetism of his scent nearly knocked Lauren over when she answered the door. She put her hand to her chest and took a step back.

"Sorry. I forgot the Old Spice."

"Don't apologize. You smell...great." She rested her hand on the foyer table to steady her wobbly legs and stole a glance at Smokey, who was doing pirouettes.

"I don't want to make this difficult for you, Lauren."

"Hey, I'm the one who wanted to talk." She turned to face the table and the mirror above it. She thought she could put some distance between them by talking to him in the mirror, but she'd forgotten he had no reflection.

"Do you know what you look like?" she asked.

John laughed. "I've had many portraits painted over the years, beginning with one by Hans Holbein during King Henry's reign. Nothing in the past hundred years, but I doubt I've changed. Was that first on your list of questions?" He nodded to the yellow legal pad that Lauren was now hugging like a Teddy bear.

"Yes, that was on the list. Would you like something to drink before we get started?" She'd told herself she needed to approach this meeting for what it was...a fact-finding mission. She hoped she could keep her cool.

"Sure, anything red," he answered.

Lauren turned for the kitchen, while John sat in one of the two plaid wing chairs. She was glad he hadn't chosen the couch. She checked her reflection in the toaster. Not good. Her flush had crawled from her chest to her face, and she looked like she'd spent the day at the beach. She pressed an ice cube to her forehead and took several cleansing breaths; in through the nose, out through the mouth. She emerged from the kitchen with two glasses of cranberry juice and her legal pad tucked under her arm. Smokey was already curled up on John's lap.

Setting the tray on the ottoman, she settled in the opposite wing chair, trying to look nonchalant by crossing her legs. She picked up her legal pad and pen and positioned her tiny reading glasses near the tip of her nose. "Let's begin, shall we?"

"Shoot."

"All right, first things first. How did you become a vampire?"

"It was during the reign of King Henry VIII, and I was a barrister under the tutelage of Sir Thomas More. England and France were on the verge of war, and the French ambassador, who was a vampire, needed a spy in England. He wanted me to eliminate anyone in Henry's circle who was unsympathetic to France. When he ambushed me, he chose the wrong man."

"Weren't you angry?"

"I was furious, but once I realized what I had become, I had to make the best of a bad situation. Isn't that a phrase from a song by Gladys Knight and the Pips?"

Lauren laughed, and then quickly tapped the point of her pen on the legal pad to resume her inquest.

"How old are you?"

"I've been thirty years old for five hundred years."

"Do you have to sleep in a coffin?"

"No, not here in Orlando, but it's a force of habit. I've lived in less secure places over the years, and the coffin provides safety. I have an alarm system in the house, so I could sleep in a bed. Besides, there's no one to threaten me here. Unless organized crime finds me."

"How could they hurt you? I mean, you're immortal, right?"

"A stake in the heart would do me in, and I wouldn't fare well headless, either. Other than that, gunshots have no effect, and I heal quickly from stabbings. Organized crime, however, has its ways of getting to people. I'm very cautious about who sees me when I'm hunting."

"What is it with you and animals?"

John smiled. "Vampires have a natural kinship with animals because of our heightened senses, but we don't like wolves. Wolves and vampires are sworn enemies."

"I've read that many vampires live relatively normal lives, working at jobs during the day. Have you thought about leading a more human existence?"

"I'm thinking about it now. I'm actually studying for the Florida Bar Exam."

"Really? I imagine there've been many changes in the law over the past five hundred years." Lauren uncrossed and recrossed her legs for the next question. "Tell me about your first wife."

John paused, and Lauren saw the expression on his unhumanly handsome face change from relaxed to pained as he closed his eyes and squeezed the arms of his chair. "I killed her."

Lauren's hand went to her throat.

"Let me explain." He took a deep breath and began. "Her name was Catherine. She was a lady-in-waiting to Anne Boleyn. I had only been a vampire for a few months when I met her. It was fall, and King Henry had moved the court back to Whitehall for Christmas." Lauren could almost see the memories flooding back in John's pained expression. "I can still remember the first time I saw her, clad in the ermine furs that set off her green eyes—"

"Wait. Did you make her a vampire against her will?"

"No, she wanted to join me, but I was inexperienced in human nature. I assumed any woman I chose would follow

Love Fang   Susan Blexrud

the path I'd chosen, protecting the innocent and preying only on criminals and convicts. The Tower of London was rife with political prisoners, and dying from a vampire's feed was a much more humane way to go than being drawn and quartered. But Catherine's taste was for children. Looking back, the signs were there, but I couldn't see them. She always had a bevy of children around her, and she was particularly fond of Prince Edward and Princesses Mary and Elizabeth. She would have changed the course of history had she sunk her fangs into any of that tender Tudor flesh." John paused.

"What happened to Catherine?"

"I tried to rehabilitate her, but she'd had too much young blood to change."

"How did you kill her?"

John shuddered. "We slept in a family crypt at Lambeth, just outside of London, and one morning after she retired, I kissed her gently and then drove a stake through her heart. I should have cut off her head, too, but I couldn't. She's buried at All Hallows by the Tower." He closed his eyes and sighed. "I hope she's at peace in death, but she couldn't be allowed to walk this earth and continue to take young, innocent lives."

Lauren paused before her next question. "Did you love her?"

"She was my life." John swept his fingers through his hair, and Lauren longed to rush to his arms and comfort him for making him remember. But she thought better of it.

"I'm so sorry, John."

John hung his head, and when he looked up at Lauren, she saw such sorrow in his eyes. And then she saw something else that seemed to well from deep inside him. It was love.

"Is there any way we could have a relationship without making me a vampire?"

"No. It wouldn't be enough, Lauren, for either of us. Your scent is embedded in me now, and mine in you. The more we see each other, the stronger our attraction. You'd have a weak moment and succumb when you really weren't sure, and my animal would overwhelm me. I won't take you like that."

Lauren rubbed her arms.

"Did I frighten you?" John asked.

"No." Lauren closed her eyes. "I'm...turned on."

"It would be better if I didn't know that."

"How can you be sure I wouldn't become a monster?" she had to ask.

"I've never been surer of anything." And then he was gone.

* * *

John went straight home. Though he was hungry, he needed to collect his thoughts before launching into the evening skies. He walked through the house to the sliding glass doors that spanned the large garden room. Leaning against the door jam, he surveyed the manicured lawn, reminiscent of his ancestral home in England. There, a maze of pruned rose bushes took center stage, and he'd wiled away his youthful summers on the croquet lawn, oblivious to his fate. Here, a gazebo with a stone walk leading from the house was the main attraction. A full moon shone through the gazebo tonight. Passion vines, sparkling from the aftermath of a brief rain, crept up the sides and met on the roof of the hexagonal structure. Passion vines. Passion. Damn, he'd fallen hard. He could feel every breath she took.

Doreen entered the garden room from the kitchen, where she'd been moving things around, not cleaning. She tapped him gently on the shoulder, letting him know she was leaving. "See you tomorrow. Anything you need before I go?"

"Could you wrap up a certain dentist and deliver her to my arms?"

"How'd it go?"

"She's conflicted." John sighed. "I know she wants me,

but she has to weigh her very nice life against a big unknown. And the more I see her, the harder it is for me to keep my hands off her."

"So, what's your next move?"

"I wait. I hope. I stay busy."

"Do you need help with review questions for the bar exam?"

"Tomorrow, Doreen. Tonight, I have to avenge the city."

* * *

Rosetta was reading the newspaper when Lauren shuffled into her office at eight a.m. "Did you see this morning's paper?" Rosetta asked.

"No, and I don't want to. Just tell me he's safe."

"He's safe. Sure you don't want the details?"

"No, it'll just prolong the agony."

Elaine, the receptionist, interrupted to say that Mrs. Brady had arrived for her follow-up and that Rosetta had a telephone call.

"Take the call, Rosetta. I'll visit with Mrs. Brady for a few minutes."

"This is Rosetta." She answered the phone.

"Hi, Rosetta, this is Doreen, Mr. Wright's assistant. Remember me?"

"Of course. Things used to be on pretty solid ground until Mr. Wright graced our office. Now it feels like the cleanup after a tsunami. How long ago was that?"

"It was two weeks, three days, and seven hours, but who's counting? Listen, I can't take it any longer. It's time to bring out the big guns."

"What did you have in mind?"

"Can you have lunch tomorrow?"

"Sure. I'm pregnant, so I'm into quantity."

"I don't have that excuse, but quantity works for me,

too. How about Steak n' Shake at noon?"

"See you there."

Over double cheeseburger platters and chocolate milkshakes, Rosetta and Doreen put their heads together to formulate a plan.

"She likes basketball, right?" Doreen asked. "What could be more neutral ground than an Orlando Magic game? I won't have any trouble getting Mr. Wright to go, but do you think you can convince Dr. Marsh?"

"I think so. I'll call you tonight."

"You and your husband can come, too, and I'll bring my husband, Bill. She'll be heavily chaperoned."

When Rosetta returned to work after lunch, she had a few minutes to set up instruments for the next patient, and she took the opportunity to talk with her boss.

"Please don't think I'm meddling, because this wasn't my idea, but I think it's a good one."

"Rosetta, what are you talking about?"

"I went to lunch with Doreen today. You know, Mr. Wright's Doreen."

"So, you two are what, co-conspirators?"

"Yeah, something like that. And she says he's as miserable as you. And we thought that you two have to give each other another shot. And so we thought we should all go to the Orlando Magic game on Saturday night. What d'ya think?"

Lauren rolled her eyes, looked up at the ceiling, and then back down at Rosetta. "That was sneaky, and haven't you had a big turnaround."

"Well, I see how unhappy you are without him, and now that I know he's the Vampire Vigilante, I have a whole new slant on the guy. So, will you go? Doreen and her husband, Bill, and Manny and I will be there."

"All right, but don't leave me alone with him. I don't trust myself."

* * *

Lauren agonized over what to wear on Saturday night. Part of her wanted to look sexy, while the safe side lobbied for a full suit of armor. She settled on a peach sweater set, brown slacks, and brown loafers with a little heel. The shell allowed a bit of cleavage, but the cardigan was there to cover things up.

Her heart raced as the elevator in the Orlando Arena took her up to skybox level. She walked around the circular corridor until she found the door with the small "Wright" plaque. Should she knock? No. She opened the door to find Doreen, beer in hand, to greet her. "Hi, Lauren. You don't mind if I call you Lauren?"

"Please, yes, I want you to," Lauren said.

"Well, grab what you want to drink from the fridge. The tipoff's in five minutes."

Lauren stepped left into the skybox's small kitchen, big enough for a sink, a few cabinets, and a full-size refrigerator.

John was staring into the refrigerator and didn't turn immediately to greet her. "What can I get you?"

"A light beer would be nice." Lauren took a deep breath, waiting for John's impending turnaround.

"I'm looking for tomato juice," John said.

"Take your time." Lauren put one hand on the sink to brace herself.

John shut the refrigerator door and handed Lauren an Amstel Light.

"This isn't going to work," she said. Her knees buckled, and John stepped toward her.

"Perhaps this wasn't a good idea."

"No, I'm glad I came, but can we go somewhere private?"

"There's the bathroom. It's the door behind you."

Lauren turned around and took three steps from the tiny kitchen into the skybox's private bathroom. John followed her and closed the door.

Lauren sat on the bathroom vanity that stretched the length of one wall, while John leaned against the door. The toilet was behind a small partition.

"I've been thinking," Lauren started. "What's the process of becoming a vampire?"

"Do you want the clinical or emotional answer?"

"Both."

"Clinically, we have sex three times with the exchange of blood." John paused. "Emotionally, we become lifemates. Each time we make love, our passion will swell to a new height of physical and emotional wonder. By the third time we make love, Lauren, your orgasm will be so intense that each wave..."

Lauren put her hand to John's lips to stop his explanation. Just touching his lips sent shockwaves to her feminine core. "I get the picture."

He kissed the fingers that remained on his lips, and then took her hand and pressed it to his heart.

"Does it hurt the blood exchange?"

"No, it's euphoric. You'll feel a bit of pressure, and then warmth spreads from the wound to the tips of your toes and fingers."

"I imagined it to be sort of a roller-coaster ride."

"There's no nausea or lightheadedness, but it's intense. The pain comes after we make love, as your blood changes. If you decide to become one with me, I'll do everything in my power to minimize your pain."

"How painful is it?"

"It's excruciating, but thankfully, short-lived."

"What would happen if we just made love one time?"

John ran his fingers through his hair. "I've been able to hold myself in check because I haven't tasted you. Once we have the first blood exchange, I won't be able to stop, and you won't, either."

Lauren felt a flush rise from her chest to her cheeks. "What about my teeth? When would I get fangs?"

"Vampires can will their teeth to become fangs as they

need them."

"That's a relief." She thought for a minute. "How would I know what to do?"

"It's all instinctual. We don't spend time and energy contemplating our inadequacies like humans do. And Lauren?"

"Yes?"

"I won't deceive you." John's eyes glowed red as he continued. "There will be many changes in your life and no turning back. No more bright sunlight...ever. No more checking your appearance in a mirror. Your computer will malfunction and your watch will stop. Your taste for blood will be overpowering, as will your taste for me. But I promise you this; I will be yours until the end of time."

John held out his hand to Lauren. She took it, and he turned her to face the mirror. Though she could feel his strong arms around her, all she saw in the mirror was her own reflection.

"Love can't be found on the surface of a mirror. It's the contentment underneath." He reached behind his back to open the bathroom door and pulled her with him into the room where the foursome greeted them.

Though the noise from the arena was palpable, her fluttering heart wasn't due to the roar of frenzied fans.

CHAPTER FIVE

A week passed, and while Lauren agonized over her decision, she kept up with John's whereabouts through the newspaper and Rosetta's conversations with Doreen. She worried that someone would track him, find out where he lived, and turn up at his house one day with a stake and hatchet. She knew the chances were slim, what with his alarm system and Doreen's wariness, but she worried nonetheless. Organized crime had ways of disposing of bodies, or maybe she'd just watched too many episodes of "The Sopranos."

Then she received a call at home one Friday evening from Doreen.

"He's gone," Doreen said.

"What do you mean, he's gone?" Lauren jumped up from the couch, where she'd been channel surfing, and started pacing her living room. "Maybe he's just out on reconnaissance."

"No, he always comes home to sleep."

"Couldn't he be visiting relatives or something?"

Lauren realized it was a ridiculous question as soon as she asked it.

"He's never disappeared like this."

"Please tell him to call me as soon as he gets home." Lauren hung up the phone, picked up one of the throw pillows on her sofa and screamed into it.

She couldn't eat. She couldn't sleep. She lost five pounds. She took Smokey on long walks. She kept her cell phone glued to her side. What if the mob was onto him?

Nights were the worst. She sat on her patio, gazing at the stars, trying to will him home. *Come back to me.*

* * *

All Hallows by the Tower was as John remembered it. More moss and lichens adhered to the stones, but otherwise, the centuries had been kind. The carving on the headstones was as readable as the last time he'd visited, some 200 years earlier. Standing over Catherine's grave on this crisp November night, John tightened his cape around him to seal off the wind and read the familiar inscription.

Lady Catherine Anne Wright
Beloved Wife of Sir John Arthur Wright
Born 1510
Died 1535

"Hello, Catherine. I felt compelled to visit you, and I hope, as I always have, that you are at peace. Was it you who bequeathed I should love only dark-haired maidens with eyes the color of emeralds? I wonder if that is your revenge, for I dearly love one now, and I fear she will never be mine."

John placed a bouquet of yellow roses at the base of Catherine's headstone and knelt in silence as the wind played with his hair and rustled the petals of the bouquet. He could hear mice scurrying in the fallen leaves, the distant call of an owl, and smell the ever present decay that humans could not detect.

"The world has changed since you were here, and I think in many ways not for the better. Countries still war with each other, and we are unkind to those we should protect. But I still believe love can conquer all, and those devoted to justice will prevail. Most of all, Catherine, I hope you will forgive me for bringing you into my world. I expected so much. Sleep, now, my fragile lady."

From the mist, a low, sultry voice said, "Do you think she can hear you?"

John twirled around to face his former wife's partner-in-crime, Amy.

"My, my, my, the years have been good to you, John." Amy floated toward John and touched him lightly on the cheek.

He recoiled from her touch. "Given your debauchery, I'm surprised the years haven't been harder on *you*," he said.

"I'll take that as a compliment." Amy licked her red lips.

"Don't. Unless you can tell me you've amended your ways, you'll receive no compliments from me." John stared her down.

"Oh, John, I'd forgotten how noble you are. Frankly, it's a worthless trait. I much prefer taking my pleasure as it comes, whether in the form of an infant or a luscious teenager. I've acquired quite a collection of young admirers."

"I'm sure you have." John's lip curled in disgust. "Do they all vie for your attention?"

"Of course." Amy blew on her two-inch fingernails, sharp as stilettos. "And they're all just as nasty as me."

"With you as their teacher, I'd expect nothing else."

Amy threw her head back and laughed. "But you know, John," she lowered her glowing red eyes to him, "there's still one man I've always wanted to taste. One man who's eluded me for centuries." She took one step forward, closing the distance between them. "But then, do I want to taste you....or kill you?"

In one swift movement, John grabbed both her wrists in one hand. "I could kill you in an instant."

"But you won't." She challenged him, thrusting her tantalizing breasts toward him.

"No, I won't, though you deserve to die." Squeezing her wrists, he pushed her away from him.

Amy landed on the cold earth, between two gravestones. "What is it about you, John? Why do you insist on being good when it would be so easy to be evil?"

"For that very reason, Amy. Being good is difficult, sometimes extremely difficult, but knowing I have to live with myself through eternity makes it worth it."

"Funny how differently we look at life." She crouched, ready to spring.

John beckoned with his hand. "Come and get me."

She sprang. It was a well-calculated move and one John recognized. The idea was to let the victim assume the strike would be for the jugular. Protecting one's face would be the natural tendency, which exposed the lower trunk to attack. John knew Amy liked the large vein in men's groins. Besides, most men would be paralyzed by any attack in the vicinity of their family jewels, and by the time Amy clamped her hot lips next to their private parts, they'd be swooning with anticipated pleasure.

John wasn't like most men. Quicker and deadlier than Amy, he jerked away from her lunge, spun, secured both her arms behind her back and held her, immobile.

"Nice try, but I'm no novice." He tightened his grip.

She winced. "Since you've rendered me helpless, you might as well have your way with me."

"You're not my type, Amy. Your scent sickens me." John closed his eyes but didn't loosen his grip. "But then again, you *are* my ideal prey. You're unscrupulous, a menace to society. I'd feel no remorse."

John felt Amy stiffen.

"Here's my condition," John said. "I want an oath, signed in your blood, that you will no longer prey on the innocent."

"You know I can't do that." Amy's lips curled in a sinister smile as four young vampires materialized out of the mist, bearing their teeth, flanking Amy.

John could take two easily, but not four.

"Let me go, and we'll let you live," Amy said.

John backed away from the four encroaching vampires, far enough to fling their disgusting leader toward them and vaporize from the deadly scene.

He landed on one of the two pediments on Tower Bridge. From this perch, a panoramic view of London reminded him of how little the city had changed. Parliament still commanded the river. Had it been five hundred years since he stood in this same location, contemplating his fate? His encounter with Amy recalled his life with Catherine. How different Lauren was. Catherine's allure was a feigned innocence, but Lauren's innocence was real. There was no deceit in her.

Oh, Lauren. Please be mine.

John slept with the bats at Westminster Abbey and spent the next several nights visiting the haunts of his youth. Before he headed back to the states, he accessed the bank vault at Barclays and claimed his mother's emerald ring, as well as his christening gown.

* * *

"Scare the devil out of me next time," Doreen said.

"I left a note in my coffin." John rummaged in the folds of the purple velvet lining to find the note he'd written to Doreen. "Here it is. I asked you to tell Lauren not to worry."

"She's beside herself. Good grief, the whole city is up in arms. You'd better get back on the streets tonight!"

"I fully intend to, but first I'll call Lauren."

Lauren checked the caller I.D. and answered on the first ring. "Where've you been?"

"Good evening to you, too. I had some unfinished business in England."

"I couldn't sleep or eat."

"I'm sorry. I didn't intend to worry you."

Silence.

"I miss you," Lauren said.

"I miss you, too. I'd give up my immortality in a heartbeat to be with you, but there are no reversals of my misfortune. I can't become mortal for you. As much power as I have, you hold our future in your hands."

"It's all I think about."

"Good, but do me a favor. In those recesses of your heart where thinking can't reach, *feel it*, because I brought my christening gown back from England in the hope that a child of ours would wear it."

"I'm coming over."

Lauren drove too fast down the uneven brick road that led to John's Victorian house, bumping her head on the roof of her Miata in her rush to get there. Many of the old streets in town had been re-bricked, but this was one of the original 1800's roads and had once been the Victorian's private driveway. His house stood out, a white behemoth amidst Mediterranean villas, French manors and brick Colonials. She pulled into the circular drive, lined with boxwoods, remembering the home as it had been when she and her middle school friends considered it haunted. The paint was cracked and peeling in those days, and the attic was home to bats. Today, it shone with fresh paint, restored windows, and a new shingle roof. She'd always loved the turret. At age thirteen, on a dare, she'd climbed the winding stairway to its top where her reward was an expansive view of Lake Osceola. Now, like long ago, Lauren walked up the steps to the broad porch and double front doors, which were framed in Tiffany stained glass. The pattern was irises in the same deep violet as John's eyes.

John opened the door before she rang the doorbell. She thought he would pull her into his arms, but instead, he turned her around and led her to a white wicker chair on the porch. He took the chair opposite her and leaned forward. She saw him move to rest his hands on her knees, but he stopped, clenched his fists momentarily and placed his hands on the arms of the chair. She'd anticipated his warm touch through her cotton capris, and she was disappointed when he pulled back.

"Lauren, I know you came over to surrender, but I feel that I coerced you."

"No, you didn't coerce me. I've been hurting so much because I was trying not to love you, but I realized that if I put the hurt aside, what was left was real love."

"No, my darling. Listen. I know you want children, and I shouldn't have told you about the christening gown. I used something I knew to be true about you to influence you, and I can't make you mine under those pretenses."

"Do you know everything about me?"

"Not everything, but some of your history has come to me in dreams."

"Like what?"

"I know you were an only child. You had open heart surgery when you were three. I suspect your surgery is one of the reasons your scent is so intoxicating to me because your heart has been exposed. And, I know your parents died in a car crash when you were a teenager."

Tears welled in Lauren's eyes, and John said, "I'm sorry. I shouldn't have made you remember."

"It's been twelve years since my parents died, but it's still painful," she said, wiping her hand quickly across her eyes. "What if there are things I don't want you to know?"

"If you become a vampire, you can block the things you want to conceal."

"So, if we were married, and I wanted to know the sex of our unborn child, I could find out but still keep you guessing?"

"That would be unfair."

"I love you, John."

"I know, Lauren, but I won't make love to you tonight."

"How about a quick tour of the house?"

He looked at her under his eyelashes. "No. You're not ready to handle the animal in me."

"Are you trying to frighten me?"

"I mean it, Lauren. You need to leave...now. I have self-control, but there's a limit."

CHAPTER SIX

Three nights later, John stopped at home briefly after his first feed to send a quick message to the Orlando Police Department. He almost missed the note Doreen had left on the hall table: "Call Lauren."

Lauren answered on the second ring. "I'm glad I caught you."

"What's up?" John took a deep breath and waited for Lauren's reply.

Her tone sounded expectant, hopeful. "Are you heading back out?"

"Yes. Want me to stop by?"

"Please."

"I warn you, I'm a bit grubby."

Two minutes later, Lauren opened her front door to find John in black jersey shorts and a tight black t-shirt.

"That's your definition of grubby?" Her hand went to her heart.

The screen door separated them, and just as Lauren

moved to open it, John said, "Is there a latch on this door?"

"Yes," Lauren answered, a puzzled look on her face.

John squeezed his eyes shut. "Lock it."

"You want me to lock you out?"

"Yes, hurry." John spoke through clenched teeth.

Lauren flipped the latch shut.

"Now," John said, "don't move. You'll stir the air." He backed up four steps and planted his feet, shoulder width apart. He was breathing heavily. "You're bleeding," he said, finally. His red eyes glowed in a penetrating stare.

"No, I'm not," Lauren started, and then said, "Oh, you mean...my period?"

"Yes." John squeezed his eyes shut. "Your already delectable scent is even more so. Just don't move."

"I locked the door." Lauren squeaked.

"Like that would stop me." John took several deep breaths. "I could be inside you with my teeth in your neck before you had a chance to gasp." He pinched the bridge of his nose between his fingers. "I need a distraction... Sing something...stupid."

Both of them stood, frozen in time, and then Lauren began, "She wore an itsy-bitsy-teenie-weenie, yellow polka dot bikini..."

"Good, keep going," John said.

"...that she wore for the first time today. An itsy-bitsy-teenie-weenie, yellow polka dot bikini, and in the locker she wanted to stay."

John unclenched his fists, though he didn't move.

"Better?" Lauren asked.

"Much, thanks."

"I guess that means that if we were married, you wouldn't consider my period off limits for sex?"

"Hardly."

"Are you going to stand there in my front yard all night?"

"It's not safe for me to be close to you. Why did you

want to see me?"

Lauren hesitated, and then asked, "Would our children be immortal?"

John smiled. "Yes, Lauren. Vampires beget vampires."

"There's something oddly comforting about that," she said.

John blew her a kiss and disappeared into the night.

* * *

Lauren had a full workload through the week, which helped keep her mind occupied. Every minute she wasn't with a patient brought her back to her last encounter with John. He was a vampire, yet he was the most moral being she'd ever met. One thing was clear. She loved him.

She unloaded her woes on her friend, Meredith, over lunch. "He's just so unusual. I'm not sure I could adjust to his quirky lifestyle." Quirky didn't begin to explain, but Lauren wasn't about to tell Meredith the whole truth.

"What you need is a distraction," Meredith said. "I think I have a major hunk to fit the bill."

"No, not another of your blind dates."

"This guy's different."

"They've all been different, Mere. There was the accountant who wanted to do my tax return, the actor who tried to sing to me at dinner, and please, no more lawyers."

"You'll love this guy. I swear. He's a landscape architect. You know, into the soil and all."

"I'm not up for it," Lauren said, "but one more night of obedience training with Smokey isn't appealing, either."

"Excellent. You won't be sorry."

Truth was, Eddie Manning was kind of cute. Years of the Florida sunshine had caramelized his skin into a rich bronze, and his sandy hair was sun-bleached and untrainable in an attractive sort of way. His blue eyes sparkled, revealing premature crow's feet. Why was the same thing that would send a woman to a plastic surgeon appealing in a man?

They met on neutral ground, the rose garden in Central Park, close to Meredith's dress shop. Warm and genuine, he extended his hand to Lauren. "Very nice to meet you." He smiled, displaying straight, and very human, teeth. "I thought we'd try the new Asian fusion restaurant on Park Avenue. Sound good to you?"

Throughout dinner, Eddie regaled Lauren with stories of his landscape expertise. It would have been boring, but the tales of his topiary work at a local tourist attraction were pretty amusing.

"Would you believe you could fashion an elephant from a podocarpus?" His eyebrows flew up with his question.

Lauren was actually starting to enjoy the evening. Into her second glass of wine, she relaxed into listening to his stories and even laughing at appropriate moments. She wasn't into sharing anything about herself. The last time she'd done that...

"Why so suddenly serious?" he asked.

"Sorry," she said, "it's nothing you said. I just have a lot on my mind."

"You were displaying that gorgeous dimple, and then your smile faded."

"Just a momentary thought about a patient." Lauren smiled again.

"That dimple is very enticing."

Lauren considered the handsome face across the table and wondered what kissing him would be like. She supposed a point of comparison couldn't hurt, and then the thought depressed her. She didn't need to compare; she already knew no one could kiss like John.

"Oops, that dimple disappeared again." He frowned.

As the waiter cleared the dinner plates, Eddie said, "How about a walk around the park?"

"Sure," Lauren said.

The air was unseasonably warm for early November as

the couple strolled to the Emily Fountain. Gazing at their reflections in the clear water, Eddie said, "There's something I wanted to ask you." He hesitated. "Would you be interested in trading services?"

"Excuse me?"

"Well, I'm in need of a root canal, and I've got two beautiful ligustrum trees that could frame a front door."

Was he serious? Lauren extended her hand. "I have an early appointment tomorrow morning, and I really should be going. Thanks for dinner." She turned on her heel.

"Did I offend you?" Eddie called to her retreating figure.

"No," she said, over her shoulder, and then she turned, now about ten feet from him. "You just brought to mind the big difference between seeing someone for what they do versus who they are. I should thank you. I *do* thank you." She strode to her car, not one bit interested in looking back to check his reaction.

Crossing Morse Boulevard into the second block of the park, the screech of tires turned her attention to two cars in the parking lot of the old post office building across the railroad tracks.

With the retail shops and businesses long closed and restaurant business along the avenue winding down on this slow Wednesday, Lauren was the only spectator as men emerged from the two cars, and one pulled a gun. She shrank behind a hedge for cover, not willing to risk the consequences of witnessing this scene. She grabbed the cell phone from her purse and quickly dialed 911 for the Winter Park Police Department. She easily described the exact location and took their advice to stay under cover. They were on their way.

Lauren shivered as one man struck the other with his gun barrel, and then an accomplice in the car began firing. Lauren checked the second hand on her watch, hoping the response time would match the two minutes the city prided itself on. Suddenly, something dark and ominous flew onto the scene, catching the assailants off guard. Guns from both cars began firing at what looked like a big black cape. Lauren clamped her hand over her mouth as she realized it was John. He moved silently to disarm the men, throwing the two who were outside the car onto the pavement, which knocked them unconscious. He swiftly extracted the remaining two men from each car. One man fired his gun point blank at John, who swatted the gun away, wrenched the man's neck, and sunk his teeth in. The other man threw his arms up in surrender. A small whimper from the backseat of the second car alerted John to a little girl huddled against the car door, her eyes buried in a big Teddy bear. He gently gathered her into his arms just as two police cars careened onto the scene. Kissing her head, he whispered to her, and then set her down to run to the policeman who was getting out of his car. Saluting the police, John leaped into a nearby tree, and then fluttered away as a bat.

Lauren's heart was racing as she tried to process the scene she'd just witnessed. So that's what he does. Amazing.

CHAPTER SEVEN

On Thursday afternoon, preparing for her two o'clock appointment, Lauren heard Rosetta murmur a weak "Help" from behind the lab door.

She rushed in to find her trembling assistant standing in a puddle of water and clutching her huge belly.

"Oh my gosh, you're in labor," Lauren said.

"Tell me something I don't know," Rosetta said, wincing.

"Have you timed your contractions?"

"This is different from the last five times. I was fine, had my usual enormous lunch, was just lining up instruments for the afternoon, and BOOM! It feels like one big contraction. I don't know if I can make it to the hospital."

Lauren took Rosetta's elbows and gently walked her to the one chair in the room. "Don't move. I'll call the ambulance."

"*Presura!*"

"Yes, I'll hurry."

After Lauren called 911, she had Elaine re-schedule her

afternoon appointments. The ambulance arrived in three minutes and loaded a moaning Rosetta. Lauren rode with her to Florida Hospital's Emergency Room. She alerted Rosetta's obstetrician on the way, and he met them in the E.R.

At two-o-seven on Thursday, November 12, Emmanuel Jose Gonzalez entered the world on a gurney enroute to the delivery room. Lauren held Rosetta's hand, and the doctor caught the baby, practically in mid-air. As little Emmanuel was cleaned up and placed in his mother's arms, Lauren and Rosetta cried together.

"Why you cryin'?" Rosetta teased. "I did all the work."

"I've never been this close to a miracle." Lauren dabbed at her eyes with a box of hospital tissue.

"Oh, honey, your day will come."

Manny and the rest of the Rodriguez brood bounded into Rosetta's room with a box of chocolates and flowers from the hospital's gift shop. He took one look at his new son, gathered him in his arms, and said, "Welcome to the world, Speedy Gonzalez!"

* * *

Lauren stayed at the hospital until six o'clock, when Rosetta's parents arrived from Miami. She drove home, exhausted yet exhilarated, took Smokey out for a brief watering, and then collapsed on her couch. There was one person she was dying to share her day with.

"Lauren." John answered his phone.

"Rosetta had her baby...a little boy...Emmanuel Jose Gonzalez...he's adorable." The words spilled from her.

John laughed. "I want the whole story."

"One minute she was in the office, preparing for our next patient, and the next minute we were in the ambulance. I thought she'd have the baby on the way to the hospital. I'm still in a state of shock." Lauren started to tear up again. Happy tears. "It was amazing...a miracle."

"Yes, babies are."

"He's beautiful."

"Can I see him?"

"She'll probably go home with him on Saturday. I thought I'd take dinner over on Sunday. Want to go with me?"

"Absolutely."

"Is six o'clock too early?"

"No, I'm getting used to daylight hours, little by little."

"Great, I'll pick you up. I...I've missed you."

* * *

Lauren cooked all day on Sunday. She wasn't skilled at Mexican cuisine, but she wanted to make something the whole family would eat and figured ethnic was best. Amidst the pots of simmering beef and chicken, and the aroma of corn tortillas and guacamole whirring in the blender, Smokey's nostrils were perpetually flared.

"How about a Mexican hat dance?" she asked her Chihuahua.

When she'd finished the preparations, she took a long shower, shaved her legs, and then dressed in a turquoise peasant skirt and blouse that she finished with a chain belt and dangly earrings. She was feeling reckless, so no bra. She gathered her thick hair in a clip, with tendrils framing her face. She wore yellow sandals, with her red toenails in plain view.

She'd bought a donkey piñata for the kids to keep them busy and provide some adult time for Rosetta and Manny, and she included a big bottle of Jose Cuervo Gold Tequila as the piece de resistance.

Pulling into John's driveway at exactly six o'clock, she didn't need to honk. He was waiting for her on his front porch with two wrapped packages in his arms.

"What you got?" she asked, leaning over to the passenger side to open his door. She was glad she didn't have to get out of the car. The sight of him in a black linen shirt, open at the collar, and tight jeans was something one should be seated for.

"I found something unique for the baby on the Internet and had it overnighted," he said. "The other gift is from Doreen. Whatever it is, she said it's an absolute necessity."

"Want the top down?" she asked.

"Yes. The wind will help dissipate your scent, which is particularly alluring tonight."

Lauren unlatched the two clamps to her car's convertible top, reaching across John to access the clamp above the passenger seat. Her breast brushed his shoulder, and she bit her lip to stay in check.

"Unless you're ready for me, you're going to need to keep your distance," he warned.

"Sorry. I'm not trying to make this any more stressful than it already is."

"Really? In that sexy outfit? Could have fooled me."

Lauren took a deep breath. "You're right, and I'm sorry." She touched John's arm, but he put her hand back on the steering wheel.

"Lauren, do you understand that if I wanted to take you, you'd have no recourse. You may think you could kick and scream, but I'm lethal."

"Maybe that's what I want...for you to take away my choice."

"Never...ever...say that again." John glanced in the back seat of the Miata and grabbed Lauren's gym bag, which he rifled through, extracting a white sports bra. He crumbled it in his hand and dropped it in Lauren's lap. "Put it on. The sight of you bouncing around bra-less is dangerous."

John looked out the window at the Florida sky, preparing for a spectacular sunset. Twilight had just triggered the lights of the antique street lamps as they rode the remaining distance to Rosetta's house in silence.

They parked at the curb since Rosetta's driveway was

littered with children's bicycles and Little Tykes' cars. They made several trips to unload the food and gifts. On the final trip, to the delight of Manny and Rosetta's shrieking children, John brought the piñata. Lauren put her convertible top back up, and then hurried to the kitchen to assemble four margaritas, one virgin style for nursing Rosetta. The adults led the children to the backyard where Manny hung the piñata from a large Magnolia tree. He brought four plastic baseball bats from the garage and handed them to John to disperse to the children.

Four-year-old Theresa was allowed to take the first swing, which had no effect on the purple, yellow and green donkey. John put his hands over hers, and the second swing landed a blow to the donkey's abdomen, spewing the first rush of candy on the grass. From there, it was a free-for-all as Ten-year-old Alberto, eight-year-old Selma, and six-year-old Fernando swung vigorously at the piñata to expel every piece of candy. Lauren held a clapping and wiggling Delora, who was almost two. After the first rush of excitement, she handed Delora off to John, and she and Rosetta went back to the kitchen. Baby Emmanuel had just awakened, and Rosetta brought him into the kitchen to nurse while Lauren set out the plates of food.

"Look at him with the kids." Lauren observed John from the window above the kitchen sink. Led by John, the kids sorted their candy on the picnic table according to the color of the candy wrappers. Lauren could hear John quizzing the children on their colors in English and Spanish and congratulating them on their performance.

"He'll be a good father," Rosetta said.

Lauren continued to watch him. "I didn't even know he could speak Spanish."

"He's full of surprises," Rosetta said. "Think how interesting your life will be."

"You say that as if it's a foregone conclusion."

"Isn't it?"

"Almost." Lauren's nipples hardened as she considered, for the thousandth time, an eternity with John.

"I sure wouldn't let him go." Rosetta rocked her satiated baby, whose eyelids were growing heavy.

"Know something, Rosetta? You're absolutely right."

Lauren found brown paper lunch bags, wrote each child's name on a bag, and took them out to the backyard. She'd intended to put the bra on, per John's instructions, but that wouldn't be necessary now. While Manny returned the baseball bats to the garage, and the children scooped their candy into their bags, Lauren slipped her hand into John's and squeezed it.

As he looked down at her, she said, "I'm sure."

He gathered her in his arms and kissed her hair. "Was it my command of Spanish?"

"No, it was that sexy donkey."

"Right." He traced his finger around her lips, and then brushed his thumb over her erect nipple. "Later."

They re-joined Manny and Rosetta in the kitchen, where John excused himself from the meal. "I'll be back in an hour or so," he said to Rosetta, and then he was gone.

"That disappearing act could take some getting used to," Rosetta said.

"It has its advantages. I'll spend less time in the kitchen."

"You have a point."

They fed the children first, and then took their plates to the round dining room table where Lauren had created a buffet. After dinner, Manny tended to the children's baths and pajamas, while Lauren and Rosetta cleaned up the kitchen.

John returned at nine o'clock, materializing on the living room couch just in time for the presents. Lauren thought he looked particularly fit, though he sneezed a few times.

"Sorry," he said. "Something must be blooming out

there."

Rosetta opened John's present first. Looking into the box at the collapsed mobile, she withdrew it slowly to reveal rows of flying bats with blue ribbons around their necks.

"I made sure I had the boys' version," John said. "Crank it up."

Rosetta turned the key on the mobile's music box, and a chorus of "Bring Back the Bat" played.

"Too cute," Rosetta said. "Thanks so much." She untied the hot pink ribbon on Doreen's gift.

"She obviously didn't observe the 'blue for boys' rule," Lauren said.

"Doreen has her own rules for everything," John said.

Rosetta's hands emerged from the box with a breast pump in one hand and a sexy Victoria's Secret teddy in the other. "I don't have to ask which comes first."

They all laughed, and then John said, "It's getting late."

Lauren retrieved her purse from a chair in the kitchen, and as she and John walked to the door, Rosetta slipped the teddy in Lauren's purse. "You'll need this sooner than I will," she whispered.

Driving away, Lauren asked, "Your house or mine?"

"Smokey could be a distraction," John said.

"I'm beyond distraction, but let's go to your house."

"Good. No doubts then?"

"No, not one." Lauren sped up a bit. "I need to stop home for a minute and let Smokey out, though. I'll come back tomorrow morning to dress for work."

"Sounds like a plan."

John waited in the car while Lauren tended to Smokey. She also picked up her toothbrush, toothpaste, and a few other personal toiletries.

He put in a quick call to Doreen.

"What's up?" she answered.

"Are there sheets on my bed?"

"Woo-hoo! You bet...lilac satin ones. And there are silk boxers in the top drawer of your dresser."

"Thanks, Doreen. I owe you one."

"One? I've lost count of how many you owe me. Oh, and...ah, hell...I'll just come out with it...there are condoms in the nightstand, ribbed for extra pleasure."

"Don't you think that's a bit personal?"

"When have I ever worried about getting personal?"

"True. And Doreen, I may not have had sex for a long time, but I'm aware of twenty-first century contraception."

"Okay, Mr. Boy Scout."

CHAPTER EIGHT

Lauren drove the speed limit on the way to John's house. She figured this wouldn't be a good time to get a ticket.

John punched in the code to his alarm system on a key pad outside the front door, and they entered the massive foyer.

"I believe this is where I ask if you need a few minutes to get ready?"

"Hmm, sounds like a line from a romance novel, but yes, where can I change?"

"My bedroom and bath are up the stairs. First door on the left."

Lauren walked slowly up the winding staircase, taking in the family portraits of Wrights that lined the stairwell. His bedroom smelled faintly of vanilla and lavender. The furniture was heavy and ornately carved, and the huge canopy bed faced a Palladian window with a view of the garden. There were fresh irises in a Waterford vase on the nightstand. She turned on a small lamp, catching her reflection in the mirror above the dresser. She thought briefly about the coming changes. Her heart was beating fast, but it wasn't from fear. She'd made the right decision. She was sure.

She changed in the bathroom. The teddy was a perfect fit: black, with tiny pink rosebuds framing the plunging neckline and hi-cut legs set off by lace. A thin pink ribbon crisscrossed the bodice, creating a corset effect. She'd never owned anything even remotely like it.

John was waiting for her. "Come...here."

He'd already turned down the bed, and as she walked toward him, he unbuttoned his shirt, and then lighted a lavender scented candle on the nightstand. "Doreen didn't miss a beat," he said, pointing at the candle.

He unzipped his jeans, stepped out of them in one fluid motion, and stood before her in black bikini briefs, his erection prominent.

He took her hand and placed it on his chest. She felt his pulsating warmth and let her hand drift down to his rippled stomach muscles. His breath was calm, regular and very deep, like a big slumbering tiger, only he wasn't asleep. She slipped her hands under the elastic of his briefs and eased them over his erection and off his tight butt.

"Lest I assume too much, will you marry me?" His eyes glowed red.

"Read my mind," Lauren said.

He swept her into his arms, this gossamer angel in a devilish teddy, and placed her gently on the bed, fluffing the pillow behind her head.

"Don't be afraid, Lauren. This will be intense, and you'll feel the animal in me, but I won't hurt you."

He hovered above her, allowing his erection to tease her thighs. Gently, he lowered himself to her, kissing her open lips, performing a dance with his tongue as he explored her mouth. He pulled back then and lowered his head to her breasts, easing the straps off her teddy as he took each breast in turn into his mouth, suckling until she moaned with desire.

A deep growling began to roll from John's chest, and he

pulled Lauren's teddy down her body and flung it from the bed. He opened the small drawer of his nightstand and took out a condom, which she took from him, opened the wrapper with her teeth, and slowly unrolled on his erection. Kneeling between her legs, he massaged her thighs and teased her feminine core with his thumbs. He lowered his head to her and rhythmically licked her aroused bud. She arched her back, and he bent her knees up to his chest, slowly spreading her legs. He threw his head back as he entered her, and then he eased his hand behind her head, tipping her chin gently to the left. In one swift movement, he sank his fangs into her neck, and the intimacy of his action spread to her core. She had the weightless sensation of floating in tingling warmth. With the overpowering rhythm of his thrusts, she surrendered to his animal. Her climax overtook her as he plunged deeper into her sheath and held her neck in his mouth. When the waves of her climax subsided, he sealed the small puncture wounds with his tongue, and then slowly eased out of her.

He brushed her cheek with the back of his fingers, and then kissed her temple. "Do you thirst, my love?" he asked.

"Yes, extremely."

"Then take me as I took you."

He turned her to her stomach, propping a pillow under her hips. He brought his wrist to his mouth, bit into his flesh and offered his wrist to her. She grabbed the back of his hand and clamped her mouth over the wounds he'd created. He wrapped his other arm around her waist and entered her from behind, pumping into the depths of her. He came with the knowledge that his blood and his abiding love now coursed through the woman he would love for eternity.

He rolled onto his back and pulled her on top of him, holding her close.

"And you tell me it gets better? I find that hard to believe." Lauren rested her cheek on his broad chest.

"Hard is the operative word, and yes, it gets better."

He carried her to the second-story porch, which

overlooked the lake, and rocked her as the pain of their blood mingling hit her. She clung to him, and he held her close, whispering in her ear, "My love, my forever love."

* * *

A December wedding in Florida meant poinsettias, and lots of them. Doreen lined the walk leading from the house to the gazebo with the brilliant flowers, which she'd alternated in shades of red, pink, and white. She wasn't oblivious to the fact they were hypoallergenic.

At twilight, a radiant Lauren dressed in candlelight satin walked toward John on rosebuds scattered by Doreen's youngest granddaughter, Kelsey, and Rosetta's Selma. The girls beamed in their pink velvet, while Selma's brother, Fernando, endured the indignity of being ring bearer.

John took his mother's emerald ring and slipped it on Lauren's finger, and then bent to kiss her. Her beautiful green eyes glowed red and a low growl rose from deep within her.

~~~~

FANG SHUI

CHAPTER ONE

John brushed his lips across my neck and whispered in my ear. "She wouldn't dare show up on our wedding day."

"After the note I got this morning, I wouldn't put anything past her." I chewed on the inside of my cheek.

The "she" in question was Amy Rothbart, partner-in-crime to my husband's deceased first wife, Catherine. Amy was wreaking havoc in London, assembling a posse of new, young vampires. In fact, Amy being in London was the reason we would be honeymooning in Italy, rather than England.

"Lauren, you have nothing to worry about." John tucked an errant curl behind my ear. "She's dangerous in London where she can orchestrate her thugs, but she can't touch us here in Orlando. Her vampire boy-toys are too young and inexperienced to function outside their home turf."

"And you've got your own newbie to take care of." My hand slid from around his waist to squeeze his tight butt, and I displayed a flash of fang.

His eyebrows shot up. "Be careful, there are humans present."

"Ah, but these humans are enlightened." I was referring to my dental hygienist and good friend, Rosetta Gonzalez, and John's personal assistant, Doreen Adkins. Rosetta and Doreen had played Cupid on more than one occasion for John and me. Today, they were here in full force with spouses, children, and grandchildren in tow. I smiled at my extended family; all gathered in the backyard of John's, and now my, Victorian home. I felt loved and supported, and as a new vampire, I needed all the reinforcement I could get.

On this most perfect day, however, the note from Amy was threatening my happiness. Arriving via certified mail, it read: *This is a warning. Watch your back. When you least expect it, I'll be at your throat, and even John won't be able to save you. Have a nice day! Amy*

Nice day, my ass. My lips curled in a pout.

"That is not allowed." My new husband seemed to intuit my mood. "When we get back from our honeymoon, I'll take care of Amy, once and for all." He wrapped his strong arms around me from behind and rested his chin on my head.

I leaned into him. "I can't help it. I've never been threatened before."

"Surely you've had a patient who was less than happy with your handiwork at some time in your illustrious career," John teased.

"Dentistry isn't on the list of high-risk professions." As I thought about it, I had to admit, "I did have a woman once who was disappointed her root canal didn't come with a face lift."

John laughed. "I believe it's been five minutes since I told you I loved you."

"Why don't you show me?"

John turned me to face him. He twisted a tendril of my hair between his fingers and gently tugged to bring my face up to his. Kissing my forehead, he then traced his lips from my ear to my jaw. He blew his intoxicating breath across my eyelids, and I closed my eyes as his arm circled my waist. He splayed his hand on my lower back, tipping my pelvis to the most erotic location on his anatomy. I parted my lips in response, and he drew my bottom lip into his mouth to suckle briefly before closing his sensuous lips on mine. He explored my mouth with his tongue while his hand caressed the back of my neck. I lost all sense of place and time in his kiss, and then everything went black.

I opened my eyes to find my head in John's lap. "I fainted again, didn't I?"

"I'll always be here to catch you. Just breathe, Lauren."

I took several deep breaths and pressed my hand to my racing heart. "Jeez, I think I swoon more now as a vampire than I did when I was human. I'm hopeless."

"No, you're extraordinary, and I adore you." John took my hand from my heart and kissed each fingertip.

Doreen shook her head and tapped her watch. "Too much of that, and you'll miss your plane." She crossed her arms and peered down at me.

John's wacky assistant had outdone herself with preparations for the wedding. She'd lined the stone walk from the house to the gazebo with poinsettias in pink, red, and white. A harpist played Debussy in the gazebo for the ceremony, and the cuisine included iced jumbo shrimp and stone crab claws flown in from Joe's Stone Crab in Miami.

And then she moved on to her personal decor. She replaced the bar stud in her eyebrow with a diamond, dyed her spiked hair purple to match her lavender "best man" dress, and sported tiny wedding cakes painted on each of her ten fake fingernails. "Seriously," she reiterated, "you guys need to get moving."

John eased me to standing. "Knees still wobbly?" he asked.

"No, I'm fine. I'm getting hungry, though." As a new vampire, my taste for blood was insatiable.

John chuckled. "There's a carafe on the bedside table." He pulled me close. "You'll need your strength for the honeymoon." Since my transformation to vampire, John had been double feeding on his crime-stopping rounds, and then returning home to feed me. He'd become aroused when I bit into his neck, but he'd hold himself in check until I'd fed. I was concerned that I was taking too much blood, but John said not to worry. "I won't let you kill me," he teased. Until I was fully trained, which he promised would be his first priority following our honeymoon; he wasn't comfortable having me on the streets tracking down criminals with him.

I kissed him quickly on the cheek and headed for the bedroom to change out of my wedding gown. Rosetta, my perfect maid-of-honor, accompanied me. Not only did I love her like a sister, but she'd been through so many weddings with her huge family that she had the details down pat, including owning a tool for unbuttoning the fifty buttons down the back of my gown.

I shivered as I stepped out of my beautiful gown and stood in only my lace chemise.

"You cold, Honey?" Rosetta asked.

"No." I bit my lip. "I can't stop thinking about Amy's note."

Rosetta patted my arm. "You think that big hunk of a husband would ever let anything happen to you? He's like having an Uzi and an armored tank at your fingertips. And what about you? Don't you have some of those special vampire abilities?"

"There's a learning curve. I feel stronger, but I don't know how to use my powers yet. Amy's been a vampire for half a millennia. She's lethal." I walked to the large Palladian window that overlooked the backyard. John, resplendent in his form-fitting tuxedo, had organized Rosetta's children in a relay race. My little Chihuahua, Smokey, was trying to keep up. The sunset over Lake Osceola provided just enough light for the spirited children, who'd been amazingly well-behaved throughout the ceremony. Even Rosetta's son Fernando, the ring bearer, hadn't fidgeted. Rosetta joined me at the window and put her arm around my waist.

"Amy couldn't possibly be as strong as John," Rosetta said.

"Not one-on-one, but she's assembling an army. She's afraid of John. He killed Catherine because she was preying on children, and Amy was Catherine's apprentice. She wants to avenge Catherine by eliminating me."

"I can't picture John killing his wife," Rosetta said.

I closed my eyes, recalling his deep pain when he told me the story. "It was horrible for him, but she was so evil. She'd steal a baby from his mother's arms. She devastated whole families throughout London, and now Amy's on the same rampage."

Rosetta shuddered--she had six children of her own-- and then she nodded out the window at John. "Honey, I still don't think you have anything to worry about. You've got the 'Vampire Vigilante' on your side."

My husband had earned his moniker from *The Orlando Sentinel* for his campaign to rid Orlando of violent crime. We'd made a pact that when we married, we'd meet halfway. He'd live a more traditional human existence, and I'd learn how to disarm criminals and go straight for the jugular. I figured it was a fair compromise. He was acclimating to daylight hours and studying for the Florida Bar Exam, refreshing the legal skills he'd honed five hundred years earlier as a barrister for King Henry VIII, and I was trying to control my energy field so the washing machine wouldn't lurch into spin cycle every time I entered the laundry room. I was also gearing up to leap from tall buildings without crashing onto the pavement. My education was a bit more treacherous than his, but my vampire body was much sturdier than the soft human one I'd lived in the first thirty years of my life. My recently-acquired durability gave new meaning to the physicality of sex. John was tender and loving, but he could also ravage me in ways my human body could never have withstood. Yum.

Again, I shivered, but this time it was in anticipation of our honeymoon.

* * *

The flight from Orlando to New York's JFK was on schedule and uneventful. Our Air France flight was delayed by several hours, but the impeccable service on this premier airline made up for the delay. There were only three other passengers in first class. We toasted each other with champagne, though we barely sipped it. Now that blood was my preferred drink, everything else paled in comparison.

"Ever heard of the Mile-High Club?" I asked my new husband.

"Yes, I have, and you've got to be kidding me."

"We could get a jump on Venice," I suggested, squeezing his taut bicep.

"Mrs. Wright, I'm shocked." His eyebrows flew up in what I assumed was mock horror.

"I bet the bathrooms in first class are big enough for two." I fluttered my eyelashes.

"I don't want the memory of our first wedded lovemaking to be the washroom on an airplane." He didn't ditto my fluttering.

"You have a point." I slid down a few inches in my seat. "I'll retract my horns."

John laughed and touched my cheek. "Let's save the ravaging for our room at the Londra Palace." He turned and squared his broad shoulders toward me. "I hope you know how important it is to me that everything be right...this time."

"Are you worried for one millisecond that I'll turn out like Catherine?" I was incredulous.

"No, my darling." John took my hand and massaged my palm. "You could never be evil, but I didn't pay attention with Catherine."

"Sorry, I'm not following."

"Catherine's desires overwhelmed her. She had no self-control."

Okay, now I had to laugh. "Are you equating my desire for you to her penchant for eating children?"

"Only in terms of self-control." He looked at me from under his eyelashes.

"All right, I'll show you self-control." I folded my arms across my chest and stared out the airplane window at the cloudless sky.

"Now you're being childish." He pinched my cheek.

"You *are* five hundred years older than me."

"Darling, I know this is difficult for you. You've been a thinking, feeling being, and now you have to reconcile what you think and feel with instincts that are beyond the realm of the human." John took my chin in his hand and locked eyes with me. "For instance, your eyes are glowing very red now, and you're going to need to control that."

"I feel like a bunny who knows exactly where a very large carrot is hidden."

John laughed. "Interesting analogy, but a cucumber would be more appropriate."

I slumped in my seat and covered my eyes with my hand.

"I'm sorry, Lauren. I've forgotten what it was like to be new. Your cravings go with the territory, but can I tell you something?"

I peeked through my fingers, conscious that the stewardess might notice my illuminated eyes. "What?"

"I saw this coming."

I straightened up in my seat. "How?"

"Well, that state-of-the-art vibrator was a clue. Frankly, I hope the real thing hasn't been a disappointment. In spite of my considerable powers, I can't thrust, tickle, and spin at the same time."

I let loose an embarrassed chuckle. "How did you know about my vibrator?"

"Smokey was digging for something between the couch cushions one evening. Imagine my surprise when I thought I'd be retrieving a dog toy and found your toy, instead."

I groaned and felt myself blush.

"Don't be embarrassed. Dealing with your libido was a challenge I looked forward to."

"So you knew I was going to become a raving animal?"

John chuckled. "I knew your focus would be on me and our union, not on roaming the streets looking for young blood."

"Like Catherine?"

John closed his eyes. "Yes."

"Weren't you taking a chance with me?"

"No." He didn't hesitate to answer. "I've learned a lot about human nature over the years, and I knew when we met that your character was moral and strong. Your libido, on the other hand..."

"I know...needs some restraint." I pursed my lips.

"Well, not *too* much restraint." He reached over, unlatched my seat belt, and pulled me onto his lap.

"You know, if we asked for a blanket, I could hike up my skirt and..."

"Lauren, behave. We're almost in Paris." He wrapped his arms around me and tucked my head under his chin. I settled into my husband's broad chest, but I was too turned on to get comfortable.

The pilot announced preparation for landing, and the stewardess in first class readied the galley. John returned me to my seat.

With the delay in New York, we missed our connection from Orly Airport to Venice. We sipped on champagne in the airport bar, and then I found the ladies' restroom to freshen up before the next flight.

As a new vampire, I was still getting accustomed to not having a reflection in the mirror. I was alone in the bathroom, which was convenient since I didn't want to freak out anyone who might be standing at the sink. I brushed my teeth and reapplied my lipstick before I heard the door open.

"Hello, Lauren." The voice was smooth as silk.

I looked in the mirror but saw no one behind me. Then it hit me.

I turned to face my adversary. "Hello, Amy."

DCL Publications, LLC

CHAPTER TWO

There she stood, in all her blonde glory, five feet from me. She wore a chartreuse spandex jumpsuit with a wide Louis Vuitton belt cinching her tiny waist. She probably had a good three inches on my five-foot, six-inch frame.

She laughed and took one step forward. "Well, this was easy. Won't your husband be surprised when you don't return? He'll think you got cold feet and bolted."

I backed away as far as I could, which was one step into the sink behind me. "Let's talk about this."

Amy touched her chin with a stiletto fingernail. "Sorry, I'm too hungry to talk." She bared her teeth, displaying an inlaid diamond on one lethal incisor.

"Why kill me? Need any dental work done? How about a root canal? Anything else I can do for you?" I was really grasping at straws here.

"Well, you could give me John, but somehow I don't think he'd comply. I am curious, though. Catherine used to rave about what a great fuck he was. How would you score him?"

Stall…stall…stall. She could kill me in an instant.

"Come on, sweetheart. Out with it." She examined her fingernails, which seemed to grow as she contemplated them. "I stationed the 'Restroom Closed' sign at the door, but I don't have all day."

"You're the last person I'd share intimate details with."

Amy laughed. "At least tell me how big his dick is."

I'd been a vampire for one month, and intimidation was not a skill I'd acquired yet. I'd just have to fake it. "I guess size would be important to you. Rumor has it that the cavern between your legs is even bigger than the one between your ears."

Amy bristled, as I'd hoped she would. "Aren't you tough?" She began to pace like a cat in her black Diesel sneakers, closing the distance between us. She stopped, close enough to claw my face. "You bear a striking resemblance to Catherine. John always was a sucker for green-eyed brunettes. It will almost be a shame to ruin that beautiful mug."

I couldn't fight her. She was much too skilled in vampire tactics. If I could just catch her off guard.

"*Attends!*" A voice yelled from outside the door. My French was shaky, but I got the gist of what the deep voice said, which went something like, "You're not scheduled to clean this bathroom for another hour."

I didn't hesitate. As Amy turned her head to the door, I ducked left and screamed.

She directed a loathsome glance at me for one brief moment, and then she was gone. In the wisp of chartreuse mist she left in her wake, I heard her say, "You're toast."

The attendant rushed in to find me huddled in the corner, clutching my purse and shaking.

"*Etes-vous d'accord?*"

"*Oui.* I thought I saw a rat."

He laughed. His English was obviously better than my French. Tipping his official-looking DeGaulle hat, he offered a hand to pull me up. I accepted his assistance and noted the name on his badge, Claude Bisson.

"*Merci beaucoup, Monsieur Bisson*," I said.

"*Mon plaisir, madame.*"

He steadied me as I regained my composure and wobbled from the bathroom.

I found John in a black leather Barcelona chair, reading *Le Monde*. As acute as his senses were, he'd totally missed the appearance of Amy.

"In another minute, I was going to begin a search," he said, casually. "What took so long?" Then he looked at my ashen face. "Darling, what's wrong?"

"Amy." I squeaked.

"Here?" John jumped up from his chair and grabbed my shoulders.

"She's gone now." I trembled.

John pulled me close and buried his face in my hair. "I am so, so sorry." He eased me into a chair and sat across from me, taking my shaking hands in his.

"I've been an idiot." John said. "I knew Amy was the master of surprise, and I should never have let my guard down. My God, I could have lost you." Now, John was the one who trembled.

"No, John, how would you ever guess she'd accost me in Paris? This is not your fault." I told John what Amy had said to me. "Thank goodness that attendant came when he did."

"Lauren, don't you see? I've been so distracted by the humanness of our love that I've neglected my animal instincts. I should have sensed Amy's proximity."

"John, please don't blame yourself. All couples have a period of adjustment. It's a balancing act, like feng shui. Only in our case, it's fang shui." I smiled; he didn't.

"I'm not letting you out of my sight, and we need to begin your training now. You were lucky today because Amy stalled. Next time, she won't ask questions first." John took my chin in his hand. "Look directly into my eyes."

His violet eyes and thick black eyelashes had captivated me since the first time I saw him, draped for a dental procedure at my office. Today was no exception as I melted into his gaze. "Kiss me," I said.

He smiled briefly. "Later." He did that two-finger, my-eyes-to-his-eyes thing. "Don't turn your head. Just move your eyes as far left as possible and tell me what you see."

I strained to extend my peripheral vision. "I see a magazine rack." I smiled proudly.

"Is that all? You can't see the candy counter?"

"No, should I?"

"Yes. Turn your head and look."

A teenager was shoving whatever he could pilfer into his pockets while the clerk had his back turned.

"It's all practice, Lauren. Think about your eyes disappearing into your head as you look right, left, up and down. Imagine the world at three hundred sixty degrees. You have the capabilities. You just have to use them. Now, let's walk." He offered his hand, and we started down the long concourse.

"Can we do this without attracting attention?" I asked.

"Everyone's hurrying. They won't notice that our feet don't touch ground."

John squeezed my hand. "Okay," he began. "You're a runner. When your legs are in motion, do you consider the pavement or the movement?"

"Both?"

"Forget the pavement. Think about the spiraling movement of a machine, how wheels turn in a fluid motion. If you lift your knees, you can begin to propel yourself without touching down." He took my elbow, and suddenly we were gliding together down the concourse. We covered about one hundred yards levitating a few inches above *terra firma*.

"How far can we go like this? Miles?"

John chuckled. "Unfortunately, a few hundred yards is about the most distance we can cover at one time. It's not meant for transcontinental travel, but it's handy, particularly in a crisis."

When the intercom heralded boarding for our flight to Venice had begun, I said to John, "I can't say I'll miss Paris."

As we settled into our seats and the plane taxied down the runway, I finally breathed a sigh of relief.

John took my hand and flashed that intense look that got my heart going. "Someday, we'll come back to Paris, but I'll make sure Amy is no longer in this world when we do."

I scrounged through my big Gucci purse (Meredith had insisted I carry Gucci to Venice), to find my Laurell K. Hamilton paperback. I looked forward to catching up on the antics of Anita Blake, vampire hunter. Since she only hunted bad vampires, I considered her in my camp.

John pulled out his laptop. "What was the name of the attendant who rescued you?"

"*Monsieur* Claude Bisson," I said. "Why?"

"Since he made my eternity, I think I'll make his day."

I looked over John's shoulder as he accessed Google and searched for the address for Orly.

"What're you doing?" I asked.

"I'm going to send *Monsieur* Bisson a small token of my appreciation. Enough for him to retire on."

"I forget how rich you are."

"It's how rich *we* are, my love. And money can't begin to repay him."

* * *

Late December in Venice was perfect for us. While the rest of the world chose summer in Venice, we had the ancient city relatively to ourselves. No lines for romantic gondola rides and no queuing to get into St. Marks. And with the overcast skies of winter, we could sightsee without the threat of sunlight searing our sensitive eyes.

I'd always been a night person, but with my new

strength, jet lag was a thing of the past. There'd be no napping necessary. Besides, I was anxious to get into bed for other reasons.

As I entered our huge suite from the bathroom, dressed in my sexy new teddy, John interrupted my approach. "Stop, and close your eyes for a moment."

"Okay..." I waited for instructions.

"Instead of walking to the bed, imagine being on top of me. When you move, think of where you're heading, and you'll propel yourself in a split second."

I squeezed my eyes shut and pictured myself in his loving embrace. Though I'd seen John cover ground like this a thousand times, this was my first attempt.

"Oof." John coughed as I thumped into him. "Excellent. You'll learn to lessen the impact in time."

I wrapped my arms around his neck and began nibbling on his ear.

John clutched my buttocks in his large hands and positioned me for his entry. He traced my lips with his velvet tongue, and I opened my mouth eagerly. Nobody kissed like John. Where other men felt they had to strangle you with their tongue, John orchestrated a slow, erotic dance with his. He circled my tongue, enticing it into his mouth where he caressed it with strokes of sheer physical genius. I opened my eyes briefly to catch his violet eyes turning the rich, blood red color that signaled his arousal.

Knock! Knock!

"Ignore it," my husband whispered, his already baritone voice huskier than usual.

I inhaled his heady scent and returned to my nibbling.

Knock! Knock! Knock! Knock!

"We know it's not room service," I said.

Knock! Knock! Knock! KNOCK!

John turned his head and yelled at the door. "Hold on!" He looked back at me. "I'm in no condition to answer the door." His flagpole erection was impossible to disguise.

I smiled at him, rolled off the bed, did a flash to the door (John gave me a thumbs up on my skill level), and peeked through the fisheye peephole. At first I thought it was Brad Pitt, the resemblance was so striking. The man was dressed in a black suit, lilac shirt, and kaleidoscopic tie.

"John, are you going to open this door or not? It's been a good two hundred years since we talked. You can make love later." He spoke English, but with a strong Italian accent.

John covered his eyes with his hand. "Are you alone, Lucianno?"

"Yes, yes. Let me in."

"Just a minute," John said.

I took one of the hotel's plush terry robes from the closet and extracted another one for John, which I threw to him on the bed. John's manhood was now at half mast, so he was safe for company.

John opened the door and embraced his friend. "Your timing leaves much to be desired."

"There's always time for *that*." I watched Lucianno's eyes undress me. "Who's your treat?"

"Since you must have ascertained my whereabouts from airport security, you should know that this is my *wife*, Dr. Lauren Marsh Wright."

Lucianno addressed me. "Sorry, I meant no disrespect. For as long as I've known your...husband... (he choked on the word)...he's been careful not to become *involved*."

I looked at my darkly handsome husband, and then back to his blonde counterpart. "Apology accepted." I took John's hand, squeezing it. "He just hadn't met the right woman."

Lucianno laughed. "I never thought he'd succumb to matrimony again. My congratulations! I have managed to avoid that fate by only tasting each woman one time. I leave her with a touch of animal but still human."

"You miss the best part, my friend," John said. "You never truly love."

"Yes, but how can I miss what I've never experienced? This works for me. Besides, I don't want to risk what happened with your first wife." Lucianno stiffened. "Sorry, I shouldn't have mentioned that. I seem to be doing a good job of putting my foot in my mouth."

"I know all about Catherine," I said. *And unfortunately, Amy won't let me forget.*

"Well, enough reminiscing." Lucianno twittered his long fingers together. "How about joining me for a quick caper?"

John shot me a glance. "It's up to Lauren."

I had to admit I was getting hungry. "I'm game."

John wrapped his arm around my waist. "Lauren's not hunting yet, Luc. What did you have in mind?"

"She can watch from a safe distance. I'm closing in on a drug ring. The conciliari of the two most influential Mafia families will be dining this evening at Caffe Florian. One family is in charge of imports, and the other handles distribution. They've created a huge heroin problem in our city schools, and the Venetia Polizia would like some assistance. If we knock off the conciliari, their operation will stall, at least temporarily."

"What are conciliari?" I asked.

"Lawyers, my love. They're not all upstanding citizens like me."

"Can I help?"

"Perhaps." Lucianno tapped his index finger to his lips.

"No direct contact," John said. "She's not trained, and I won't risk her safety."

"I was thinking more of employing her as a scout," Lucianno said. "She can keep her eyes on them in the restaurant."

"I won't let her out of my sight." John was adamant.

"Don't worry. I'll be in the alley, and you can wait out front. You'll have a clear view of the restaurant. These guys are afraid of their own shadow. They'll have bodyguards stationed fore and aft. What Lauren can do is alert us to which way they're exiting."

"How will I do that?" I asked.

"Signals. Take out your lipstick if they're moving to the alley. Put your hands on your hips if they're coming out front. Sneeze if they split up. John will relay your signal to me with this pager." He handed a small beeper to John. "Beep me once if you need help and twice if they split up. If they're heading my way, just get your ass out back."

"And then what?" I looked at John.

"We'll have the element of surprise, and we're lethal. The two of us can handle five or six men easily." John took my chin in his hand. "And you stay put."

"Just like old times," Lucianno said. "Remember when we helped Casanova escape, my friend?"

"You knew Casanova?" I asked.

John rolled his eyes, and then focused them on Luc. "That's a story I'd just as soon my wife not know, though I didn't consider him a role model like you did."

I folded my arms and tapped my foot in mock annoyance.

"Let's go," Lucianno said. "I'll wait downstairs while you get dressed, but hurry."

I turned to my husband as Lucianno closed the door. "I'm beginning to feel like there's a conspiracy to keep us out of bed."

John kissed my nose. "We'll have the whole night once we finish this little adventure. And I don't plan on sleeping until tomorrow." His violet eyes held a spark of red.

"I'm holding you to that." I moved to the closet where I chose an Anne Klein beige silk pantsuit and cashmere shawl in mocha. I dressed, slipped on my Miu Miu ivory leather pumps, gathered my hair in a loose twist and secured it with a tortoise clip. I was hopeless with fashion, but my friend Meredith, who owned a trendy boutique near my office, had assembled my trousseau. "I'm ready."

John chose a baby blue Prada shirt and a polka dot Brent Morgan tie in gray and black to set off his black Armani suit. He looked like a GQ model.

He brought me in for a hug and buried his face in my hair. "Come on. The quicker we get this done..."

Lucianno was waiting in the hotel bar, sipping a Bloody Mary, the universal vampire cocktail. He glided off his barstool at our approach.

"The restaurant's on St. Mark's Square. We can walk there in five minutes." We could have flashed there in thirty seconds, but we didn't want to startle anyone, so we needed to affect a typical human speed.

It was ten-thirty p.m. by the time we reached the restaurant, not a late hour for Venice diners, but with the off season, only four tables were occupied. Lucianno nodded to the table where the two lawyers sat, and then he and John left the restaurant to take their stations. I slid onto a stool at the bar, ordering my old standby, a Cosmopolitan. The bartender spoke English, so we chatted briefly, though I kept my eyes on the two men. By eleven thirty, they were finishing espressos and canoli. Finally, at midnight, the smaller of the two dark-haired, and may I say greasy, men wiped his mouth with a linen napkin.

I straightened my back, waiting for one of them to push away from the table. Simultaneously, four burly men emerged from a secluded table at the back of the restaurant. Bodyguards, I guessed. I watched closely as the six men talked and laughed for a few minutes. They split in two groups of three, and I looked outside to John and executed a huge sneeze. He nodded, and I watched him hit his pager to alert Lucianno. One of the men in the group that was exiting to the alley popped himself on the head as though he'd forgotten something, and the threesome that had been heading to the rear turned to join their friends exiting via the front door. I watched six men walk into the dark square with only John to subdue them.

Well, I wasn't going to just stand there.

DCL Publications, LLC

CHAPTER THREE

I can do this! I propelled myself toward John, who was about to step out of the shadows. He issued a quick, "Lauren, NO!"

"Get Luc," I said, and then turned as John disappeared in thin air. I walked toward the men, my feminine wiles in tow.

"Hi, fellas. I noticed you in the restaurant and wondered if you were up for a little fun?" *Please speak English.*

"Honey, there are six of us, and only one of you," the smaller of the two lawyers answered in English. "Got any friends?"

"Absolutely. What do you like?"

"What do you think, guys?" The diminutive lawyer looked around at his cohorts. "Want five more like her, or should we mix it up?"

One of the larger bodyguards spoke. "I like albinos."

Another said, "I like boys," to which the five looked at him like he'd sprouted the Ebola virus.

"Don't have any boys in my arsenal, but Pinky should fit the albino bill." *Pinky?* "Your place or mine?" *Where was John?*

"We're at the Russo Palace. Ring for Andre Giarelli."

"My girls like champagne."

"Honey, we got whatever you want. Don't we, boys?"

One of the bodyguards grabbed his crotch. Like I needed a visual.

"And money's no object." Andre patted his lapel. He was the spitting image of Napoleon Bonaparte.

All six of them were focused on me, and they didn't hear John and Lucianno approach stealthily from behind. "Just in case we cross signals," I said, "let me give you my card." I adjusted my cleavage, and they moved closer. The two lawyers reminded me of salivating hamsters. I had no intention of giving them my business card, but as ploys go, it was the only diversionary tactic I could muster. I glanced up to see John motion for me to keep talking.

"Where the heck are those cards?" I fumbled around in my purse, withdrew my compact, plunked it back in a side pocket and inadvertently dropped my leather card case.

Andre stooped to pick it up, extracted a card, and then handed the case back to me. "Lauren E. Marsh, DDS...You're a dentist?" It was the last thing he said.

John and Lucianno each took two of the men by the back of the neck. Wrenching their necks sideways in a split second, they dropped their victims and reached for the two remaining men. Lucianno grabbed one and sunk his teeth into his neck. With seemingly no concern for his partners in crime, the lone remaining mobster managed to elude John, hopped on a black Vespa and sped off. The whole thing had taken less than a minute. John moved to follow the retreating mobster, but he had already entered the square and was weaving around pedestrians on his scooter.

John and Lucianno moved the dead men to the alley in record time. Blood had to be fresh for consumption, and we wasted no time feeding. This was the first time I'd fed on someone besides John, and it was more than a little creepy. When we'd had our fill, Lucianno lobbed the bodies into a nearby dumpster, and we calmly walked away. I began to shake when we reached the hotel. John wrapped his arm around my shoulder and guided me to a leather couch in the deserted lobby.

"I had a moment of panic when you joined me in front of the restaurant. I thought we were going to have to let them go." John chuckled. "But you were amazing. Honestly, Lauren, you're full of surprises."

"I work well under pressure." I closed my eyes to still the shaking. "The meltdown comes later."

"It gets easier." John massaged the back of my neck with his strong fingers. "I should be angry at you for taking such a chance, but I admire your aplomb. You're good at this."

Lucianno piped in. "And I thought she was just another pretty face. Bravo!"

"You guys are giving me too much credit. You did the heavy lifting."

"Lauren, being a vampire is half brawn and half cunning." John pulled me onto his lap and hugged me close. "You've got the cunning part down."

* * *

Bodyguard Demetrio Pendaras sped through the empty square. He didn't dare return to the Russo Palace, but he didn't want to leave the city, either, so he checked into the Hotel Saturnia. He'd have a stiff drink at the bar, and then return to the scene. Maybe his boss and the other guys weren't dead. Who was he kidding? Two guys who looked like fashion models had wrenched their necks one hundred eighty degrees. Damn, they were quick. He hadn't gotten a good look at them, probably wouldn't be able to identify them, except that they were gorgeous. Under other circumstances...

The woman, though...he'd looked directly into her eyes. He'd recognize her anywhere.

He bolted down two martinis, and then rode back to the scene. It was two a.m., and the streets were deserted. He checked the plaza in front of the restaurant. Nothing. A passerby would never guess that people had died here a few hours earlier. He moved to the alley behind the establishment, where he detected fresh blood on the pavement. Then he saw the dumpster. Stacking some empty vegetable crates from the restaurant's back door, he hoisted himself up to peer in the cavernous and stinky container. In the light from a nearby street lamp, the bodies of his partners-in-crime were plainly visible, presented with a few sprigs of wilted parsley and a carrot or two. "Hi, guys. "Quite a night, eh?"

No love lost there, but Demetrio would have some explaining to do. This would kill negotiations for awhile, not to mention the distribution of drugs. Fuck. He needed this job, and it had been easy. All he had to do was look intimidating. Until tonight.

He lowered himself into the dumpster. He supposed the thieves, or whatever they were, had confiscated wallets, but he checked just in case. Rolling the bodies around, he retrieved identification and money from each victim. The attack had been so quick and so lethal that he swore the guys with the wrenched necks sported looks of surprise. With enough cash in his pocket to split town and never look back, something white and shiny clutched in Andre's hand caught his eye. He pried the stiff fingers open and smiled as he read the card, Lauren E. Marsh, DDS. Weird. Her address was Winter Park, Florida. Where the hell was that, and what was she doing in Venice? He weighed his options. He could run with the cash, or he could be the hero with his boss. This gal could be part of a rival mob ring in Florida, and he held the incriminating clue. Hmm. What was a handful of cash when there was a potential fortune to be made? And wouldn't a trip to sunny Florida be just the ticket?

* * *

I yawned, and John took the hint.

"Luc, I'm glad we could be of service. I may need you to return the favor someday."

"Anytime, my friend." Lucianno rose from the chair he'd occupied while we detoxed from our caper. Well, I detoxed. The guys handled it in stride. He gave John a two-finger salute, blew me a kiss, and bid us goodnight.

We walked to the elevator and John whispered in my ear, "I hope that yawn didn't mean you're really tired."

"Of course not. I have all day tomorrow to sleep."

Arriving on the fourth floor, we glided down the hall to our room. John unlocked the door to our suite. "Will you grant me the indulgence of carrying you over the threshold? I neglected to do it earlier, and I quite like that tradition."

He didn't wait for my reply. Sweeping me into his arms as though I were weightless, he kicked the door open with his foot. He carried me over the threshold, set me down gently once inside the room, and then backed away. "I want to watch you take your clothes off." He sat on the edge of the bed.

"Okay, but turn about's fair play." I started with my pumps. Balancing like the agile vampire I was, I lifted each foot behind me and flung the shoes to the opposite side of the room. Oops. I forgot my strength. The heel of one shoe embedded in the wall. Removing the clip from my hair and shaking my head, I let loose my dark curls to cascade around my shoulders. Next came my jacket, which I twirled in striptease fashion before dropping it to the floor. I eased my slacks off my hips and let them fall in a puddle around my feet, stepping out of one pants leg and kicking the slacks across the room with the other foot. I now stood in my lace chemise.

"Stop," John said. "Let me take it from here." He took two steps toward me and put his hands on my shoulders.

Lowering one strap of my chemise, he slipped it off my shoulder with his fingertip, and then he lowered the other strap. It didn't fall, and he traced his fingers across the lace that perched on top of my breasts. He eased his thumb under the chemise and taunted my nipple. I moaned.

"Time out," I said. "You have entirely too many clothes on." I replaced the straps of my chemise on my shoulders, stood back and crossed my arms.

I soon realized I was an amateur.

John started with his tie, which he loosened to unbutton his top shirt button. With one swift motion, he pulled the tie through his collar and circled my neck with it. He tied a perfect knot, leaving me dressed in a beige chemise and a polka dot tie. His eyes never left mine as he unbuttoned his shirt. When he reached the top of his trousers, he did a little zipper tease down and up, down and up.

"Can I be of assistance? Don't want you fumbling with that zipper." I took one step forward.

John held out his hand to stop me. "Lauren, I don't fumble." He stepped out of his black Gucci loafers, and then let his trousers fall, displaying a black thong that barely covered his prominent erection.

"I believe you've leveled the playing field."

"Not quite, my love. You're still wearing my tie." He reached out and pulled on the tie to close the distance between us. "I like the look, but it will get in the way." Honestly, I don't know how he did it, but my tie and chemise were off, and I was pressed hard against his chest.

"Part of me is screaming to be inside you with no more preliminaries."

"Are you asking for permission?"

"I'm asking how rough I can be?" He traced his lips from my ear to the hollow of my neck.

"I want you to reach the depths of me."

I felt his growl build, a low, sexy rumble that vibrated from his chest to mine. The mood was shattered as something came crashing through the window of our fourth-story suite. A rock settled on the ottoman at the foot of our bed as John flashed to the window. Wrapped in paper and secured with a rubber band, the rock revealed a note, which I read aloud to John. *I know who you are.* "Does that mean he knows we're vampires?"

"Possibly." John's eagle eyes swept the street below.

"This has to be a record. We've been married for two days, and it's been a threat a day."

"Amy is a threat. This is a warning. My guess is the local bad guys think we're a rival mob, and they want us out of their territory." John bit his bottom lip. "Bolt the door and don't answer it for anyone." He morphed to bat form and flew out the window.

"So much for lovemaking," I said to the trace of vapor that lingered in the window.

I took his suggestion a step further and moved the armoire in front of the door. Wow, that was easy. The barrier wouldn't stop a vampire, but it should definitely deter a human intruder. I was beginning to feel that if Amy didn't get me, the mob would. I put a hotel robe on and waited for John's return, assuming it would be through the window.

I didn't wait long, but this time, two bats materialized. Returning to vampire form, John and Lucianno faced me.

"Looks like another postponement of our honeymoon," I said, scowling at Lucianno.

"Welcome to the world of the undead." Lucianno turned to John. "Your wife needs a better fix on the meaning of eternity."

John circled his arm around my waist and whispered in my ear. "Patience, my love." He looked at the armoire, secure against the door. "Good job." He reached down to pick up my purse, which had slid off the bed, and handed it to me.

"Oh, no." My hand flew to my mouth as I took my purse. "I just remembered. The one lawyer, Andre, took my business card. What if the police found it?"

"Sorry. I guess I neglected to tell you," Luc said. "I am the police. Lieutenant Lucianno DiSalvo, at your service." He bowed with a flourish.

"Okay, Lieutenant Smarty Pants, what if the guy who got away found it?"

John and Lucianno did that light bulb alert thing. You know, elevated eyebrows and all. In humans, it looks like a non-verbal "Uh-oh," but in vamps it has a sinister edge, more like, "Uh-oh, somebody's going to die."

"We need to find him before he shares what he knows with his Don," John said.

"Chances are, he's still in the city," Lucianno said. "The bosses live in heavily-guarded villas outside of town, but he wouldn't go there tonight."

"I guess this is a stupid question, but can this wait until tomorrow?" I implored.

John kissed my forehead. "Sorry, love. Stay barricaded in the room. Luc and I should be able to find this guy."

I watched as my husband and his friend returned to bat form and disappeared out the broken window. I was beginning to feel like a character in a Batman movie, when what I was going for was *Shakespeare in Love*. So much for a romantic honeymoon. I pulled my robe tighter around me and looked out the window to the deserted street below. A dark figure in a black cape slinked along the storefronts at street level and then began scaling the wall under my window, just like a vampire. Just like Amy.

"Oh, shit." I backed from the window, threw the armoire away from the door and bolted into the hallway. I began banging on the doors of other suites along the hall, and I smashed the glass of the fire alarm before I took the stairs four at a time, bypassing the third and second floors and heading to the lobby. As I sprang from the stairwell, I bumped into the front desk, moving the massive structure about a foot and startling the night clerk, whose alarmed expression was probably the result of the blaring fire alarm and the fact that

I'd almost pinned him to the wall. He squeezed himself out from behind the desk.

"I smelled smoke," I said, screwing up my nose.

"Stay here, signora." He made a quick phone call to the fire department, and then turned to the stairwell.

"No, don't leave me," I pleaded.

"I need to evacuate the other guests."

Turns out, he didn't need to leave. The hotel's few guests began emerging from the stairwell and the ancient elevator. Most were dressed in the hotel's robes.

With yawns and demands for answers, the small assembly assailed the desk clerk. He did a head count and seemed to ascertain that all but one guest was now in the lobby. The missing guest was John.

The Venice Fire Department arrived seconds later. They briefly surveyed the guests for any indication of smoke inhalation, and then they hauled their huge fire hose up the stairwell, meeting my descending husband and his friend.

"*Incendio, signore*?" One of the firemen asked.

"No, there's no fire." Lucianno answered.

John rushed to my side. "What happened?"

I told him about seeing Amy and my flight from the room. I'd seen my husband's eyes turn from violet to red, but this was the first time I saw them turn black. He smashed his fist into the hotel's wall. Luckily, with the noise of the fire engine and the escalating chatter of the guests, no one heard the impact of his fist or the sound of crumbling plaster.

"I take it you didn't see Amy," I said. "Did you find the mob guy?"

"No, but we know who he is, and Lucianno is going back out now."

I looked up at the love of my life, and my lower lip began to tremble. "I just want to go home."

CHAPTER FOUR

I'd been in a funk, staring out the window of the Boeing 747. "Was that our honeymoon?" I turned to look at John. "Because I think we missed something."

My sarcasm wasn't lost on him. "You think?" He took my chin in his hand. "All right, I'm willing to make a concession."

"Don't do me any favors. I'm beginning to feel like I'm the only one with a sense of urgency."

"You must be joking. I'm about to explode from wanting you." His violet eyes smoldered. I could see the red tinging his pupils. "In the five hundred years I've walked this earth, no one has ever been as important to me as you, and our lovemaking is beyond ecstasy. If anything happened to you, I'd face eternity alone. Just looking at you, sitting there in your lacey blouse and tight skirt, the animal in me wants to tear your clothes off."

I opened my mouth to apologize.

"I'm not finished."

I closed my mouth.

"I plan to make love to you until the end of time, but I need to finish off Amy, and you're going to have to live with me being a bit distracted. Can you do that?"

"Yes, of course. Now, what's the concession?"

His expression began to change from burning intensity to a sexy smile. "Why don't you check out the lavatory?"

I did a vampire flash, quicker than the human eye could see, to the tiny airplane bathroom and back to my seat. "It'd be a tight fit."

"It is anyway."

"That's for sure."

John unbuckled his seat belt. "Last one there's...."

Tight fit didn't begin to describe it. We could barely close the door. Pressed hard against each other, I positioned my hips to grind into John's swollen member. He groaned and eased my skirt up to my waist. There was no room for me to guide him between my legs or for him to tease my sensitive bud. He managed to get his zipper down to release his engorged penis, which I sensuously squeezed between my legs. I was so wet, he could hone in on my core with no further guidance. He wrapped his arms around me and grabbed my butt, easily lifting me for his entry. And then he stopped.

"Almost forgot the requisite barrier." He squeezed his hand into his jean pocket.

"I'm happy to see you were prepared. I'll concede...you wanted this as much as me."

"It's not there, Lauren."

"What?"

"The condom I put in my pocket. It's not there."

"I don't care. I know it's a bit soon, but we want children, and—"

"No. You absolutely can't get pregnant now, not until Amy's dead. As much as she wants to kill you, she'd be even more intent if you were with child."

"Just don't finish." *Okay, that was a stupid thing to say.*

John lowered his eyebrows. His expression said it all.

"I know," I said. "That was idiotic. I'd sink to my knees, but there's no room."

"Tell me about it." John wiped perspiration from his forehead. We were both slick from the close quarters and lack of air circulation.

"We have to be the most frustrated newlyweds in history."

* * *

Demetrio stowed his Vespa in an alcove three blocks from the Hotel Saturnia. He checked the time, four a.m., and considered waiting until morning to call the Don, but he decided that the news was too important to delay.

Throwing his keys on the bureau of his single room, Demetrio sat on the bed and punched in the number that would connect him to security at Emilio Nova's villa. He insisted on speaking directly to the Don.

"This better be important," Emilio's gravelly voice oozed annoyance.

"Yessir, it is...very." Demetrio began the story by reporting the successful negotiations between the two families, negotiations that would have doubled local distribution.

He took a deep breath before continuing. He'd heard about the Don's habit of shooting the messenger, and this next tidbit of news would need to be delivered delicately.

"It was all going well, sewn up, until we left the restaurant." Demetrio paused. "And then all hell broke loose. The ambush was well-planned. They used a woman to entice us, and then these five guys appeared out of nowhere." No way was he going to admit to the Don that there were only two assailants.

"You wouldn't believe it, Boss. I managed to single-handedly kill three of them, but they massacred our whole team. Two guys and the dame got away, but I got the dame's business card. And listen to this. She's a dentist from Winter Park, Florida. Her name's Lauren Marsh."

Emilio cleared his throat. "Fuck. Good consigliari are hard to find." A pregnant pause followed, and then Emilio said, "I'll have my friend Rick Maroon in Orlando check out the dentist."

"I heard of him. He's the boss with all the inventions." Demetrio puffed up his chest at his display of knowledge.

"Yeah." Emilio chuckled. "Maroon's known for coming up with interesting gadgets to torture people."

"Maybe I should go to Florida to identify the dentist," Demetrio said.

"No, I need you here." Emilio emitted an audible yawn. "You done good, Demetrio." He clicked off.

Demetrio stretched his big frame across the bed. He stared at the ceiling for a few moments, and then he got up and pounded his chest with his fists, feeling proud as Tarzan. Time for some shut eye.

At first, the rap at the door didn't register through the fog of sleep, but when he heard it again, more insistent this time, he mumbled from the bed. "Who is it?"

"It's your worst nightmare, and you have nowhere to hide."

Demetrio bolted off the bed and peeked through the door's peephole at the devastating man on the other side. "I'm just a lowly bodyguard. You already killed the guys with the influence."

"Just give me the business card you pilfered off your boss's body, and I'll let you go. You can slip it under the door if that makes you more comfortable."

"Who are you?"

"My name's not important."

"Who do you work for?" Demetrio thought he might be able to swing this guy to his side...in more ways than one.

"I work for myself. Now give me that card."

"Are you armed?"

"No."   Lucianno removed his leather jacket and dropped it to the floor, extending his arms in a surrendering gesture. He wore a deep purple t-shirt that clung to his rippled chest.

Demetrio gasped at Lucianno's beauty, opened the door, and pointed his silencer-equipped revolver at Lucianno's chest.

Lucianno smiled. "Shoot me, if you like, but give me the card first."

Demetrio reached inside his pants pocket to retrieve Lauren's business card. He dangled it in front of Lucianno.

"Since you'll soon have what you came for, how about a little payback?" Demetrio gestured toward the bed.

"I don't swing that way."   Lucianno snatched the card out of Demetrio's hand.

Demetrio figured if Lucianno wouldn't have sex with him, he might as well kill him. He pointed the revolver at Lucianno's heart and pulled the trigger. The bullet went through Lucianno's body and lodged in the wall behind him.

"That stung a bit."   Lucianno swatted the gun out of Demetrio's hand and grabbed the huge bodyguard by the throat. He pushed him against the wall.

"I didn't need to feed again tonight, but since you've royally pissed me off..." Lucianno sank his teeth into Demetrio's neck.

Demetrio eeked out a weak, "What the fuck!" before he succumbed.

CHAPTER FIVE

Lucianno arrived in Orlando three days after we returned home. He'd promised John that as soon as he took care of Demetrio, he'd head our way to assist John with a plan to exterminate Amy and her coven. At least John and I had a few days to ourselves before his arrival. Bliss.

Our doorbell rang unexpectedly on the second night Lucianno graced our home. I opened the door to my friend Meredith, dressed fashionably as always in pink Juicy Couture shorts and a matching hoodie.

"Welcome home," she said, though her eyes barely registered me. She was mesmerized by the vampire standing behind me. I picked her chin up off the hardwood floor and turned her shoulders around to guide her out the front door. She pushed against me, resisting.

"Meredith, what a surprise!" I closed the door and pointed to a wicker chair on the porch for her to sit.

She wiggled around me and peeked through the stained glass that framed the front door.

"Who is *that*?"

I swear, she almost drooled.

"*That* is a vampire."

"Come on, Lauren. It worked for you." Meredith clasped her hands, pleading.

"Believe me, he's not like John."

The front door opened and out sprang Lucianno.

"I don't believe we've met," he said, locking eyes with Meredith.

"And you're not going to," I said, pulling Meredith down the front steps and tugging her toward her car. She slapped at my hand, but she was no match for my strength.

"Nice to meet you," she said over her shoulder as I tucked her head into her red BMW 330i.

"Drive," I instructed.

"Some friend you are." Meredith frowned at me, and then she started her car, gave me one last pout, and pulled around our circular drive. She meekly waved to Lucianno, who was still standing on the porch in all his glorious Brad Pitt-ness.

"Why'd you rush that magnificent creature off?" He crossed his arms as I approached.

"Don't even think about it."

"Too late. I've already imagined her writhing underneath me." His smile was nothing less than wicked.

"Lucianno, I'm not kidding. You touch one hair on her head, and I swear..."

"I don't have to touch her head."

"Cute. You know exactly what I mean."

"Lauren, she's an adult." Lucianno shot me an under-the-eyelashes look that wasn't nearly as endearing as my husband's.

"True, but she's not into casual relationships. You'll head back to Italy, and she'll never be the same. Is that fair?"

"Why don't you let her decide?"

"Because she's vulnerable. She's just getting over a difficult break up, and I'm afraid she'll cave to your charms.

I'd never forgive myself."

"All right, I won't pursue her," Luc said, buffing his fingernails across his slacks, "but if she makes the first move, all bets are off."

I plopped down on the front porch swing as Lucianno glided back into the house.

"Great." Like I didn't have enough problems. Quick recount. A murderous vampiress was intent on killing me. My dreams were haunted by a near miss with the Italian Mafia. Meredith's vulnerability could get her in serious trouble. I had a horny vampire to babysit, and I had to return to a full schedule of patients tomorrow, including eight-year-old Bobby Brewster who'd start screaming bloody murder the moment he walked into my office.

I propped my chin on my hand and stared at our manicured lawn, illuminated by hundreds of tiny white lights in the big ligustrum trees that lined the driveway. The front door opened again, and this time John emerged in a tight black t-shirt and black silk boxers. He held a long-stemmed red rose between his teeth. Offering his hand, he pulled me to standing, tossed the rose on the swing, and scooped me into his arms. Aah.

Carrying me up the stairs, he tossed me effortlessly on our big bed. Due to my new body density, I didn't bounce.

"We're going through condoms like they're water balloons," I teased as I watched him check the nightstand for the contraceptive supply.

"Your point?"

"Only that I look forward to feeling you, all of you, without a barrier."

John kissed my nose. "Nothing will make me happier than to see your belly swollen with our child, but you know the rules."

I made a circular motion with my hand and then slashed through it. "Amy."

"Correct. In the meantime, we can work on depleting

our condom stash, because once I get back from London..."

"That's assuming you come back." I bit my lip.

"Don't worry, my love. I can take care of Amy, and with Luc's help, we should be able to break up her coven."

"But you don't know how big her group of nasties has become. What if she has fifty vampires by now?"

"That's one of the reasons we need to get to London as soon as possible." John's brow furrowed.

"And another reason?"

"I'm as anxious to start a family as you are. Just the thought of you ripe and round is a tremendous turn on." John's silk boxers displayed an impressive bulge.

"Oh, honey, your timing is impeccable." I leaned back on the bed and opened my arms.

My cell phone rang from the bedside table, and I reached over to make sure it wasn't an emergency call from a patient. Meredith's timing, as I witnessed from my caller I.D., left much to be desired. I lobbed the phone across the room where it landed behind a pillow on the chaise.

* * *

When I called Meredith back, she still sounded pouty. "Were you trying to hide this guy from me?" I could almost hear her plunk her fists on her shapely hips over the telephone, taking offense at my protective nature. "After all the dates I set up for you? Can I help it if none of them met your standards?"

"Mere, Lucianno's not a normal guy, and even if you wanted to make the decision I made, he's not into true love."

"Given my track record with men, how much worse could it be? I have this horrible habit of choosing men who seem great at first, and then they try to change me. Look at Phillip. He started out just wanting me to change the color of my lipstick, and next thing I knew, he wanted a complete overhaul. Why can't I find someone who likes me just the way

I am?"

I knew how Meredith's mind worked, and this was going to be a tough negotiation.

"Believe me; you don't want to mess with this guy. He told me he'll make love to a woman one time, leaving her human but with a new brand of horniness. Is that what you want?" I had a sinking feeling that my appeal was falling on deaf ears.

"What I want is to throw caution to the wind."

"Meredith, after all these years, you can still astound me. You know damn well you're not a "caution to the wind" girl. Please, leave this guy *alone*."

"Just let me talk with him, for Pete's sake."

"It's not safe. You won't be able to resist him." I was doing a lousy job of communicating the danger involved. "Vamps have a way of getting what they want, Mere. I was just lucky to find one with moral fiber and self-control."

"Lucianno seems like a nice guy," she whined.

"Oh, he's charming, that's for sure, and he's devoted to law enforcement like John, but he won't hesitate to sink his fangs into you while you have your legs wrapped around him."

Meredith didn't retaliate.

"Think I don't know you? I just felt you shudder."

Meredith laughed.

"Was that a creep-me-out shudder or a turn-me-on shudder?"

"Both. Is that how you felt when you first met John?"

I smiled, remembering John's first visit to my dental office. "If you'll recall, I didn't know he was a vamp. I just saw this devastatingly handsome, funny, intelligent guy."

"Come clean, Lauren. What's it like to have sex with a vampire?"

Meredith deserved a truthful answer. "It's otherworldly. Intense. Insanely physical." Oops, I didn't want to encourage her. "And then there's the blood exchange."

"*Every* time?"

"Just the first three times, and though the sex is great, it feels like fire coursing through your veins afterwards. John cradled me and rocked me through it. After the third time, your transformation to vampire is complete, glowing eyes and all."

"It seems to agree with you. No more struggling with those extra ten pounds, eh?"

"Suffice it to say, my diet has changed. I was worried at first that John wouldn't like my new trim figure, since he'd fallen in love with the full-figured me. But luckily, he's still smitten."

"That's what I want." I could hear the dreamlike quality in Meredith's statement. "I want a man to go crazy on me."

"Believe me, it's not Lucianno. He may look like God's gift to women, but he's one shallow dude."

"Okay, sweetie, you've won the first round." Meredith sounded sincere. "I'm going to the gym to work my sexual frustration out on the elliptical machine. You're going back to work tomorrow, right?"

"Yeah. Back to reality."

"Me, too. The shop will be closed, but I'll be buried in re-stocking and inventory. Gotta start thinking about the spring sidewalk sale. Want to meet for lunch?"

"Sure. I'm not eating, of course, but I could stand a mid-day stretch."

"One o'clock at Panera?"

"You're on. And Mere? There's a great guy out there somewhere for you, it's just not Luc."

"So you say."

* * *

I'd been walking around the house in conversation with Meredith. I joined John in the kitchen when I hung up my cell.

"How bad is it?" he asked.

"I'm not sure. I think she's safe...for now."

John checked the emergency blood supply in the refrigerator, and then shut the door a bit more forcefully than necessary. "I'll talk with him. He has some admirable traits, but he doesn't know what love is. He'd leave her with no emotional attachment and an insatiable desire for sex."

I rubbed my arms to dispel the goosebumps. "I'll feel much better when he's gone. It's like having a panther in the house."

"I'll get him out of here as quickly as I can." John wrapped his arms around me. "We'll need a couple of days to strategize our attack on Amy and enlist a few more friends in our cause, and then we'll be off to London."

I rested my head on his broad chest. "It's weird. You're going off to kill a very bad vampire, and we're worried about a good vampire."

"I'd call him 'emotionally constricted.' He needs to grow up."

"After five hundred years, do you think there's hope?"

CHAPTER SIX

Following a successful night of crime intervention and feeding, Lucianno lay in bed, his arms propped behind his head, and stared at the walls in the beautiful first-floor guest suite of John and Lauren's house. He should be tired, but he couldn't get Meredith off his mind. He always got what he wanted, and he wanted her.

He looked out the window, squinting his sensitive eyes against the partly cloudy January sky. The temperature on the gazebo thermometer registered seventy-two degrees. It was going to be a beautiful day, and he needed good sunglasses to enjoy it.

He dressed in black Tommy Bahama linen shorts, a deep purple Polo shirt that hugged his torso, and black Mephisto sandals. He yelled up the stairwell to John, "Where can I buy a good pair of sunglasses?"

After a brief silence, John answered. "There's a great shop on Park Avenue. It's called Solstice. You can walk there."

* * *

Meredith pulled her car into the alley behind her Park Avenue shop, Bellisimo. She faced a busy day of weeding out her winter inventory and stocking the new Betsey Johnson apparel she'd acquired on her recent New York merchandising trip.

Rifling through her Burberry bag, she realized she'd left her shop keys on the kitchen counter at home. Damn, she was distracted. Dogs couldn't roll their eyes, but her Boston Terrier mix, Penelope, shot her a good semblance from her doggie car seat.

"Small detour, girl. Nothing to fret about." Meredith patted Penelope's round head. "Besides, I forgot your biscuits." Penelope's ears perked up at the "b" word.

Meredith shook her head as she retraced the two-mile route to her house. It wasn't like her to be scatter-brained. Lauren was the disorganized one. All through middle and high school, Meredith spent an inordinate amount of time locating items Lauren had lost in her mounting pile of rubble. They were like Mutt and Jeff. Statuesque, flat-chested, blond Meredith, and her shorter, buxom, brunette friend, Lauren. For fifteen years, they'd supported each other. When it was time to look at careers, Meredith steered Lauren and her science fair background toward dentistry. For Meredith, Lauren did the research on the best schools for fashion merchandising, which had always been Meredith's passion. She grew up idolizing Audrey Hepburn's fashion sense, but she also admired her for her involvement in UNICEF and world hunger. Now, she was living her dream. She had her own shop, and she chaired the board of Bread Basket, a local organization that fed Orlando's homeless and hungry. If only she had someone to share her life with.

She couldn't get Lucianno out of her head, nor could she stop the erotic fantasies that swam between her ears and resulted in a constant state of juiciness that was currently threatening to slide her right off her leather car seat.

* * *

Lucianno chose a pair of black Polo sunglasses at Solstice. From there, he bought an espresso at Barnie's Coffee to legitimize his seat on the wrought iron bench in Greeneda Court. He sipped on his espresso.

Looking up at the sound of a diminutive bark, he was surprised to see Meredith barreling through Greeneda Court. Luc's eyes raked her body from head to toe. She wore tight brown Bermuda shorts, a turquoise midriff-baring t-shirt, and gold gladiator sandals with her blood red toenails peeping through. And she was braless. Yum!

"What's your rush?"

Meredith swiveled on her heel, and then she gasped. "It's *you!*"

"In the flesh...well, sort of." Lucianno's lips turned up in his most devilish grin. "Got a minute? Why don't I buy you a cappuccino?"

She eeked out an, "Okay."

Lucianno knew she was acquiescing against her better judgment, but hey, he'd been here before. He strode inside the coffee shop to order the cappuccino. He watched her sitting pertly on the bench with her little dog on her lap. She was fidgeting with her ponytail, undoing the tie and regathering her hair. When she was done, it looked the same as when she'd started.

"Here." Lucianno handed her the cappuccino. "I took the liberty of adding real whipped cream. You don't look like you need to count calories."

"Thanks. Between working out and all my nervous energy, I can pretty much eat what I want."

Lucianno sat next to Meredith on the little bench, and her dog immediately switched laps.

"Lauren told me that animals like you...people." Heat rushed into her cheeks, and she looked down, taking a sip of her cappuccino. The whipped cream lip that accompanied that sip was more than Luc could take.

"Don't move," he said. He braced his hands on either side of her face and swept his tongue across her top lip to capture the frothy white mustache. "There. I could have done that with a napkin, but it wouldn't have been nearly as much fun."

"I thought your lips would be cold," she said, breathlessly. Her hand went to her heart.

Luc gently spread her knees apart and eased her head down between them. "Close your eyes and breathe deeply. You'll be fine in a minute." He massaged the back of her neck as she gulped her breaths. "And for future reference, vampires are like reptiles. Our body temperatures adjust to the surroundings."

After a few moments, Meredith raised her head and pulled Penelope from Luc's lap. "You surprised me, that's all." She clutched the little dog to her chest.

Luc smiled. "You don't look dressed for work." Again, he took in her attire with his bedroom eyes. "What are you up to?"

"My shop's three doors down, but I'm not open today."

"All the better." He tried his best to contain the devilish grin, but was unsuccessful.

"I have lots of work to do, though. I'm weeding out and getting ready for the semi-annual sidewalk sale. And then I'm having lunch with Lauren."

He recognized her lame attempt to put him off. "Just show me your shop, and then I'll be on my way. I thought I'd catch the Morse Museum. I understand they have a beautiful collection of Tiffany stained glass."

"Oh, you don't want to miss that. It's world famous. In fact, you should probably head there right now to beat the crowds."

"Meredith, I'm not going to attack you."

"You're not?" She blurted out, wide-eyed. "Why not?"

Lucianno did a double-take. "You *want* me to attack you?"

"Isn't that what you do?"

"No, absolutely not. I would never take a woman against her will."

"But Lauren said you'll make love to a woman one time and then never see her again."

Lucianno took Meredith's hand. "Look at me." His seductive eyes honed in on her as he turned on his vampire persuasiveness. "I want you. Do you want me?"

"Yes." Meredith made a little squeaking sound, like a mouse who'd just been pinned by a cat.

"Then let's go to your store."

Lucianno took Penelope's leash in one hand and motioned with his other hand for Meredith to lead the way.

He watched her bungle with her keys at the front door, and when they entered, she didn't turn the hanging sign to "Open."

"Flip the bolt, please," Luc said as he strode to the middle of the store where a rack of silk blouses shimmered in varying shades of sherbet. He fingered the luxurious silk. "You have excellent taste."

"Thank you. It started with playing dress-up when I was four years old."

"I'll bet you were adorable." He moved to a large Queen Anne desk in the middle of the store and took one of her business cards from a little holder shaped like a bustier.

"Do you really need that card? Lauren said you don't believe in relationships."

"What other words of wisdom has she imparted?" He rubbed his chin and let his eyes roam from Meredith's toes up to the tip of her nose. "You must think I'm a snake."

Meredith laughed--somewhat nervously, he thought.

Luc walked to the back of the store, where one glass door led to her office. He noted the orderly in/out boxes and the clean desk. A heavier glass door beyond the office caught his attention.

"What's this?" he asked.

"Don't laugh. It's a steam room. This building used to be a little storefront gym. When I renovated, I got rid of the sauna and whirlpool, but I kept the steam room because I use it to steam the wrinkles out of clothes."

"Is it on?"

"No. In fact, it's probably cold in there because it's vented through the air conditioning system."

Luc opened the door, stepped in, and motioned for Meredith to join him. He watched her steal a quick glance at Penelope for what? Guidance? And then she joined him in the chilly steam room.

He wrapped his arms around her, inhaling the skin at her temple, and then he took both her wrists in one hand and pinned them above her head against the tile wall. With his other hand, he traced a line down her left arm, beginning at her wrist. When he reached the juncture of her underarm, she stiffened under him.

"You should know that a boob job is at the top of my to-do list," she said.

Luc chuckled. "Take it off your list, Meredith. Your breasts are perfect." He reached under her t-shirt and gently squeezed her nipple, which immediately came to attention at his touch.

"My old boyfriend didn't think so. He kept pushing me to make them bigger."

"If I were your boyfriend, I wouldn't change one thing about you."

"Isn't it just my luck that you're not into a relationship. I've had a string of jerks, and the last one was the worst."

Luc pulled back to look in her eyes. "Would you like me to kill him for you?"

"NO! I mean, of course not. I don't care that much anymore. He wasn't right for me, anyway. All he was interested in was how I looked. He hated my involvement with the homeless. He thought it was bad for my image."

"I think it's admirable that you care about people less fortunate, but I don't want to talk about your ex-boyfriend." Luc released her wrists and smoothed his finger across Meredith's cheek. "Because I don't think I can wait another second to kiss you." His lips met hers, and as he tickled her lips with his tongue, he felt her melt into his embrace, her arms circling his neck. He explored her mouth slowly, and then he moved his hand to the little zipper at the front of her shorts, deftly slipping it down and easing his hand under the lace of her undies.

"Ah, you're ready for me," he whispered as he plunged two fingers into her velvety sheath. He moved his hand to his shorts, unbuttoning the top button, and then he did what he always did at this juncture in his lovemaking routine—he locked eyes with the woman of his desire. The lust that typically met his eyes was his final signal to lengthen his fangs for the inevitable bite. When he looked at Meredith, however, he saw an expression that stopped him in his tracks. He took one quick step back, opened the door of the steam room and flashed to the middle of her store, facing away from her.

She followed him. "What's wrong?" she asked.

"You're one of a kind, Meredith." He didn't turn around. He walked straight to the front door, undid the bolt, and stepped out of the store.

* * *

When I entered Panera to meet Meredith, she was standing in line, hugging herself.

"Really, Mere, it's almost eighty degrees today. Are you cold?"

She turned to me. Even with my dark Chanel sunglasses, I detected the look of panic in her eyes. I took her elbow. She looked like she was about to faint.

"I just saw Luc," she whispered.

"No, no, no. Please don't tell me you," I whispered the rest of the sentence, "had sex with him." I turned Meredith's head to check her neck for puncture wounds.

"He let me go." She had a look in her eyes that I could only characterize as wistful.

"Thank God. Maybe the guy has a conscience after all."

"I think I'm in love with him." Wistful seemed to be morphing into dreamy.

I laughed. "It's temporary vampire infatuation. Once you get his scent out of your nostrils, you'll calm down."

"You think?"

"Absolutely. Think of yourself as the prey that got away." I patted her hand. "It'll pass." And then I said a silent prayer.

* * *

That evening, while John was inside studying for the Florida bar exam, I sat on our wicker rocker on the front porch and watched the sunset. We'd been blessed with overcast days that made daytime maneuvering more pleasant for our sensitive eyes and provided the added benefit of bountiful clouds, which the Florida sun bounced off with colors of deep pink, peach, and violet.

As I breathed deeply, Luc rounded the corner of our circular driveway and bounded up the steps to the porch. He seemed consumed with energy.

"Thank you," I said.

"For what?"

"Don't play dumb with me. I talked to Meredith."

"Oh...that." He looked off to the sunset.

"It was noble of you to let her go."

Lucianno shook his head. "I've never thought of myself as noble." He picked up a stone off the front porch and hurled it into the sky, beyond the confines of gravity.

"Sure looks like noble in my book. What made you

stop?"

"Just as I leaned in for her jugular, I saw something I've never seen before in a woman's eyes." Luc took off his sunglasses and squinted into the twilight sky. "She looked at me with trust, and I couldn't betray her."

"Bravo!" I got up from my chair and gave Luc a big hug. "You can't know how much that means to me."

"Don't give me too much credit. I'm not sure I could resist again."

"You won't have the opportunity. Doreen made your plane reservations today. You and John leave day after tomorrow on the British Airways flight out of OIA."

"The sooner the better." Luc rubbed his palms down his black linen shorts. "I'm going for a run." He disappeared into the house, presumably to change into his running clothes.

Having recently been a sexually frustrated vampire myself, I had to admit it was more amusing from this angle.

CHAPTER SEVEN

As the time approached for John and Luc's departure, I stood at the door to our bedroom, watching John pack.

"Miss you already." Leaning against the doorjamb, I rubbed my arms and shook.

"Please don't worry, love." John touched my cheek and then returned to his packing, stuffing a second pair of jeans into his carry-on. "Luc and I will have plenty of back-up."

I turned to see Luc ascending the steps.

"Ready?" he asked.

"Yes." John zipped his carry-on shut.

Luc held his hands in prayer and looked at me. "One tiny request?"

"Supplication, Luc? Now, there's a new one."

"I don't really see how you could deny a man who is risking his life for you one simple request." He went down on one knee.

"All right," I said, rolling my eyes. "I assume this is about Meredith?"

"I need to see her before I leave."

"Well, I suppose it couldn't hurt for her to ride to the airport with us."

An hour later, Luc and Meredith were huddled in the backseat of my Volvo XC90. I drove, as John still hadn't bothered to get a driver's license. Every few minutes, I looked in the rearview mirror for any shenanigans. All I saw was Luc and Meredith staring at each other. With "mom" in the front seat, they were on their best behavior.

I hadn't allowed myself to dwell on John's departure. Since we'd returned from our honeymoon, I had a full schedule at work, and John had been in intense pre-war mode. Add to that my concern about Meredith, and I'd pushed the real life-and-death issue to the back of my mind. Now, it all came crashing in on me. My hands shook on the steering wheel.

I parked in the short-term lot at Orlando International, and we walked arm-in-arm to the British Airways counter. Luc seemed to have a glitch with his passport, and we left him with Meredith at the counter. When John and I reached airport security, he pulled me to the side and wrapped me in his embrace. I buried my head in his chest, inhaling his wonderful, musky scent.

He whispered in my ear. "Lauren, you are my life. I will come back to you." He tipped my chin up to his lips and kissed me soundly, exploring my mouth with his tongue. Sweet, sensuous, extravagant. I savored the flavors our tongues produced. We were so much more than lovers; we were co-mingled beings, inseparable through blood and sheer will.

When our kiss ended, I touched his cheek. "Be safe." He walked backwards for a few steps, blowing me a kiss before he joined Luc, and the two of them turned for the gate. Tears welled in my eyes. I couldn't move.

Meredith put her hands on my shoulders. "Come on; let's get a cup of coffee." I was far too strong for Meredith to turn me by my shoulders, but after wiping the tears from my cheeks, I acquiesced and turned toward the airport Starbucks.

In her wisdom, and knowing me as well as she did, she distracted me with her assessment of Lucianno.

"I can't figure him out." She shook her head. "One minute, he's ready to ravage me, and the next he treats me like his long-lost sister."

I sniffled and waited for her to continue.

"A few days ago in my store, he kissed me with such passion; I thought I was going to explode. Today, all he did was squeeze my hand and give me a peck on the cheek. Makes me wonder why he wanted me to come to the airport."

"I think he really cares about you, but he doesn't know how to be a boyfriend. It's kinda cute."

* * *

John and Luc settled into their business class seats. They refused refreshments. John opened his laptop, and showed Luc the schematic he'd drawn of Amy's manor house.

"Her bedroom's here," John said, pointing to the turret, "and our best chance of finding her minimally guarded will be midday. I'm sure she's increased her numbers, but since newbies have a tendency to roam, I'm estimating no more than ten or twelve in the den."

Luc stared at the screen.

"Earth to Luc. Come in, Luc," John said.

Luc rubbed his eyes. "Sorry."

"What's got you so distracted?"

"I don't know what to do with the way I...I can hardly say the word. Four letters, starts with an 'f'."

"You need a sex therapist for that, though I must say, I'm a bit surprised."

"No, not *that* word. If you must know, the word's 'feel'".

"Disquieting, isn't it?"

"That's an understatement. I'm not sure I like it."

"It's what makes life worthwhile."

"She gets to me." Luc turned his gaze to the window.

"Eternity takes on new meaning when you start living for someone else." John smiled at the thought of Lauren.

"So this is what love feels like?"

John laughed. "And none too soon. You'll fight even harder now."

* * *

Heathrow Airport was its usual chaos as John and Luc made a quick beeline for their train to London. Doreen had booked rooms for them at The Dorchester, which provided a central location for reconnaissance. John's primary London contact, Richard Cecil, greeted John and Luc as they strode into the lobby of the hotel.

"My friend," Richard said, opening his arms to the boyhood friend who'd become a vampire shortly after he had. "Seeing you again after so many years reminds me of our youth and the days before we were turned. I haven't thought about that in a long, long time."

The two compatriots flashed through the years in each other's eyes, and then Richard thumped John on the shoulder with his fist. "I understand congratulations are in order."

"Yes, who would have guessed?" Luc interjected.

"She must be very special," Richard said.

John smiled. "She's extraordinary, but I won't be able to settle into wedded bliss until Amy's out of the picture. What's the latest?"

Richard motioned for John and Luc to follow him to the richly-paneled bar just off the main lobby. Settling into a half-moon, tufted booth at a table in the rear, Richard leaned forward on his elbows to whisper his strategy. "You've arrived none too soon. Her coven is growing almost exponentially, but the good news is that though she's frequently in the company of eight or ten of her young admirers in the evenings, she rarely ventures out during the day with more than three or

150

four."

"I've got six backups coming from Eastern Europe," John said. "They're all seasoned fighters. What's her pattern?"

Richard chuckled. "Amy's a shopper. The boutiques in Knightsbridge cater to her, and of course she loves Harrods. She's typically there on Tuesdays and Thursdays. It's possible we could catch her trying on clothes in one of the designer salons. She's very trendy--likes Vivienne Westwood and Roberto Cavalli. She'll have a couple goons with her, and she's been known to have sex with them in the oversized dressing rooms. Under the right circumstances, we could annihilate everyone without causing much of a stir."

"Decapitating Amy in Harrods could prove messy. I'd thought we'd ambush her in her manor house," John said.

"A month ago that could have worked, but it's way too risky now. She must have twenty vamps living there." Richard scratched his trimmed goatee. "Harrods could work. Body bags look like garment bags. I think we can exit Harrods with the bodies draped over our shoulders."

"What about the blood?" Luc's eyes sparkled.

"We'll obviously have to consume all we can at the initial strike, before we decapitate." John ran his fingers through his hair. "I'm more concerned with attracting attention. We can corner Amy and her goons in the dressing rooms, but one good scream, and we're foiled."

"That's why I carry duct tape, my friend." Richard patted the pocket of his slacks.

John laughed. "And I'm sure you're adept at the application, but I know Amy. She'll have some diversionary tactics, not the least of which will be sexual." John centered his gaze on Luc. "No sex before decapitation."

"What do you take me for, a praying mantis?" Luc rolled his eyes.

"I know how fast you can whip that dick of yours out," John said. "Just a warning."

"I'm telling you, I've changed."

151

"Okay, I'll give you the benefit of the doubt."

"There's another possibility for an ambush," Richard said. "She has a flat in Kensington, and she's frequently there during the week, usually with only three or four backups."

"What are her evenings like?" Luc asked.

"She's a serious club hopper, which is where she's picked up many of her teenage victims. I think she's about at capacity for enlisting vampires. Most of her destruction lately has been straight kills, not turnings."

"Does she favor any of her novices?" John asked.

"Two. They're fraternal twins, a boy and girl. I'd say they're about eighteen years old. They're with her more frequently than the others, and they're cunning. Most of her newbies are nervous and shifty, but these two, Alyssa and Aidan, are sure of themselves."

John nodded, absorbing the information. "You've done a good job, Richard. Are you certain no one's seen you?"

"I'd have felt it, if they had. I've been careful not to get too close, and I have human employees who've tempered the distance between Amy and me."

"Unfortunately, Amy can sense me from miles away," John said. "She may already know I'm in London, but she doesn't know Luc." John turned to Lucianno. "Are you up for some club hopping?"

"Absolutely. I'll try not to let my *dick* get in the way." Luc rolled his eyes.

"Sorry," John said, "but if anyone can test one's resolve, it's Amy."

"I'll send my human friends at ten. They'll lead you on the club hop." Richard pushed away from the table and shook hands with John and Luc. "Good luck. You'll need it."

CHAPTER EIGHT

Luc dressed in a slate gray, Dolce & Gabbana pin-striped suit. No shirt underneath, just a long scarf draped around his shoulders and tucked into the lapels. His sculpted chest, smooth and hard as marble, shone from the deep vee created by the double-breasted suit jacket. He splashed Calvin Klein's Eternity for Men on his neck to mask a bit of his intoxicating vampire scent. He wanted to turn heads like your average gorgeous guy, not like God's gift to women. "How do I look?" He turned to John.

"Like you need to ask? Just try to get to Amy before another woman grabs you."

"I'm not interested. What's the phrase? Why go out for hamburger when you've got steak at home?"

"Weird adage coming from a vampire, but I get your drift. Anyway, if I know Amy, she'll be in your face with her hand at your crotch the minute you walk in the door. So, let's hear your spiel." John folded his arms across his chest. "And imagine her hand tightening around your balls."

"Good evening, my lovely. Care for a cocktail?" Luc rolled his tongue over his lips.

"You've almost got *me* turned on." John laughed. "It's a damn good thing she didn't see you in Venice, but remember, say you're from Florence. Don't want her to connect any dots."

"Don't worry. By the end of the evening, she'll be eating out of my hand, and I'll have ascertained her whereabouts for the rest of the week."

"I hope you don't have to screw her. Lord only knows what foul places she's been."

"I've got good condoms, just in case. If it comes to doing the dastardly deed for the sake of information, I'll rise to the occasion." Luc smiled.

John shuddered. "Here's hoping you won't have to."

* * *

Luc scanned the bar and the stairway to the second level of The Key Club. His two human companions had guessed that Amy would begin her evening here in Kings Cross, and then graduate to the Pacha and on to the SeOne. They were right about her first stop.

"Over there," Robert, the taller of his two companions, said. Luc glanced in the direction Robert indicated, locking eyes with Amy in time to see her mouth the word, "Dibs." Amy's two apprentices, one male and one female, followed her gaze and simultaneously licked their full lips.

As Amy and her two young vampires approached, Luc said, "Looks like we're one-on-one, boys."

Earl, the shorter, blond human, said to Luc, "The guy's mine."

"Where have you been all my life?" Amy asked as she extended her hand to shake and then diverted it to squeeze Luc's thigh. "I thought I knew all the vamps in London."

"Waiting for you, Beautiful." Luc could lay it on just as thick and syrupy as Amy. He removed her hand from his thigh and brought it to his lips. "And I'm not from London. Name's Marco. I'm from Florence, but I have business here."

"What kind of business?"

"Fashion. I'm here scouting for models, and you certainly fit the bill. Size 4?"

"You have a good eye, and I suspect that's not the only thing about you that's exceptional." Amy's eyes visually undressed Luc from head to toe. "Don't know when I've seen a more handsome hunk of marble." She bared her teeth.

"Slow down, Sweetheart. I don't even know your name."

"Since when has that been a prerequisite?"

"Let's build the tension a bit, shall we?" Luc wasn't about to get trapped into having sex without first getting the information he needed.

"Oh, all right." Amy nodded toward the bar

"Bloody Mary?" Luc asked.

"Sure, and the name's Amy."

Over the next hour, Luc shared with Amy that he would be in London for a week, coordinating fashion shows at Harrods on behalf of several Italian designers.

"Such a coincidence. I'll be at Harrods on Thursday," she said. Her eyes held a sinister sparkle. "I'm partial to the dressing rooms in the designer salon. They're...spacious."

"Good. It's difficult to get kinky when you're cramped."

"Oh, I like your style." Amy laughed, and then nodded to her accomplices. "Aidan and Alyssa seem to be getting on well with your friends. Why don't you bring them?"

"The more the merrier, I always say."

His business wrapped up for the night, he didn't want to linger. "I'd love to stay and chat, but I have other plans for the evening."

"I thought you'd want to hunt with me and end the evening with a nice gang bang." Amy stuck out her bottom lip.

"I'll see you on Thursday," Luc said. "Keep it tight for me."

As Luc left the bar, he reflected on how ludicrous his last statement was. He bid his human friends good evening and returned to The Dorchester.

* * *

"Piece of cake," Luc said to John as he slung his jacket across the back of the couch in their double suite. "Thursday at two o'clock at Harrods. We've got her."

"Just remember, I want to kill her."

"Okay by me, but if it comes to a choice between having sex and offing her, I'll have to beat you to the punch."

"I could always break in and rescue your virtue."

"You're a bit late for that." Luc chuckled.

"How well I know. I'll make sure the way is clear when you exit the dressing room. I'm tempted to send the back-ups home. You, Richard and I should be able to handle this."

"They need to stick around, just in case," Luc said.

"You're right. The woman's a cornucopia of evil."

* * *

John, Luc and Richard spent Wednesday going over the plans for their attack. Richard arranged for Harrods' security to evacuate the first floor. The London Police were in on the caper, too. They'd been trailing Amy and her coven, but a police kill against vampires can be a messy business; too much blood, and too many human casualties. They were satisfied to monitor the action, not participate.

Luc would meet Amy at the first floor designer studio, which was actually one flight up from the ground floor. His two human companions would keep Aidan and Alyssa amused while he and Amy found a dressing room. John and Richard would ambush and kill the vamps, and then join Luc in the dressing room to dispose of Amy. The guys from Eastern Europe would be stationed along the exit route, which led down the escalator, through the busy restaurants and cafes, and out to Hans Road. Sounded good on paper.

They spent Wednesday night on the streets, overfeeding to bolster their strength for Thursday's caper. Arriving at Harrod's at ten a.m, they did a final run through. At two p.m., Luc strolled into the designer studio in black jeans and a deep purple cashmere sweater. He threw his leather jacket over a tub chair as he approached Amy, who sensed his presence and turned from the gossamer chartreuse gown she was fingering on a mannequin. Luc immediately noticed that not only did she have Aidan and Alyssa with her, but she'd brought another three novices.

"Did you want an audience?" Luc nodded toward the three young vampires.

"They've been particularly good. Or nasty. Depending on your perspective. Anyway, I promised them a treat. The security guard told me we have the floor to ourselves. The store personnel are in some sort of meeting, and they aren't allowing customers on the floor for another hour, but of course, I'm not the average customer. Isn't that convenient for us?" Amy licked her lips. "You don't mind my young friends watching a couple of pros get it on, do you?"

Luc quickly processed the threat. His human friends could keep the two more dangerous vampires occupied in the salon. The novices wouldn't expect a kill, so he'd have the element of surprise, but killing Amy would take some finesse.

"Let's show them how it's done," Luc said. He held his hand out to Amy and pulled her toward the dressing room. The three novices followed.

Luc's eyes darted around the dressing room as soon as they entered the gilded French door. A huge, skirted ottoman in candlelight silk anchored the hexagonal room. The walls were lined with mirrors, but there would be no reflections from the current occupants. He closed the door.

"This is one show I would have enjoyed watching," Amy said, gesturing toward the mirrors. "I'll just have to take your words for it," she said to her accomplices, who had stationed themselves around the ottoman.

Luc had knives tucked into sheaths at the inside of his wrists. His original plan had been to wrench Amy's neck, and then cut off her head with the knives, but he knew he wouldn't have time to sever her head with the other vampires bearing down on him. As he assembled plan B in his mind, he hoped an initial strike on Amy would subdue her long enough to kill the other vampires before he had a chance to finish her off. Oh well, here goes.

Amy reached for Luc's crotch, and he realized he'd need to concentrate on the task at hand. Damn. She wasn't the least bit appealing. Amazing the damper real love can put on a formerly indiscriminate libido. But if he couldn't get it up, he'd never be able to catch her off guard. He closed his eyes and envisioned Meredith; her softness, her vulnerability, and her readiness for him. He ached to hold her, to make her his, and he swelled in response to his erotic thoughts. He opened his eyes, gauging the proximity of Amy's accomplices, who were encroaching on the ottoman.

"Back up, kids," he said. "Your boss is going to need some writing room." He smiled at Amy. "Let's get you out of that spandex, shall we?"

Gold zippers crisscrossed Amy's clingy black turtleneck. Luc hooked his finger in the zipper loop that started just below her left jaw. He pulled, and the zip meandered diagonally across Amy's body to end at her waist. Luc gave a final yank, freeing Amy's bouncy breasts and eliciting a low hiss from her.

"That's about all the foreplay I need," she said, pulling Luc hard against her, and then tumbling back on the ottoman.

Luc slipped his hand inside the waistband of her tight fuchsia sweatpants and yanked them down to her knees, disabling her legs.

"Close your eyes," he whispered seductively in her ear. She did as she was instructed, simultaneously grappling for his zipper. While her hands were occupied, Luc tipped her head to the left to nip at her neck. From his peripheral vision, he saw the novices undressing. One young female vampire was massaging her bare breasts, while the lone male in the threesome had unleashed his penis to dangle it in front of the other female, who was kneeling before him, poised to take him in her mouth. Luc figured they'd never be more occupied than they were at this moment.

The only noise was the quick crack of Amy's neck when he wrenched it. She flinched, and then collapsed on the ottoman. The young male was the first to notice his boss's distress. He leaped on Luc's back and sunk his teeth into his neck. The female who'd been copping a self-feel aimed for Luc's penis, and he turned his attention to the impending crisis.

The male stayed attached to Luc's neck, trying to weaken him from blood loss, as Luc grabbed the vampire in front of him and flung her into the other female, who had been too surprised to make a move. Both vamps shook off their collision and leaped at Luc, just as John and Richard came through the dressing room door and Amy readjusted her wrenched head to join the fray.

Richard grabbed the young male by the back of his neck, and he immediately disengaged his teeth from Luc. John lunged for Amy. If looks could kill, Amy displayed evil incarnate. Her lips curled back over her teeth, and her eyes glared black and bottomless at John. There was no need for words.

She leaped at John's groin and sank her teeth through his jeans and into his upper thigh. She grasped him by the hips, probably assuming he'd be slow to move with his family jewels in such close proximity to her teeth. Not so. John grabbed her blonde ponytail and yanked her head back. She came away from his thigh with her smile wrapped around a hunk of John's flesh. He seemed to ignore the pain, snapping his right arm down to extract a wooden stake hidden in his sleeve. He plunged it deep into her chest. The blood shot out from her wound like spray from a high-powered fire hose. It splattered against the mirrors in the dressing room. The novices, realizing their leader was done for, froze and began to beg for mercy.

"Sorry," Richard said. "You sealed your doom with Amy."

Luc, Richard and John each took a novice, quickly slit their throats and decapitated them with obsidian blades. They changed into Harrods' janitorial suits, which Richard had stashed a day earlier outside the dressing room. When they emerged from the blood-soaked room with the body bags, they strode to the down escalator, and then calmly walked through men's shoes & accessories, Harrods souvenir arcade, the perfumery, and into the maze of restaurants and cafes on the ground floor before exiting out door eleven and slinging the body bags into a dumpster outside the restaurant entrance.

CHAPTER NINE

"Hello, John? Are you all right? Is Amy dead? How's Luc?"

"Is this Lady Lauren Wright?"

"Huh?"

"Seems the British government forgot they knighted me five hundred years ago. They want to do it again, or at least, Scotland Yard is pushing for it."

"Amy's...?"

"Yes, my love, she's dead, and her coven is broken up. Luc, Richard, and I killed Amy and her lieutenants, and my friends from Eastern Europe took care of the rest of her coven at her manor house."

"Thank God! When are you coming home?"

"How does tomorrow night sound?"

"Fabulous. I'll be at the airport with bells on."

"And nothing else?"

"I wish." I was so turned on just thinking about his return that I began to pace the kitchen floor.

"Luc'll be with me. He wants to see Meredith again before he heads back to Venice."

"Do you think it's safe for her to see him?" John chuckled. "Yes, I do."

* * *

Meredith and I waited at the end of the international concourse at OIA. The flight was just a few minutes late, but every moment of delay made me more anxious to see John.

A wave of passengers turned the corner, and my heart raced as I looked for John and Luc. Several minutes passed, and the first wave dispersed into the crowd of waiting relatives and friends. My heart sank as the lull in deplaning passengers seemed to stretch for hours. Then, in the blink of a vampire's eye, John and Luc waved to us.

"Here come the two most handsome men on the face of this earth," Meredith said.

"And they're ours," I added. I wanted to flash to John instantly, but I kept my instincts in check and opted for a quick human walk. With just a few feet between us, I leapt into his arms. He dropped his laptop and spun me around. When he set my feet down, he asked, "Will you faint when I kiss you?"

"Depends on how good a job you do."

He bent his head, and I closed my eyes as his lips brushed my mouth. He parted my lips gently with his tongue and began his sensuous exploration, tasting and branding the crevices of my mouth. Laying claim to me. When I opened my eyes again, John was carrying me to baggage claim.

"Did I miss anything?"

John chuckled. "Just wait 'til I get you home."

"Shall we burn the condoms first?"

"I assume you mean that metaphorically." He smiled, and then grabbed his Hartmann tweed luggage from the baggage turnstile. "We'll flush them." He took my hand, and we headed for the parking garage.

* * *

I'd been so focused on John, I hadn't paid any attention to Luc and Meredith. Now, as I settled behind the wheel of my Volvo for our drive home, I adjusted the rearview mirror and caught a glimpse of them in the backseat. Luc was studying Meredith with his touch, tracing his fingers across her eyelids and down her nose, outlining her lips with his thumb. He seemed to be drinking her in, and she looked like putty under his touch.

John had told me that Luc really cared about her. I only hoped he'd allow her to make her own decision without undue vampire influence. We're a seductive lot. How else could we hone in on human necks with so little protest? John could have had me so easily, but he tempered his instincts and bided his time. Would Luc be as patient? I knew Meredith was smitten, but would her infatuation overrule her head? Bottom line...did she really want to become a vampire?

* * *

When we pulled into our circular driveway, I left my car parked behind Meredith's. John and I went into the house while Luc and Meredith went through the house to the gazebo in the backyard. I watched them sit together on the loveseat there.

"I know exactly what you're thinking," John said, as I chewed my lip and looked out the window at our friends.

"Okay, since I can't read your thoughts, what am I thinking?"

"She's a woman in love. Let her body and intuition do the work. That's how you made your decision." He wrapped his arms around me from behind and nuzzled my hair.

"I just can't picture Meredith as a vamp."

"She'll be even more stunning."

"That's true." I turned in my husband's arms.

"Besides, we may be getting ahead of ourselves," John said. "I know Luc cares about her, but I don't know that he's ready to commit to an eternal relationship."

"But she's not in danger, right?"

"Not unless she pricks her finger on a rose stem, and the smell of her blood overpowers him."

"Jeez, I better get them out of the garden."

"Lauren." John lifted my chin to look in my eyes. "Leave them alone. I don't want to waste one more minute." My husband swept me into his arms and carried me up the stairs. He began peeling off my clothes on the ascent, unbuttoning my blouse, unzipping my slacks, throwing my shoes off the balcony. The man was deft with his aim. Both shoes landed in the pot of the huge Robellini palm that anchored the foyer. By the time we reached our bedroom, I was down to my bra and panties.

John peeled the lace cups of my bra from my breasts and propped them on top of my underwire, exposing my breasts in a fashion that had them standing at more attention than usual. He sank to his knees in front of me and hungrily took a breast in his mouth, twirling his tongue around my nipple and then suckling me like a starved infant. He kneaded my other breast with his fingers and with his other hand, caressed my buttocks and slipped his fingers under my lace thong.

I was already wet and swollen as he wedged his fingers between my thighs and rubbed my sensitive bud, gently at first, and then with an urgency borne of his increasing need.

He moved his head down my body and proceeded to unfold me in a sensuous play of his hands on both of my thighs and his thumbs spreading my feminine lips to expose the core of my passion. He pulled up gently on the folds to bring my bud to his mouth, but before he began to circle the most erotic part of my body, he looked up at me and said, "I love you, Lady Wright, and tonight I will take you to new heights of pleasure. Open yourself to me now. Hold nothing back."

His tongue touched me softly with a long, sensuous lick, ending at my engorged bud, and then circling the point of my pleasure until my legs began to shake.

"John, please stop. Just for a minute. Stop, and let me catch my breath." I tried to ease his head away from my body, but he was too strong.

He looked up at me. "Close your eyes and breathe, Lauren." He resumed the rhythmic, erotic waves, opening me.

I gave myself to his strength and his love, trusting him completely. He lifted me, placed me gently on the bed, and then resumed his exploration. I closed my eyes and dug my nails into the sheets. If I'd chosen John for my hold on reality, he'd have had puncture wounds. My climax came in a shudder that nearly levitated me. John wiped his mouth across my thigh and slowly crept up my body, propping one hand under my hip and the other behind my neck.

"Now, my love, you will come again, but this time, hold on to me."

I wrapped my arms around his neck and brought his lips to my mouth. He entered me, and I embraced his manhood, squeezing him tightly to welcome his thrusts. He began rhythmically moving inside me, skin to skin. The feel of him was so intimate, so erotic. More than ever before, our union blended our bodies, and the thought that we might be creating a new being to love and cherish made our lovemaking all the more poignant. As I relaxed into John's sensuous rhythm, he began to swell. Without the condom, he seemed bigger. He reached my womb and filled me in a way he never had before.

"Wrap your legs around me," he said, raising my head off the pillow.

I was lost in the sheer size of him and the undulations of our bodies, moving as one.

Again, he swelled as his climax overtook him and he spasmed in my arms. His orgasm set me on fire, and my sheath clutched him in waves that kept us conjoined. When we finally relaxed in each others' arms, I punched him on the shoulder.

"Ouch. What was that for?" He rolled to his side and propped himself on one elbow.

"How did you do that?" I asked.

"What?"

"Make yourself bigger."

"It's a vampire thing. I couldn't do it with a condom. Too tight a fit as it was." He laughed. "Besides, if you'd known I could swell, you'd have disposed of the condoms prematurely."

"I wouldn't have done that."

"No?"

"Well, maybe not."

* * *

Twilight bathed the gazebo in a soft glow as Luc and Meredith held hands on the wicker loveseat.

"I don't get you," Meredith said, wrinkling her nose.

"What's not to get?" Luc looked at her, unblinking.

"I can't figure out whether you're just amused or if you *really* like me?"

"Oh, I *really* like you." Luc started to slip into his irresistible vampire gaze, but caught himself and looked past Meredith to the lush garden outside the gazebo.

"Where do we go from here?" Meredith asked, swatting at a mosquito, and then folding her legs up to hug her knees under her chin.

"I don't know, Meredith. I know that the meaning of life became much clearer to me after we met, but I'm not sure what that means for us. Whoa. *Us.* I've never used that word before."

"Could you be more vague?" Meredith smiled. "I'm kidding. I have no clue what you mean."

"How about this...the only truth I've ever known is you. I feel like I've been playing at life, toying with women, for a very long time."

"And you don't want to toy with me?"

"No, Meredith. I want to cherish you. I also want to make love to you even more than I want your blood."

"But you do want my blood."

"Oh, yeah."

"I'm not sure I'm ready for that." Meredith squeaked. "Perhaps I should go home now."

"Probably a good idea."

"I'll risk a kiss goodnight."

Luc smiled. It was the kind of seductive smile only a very experienced kisser would dare at a moment like this. "My pleasure," he said, rising from the loveseat and holding his hand out to Meredith. She put her hand in his and he pulled her up. He whipped out a handkerchief from the pocket of his grey wool slacks. "I want to taste you, not your lip gloss." He took her chin in one hand and deftly blotted her lips with the handkerchief. "Ready?" he asked.

"As I'll ever be." Meredith closed her eyes.

Luc weaved his fingers into the hair at the base of her neck and held the back of her head securely in his hand. He kneaded her scalp with his fingers.

"Open your eyes, Meredith."

She fluttered them open. "What?"

"I want you to know that as vulnerable as you feel right now, I feel just as vulnerable."

"I doubt that." Meredith's erratic breathing spoke louder than her words.

"My vulnerability is to keep myself from taking you. Do you understand that?"

With their lips only inches apart, Meredith said, "You keep track of your vulnerability, and I'll take care of mine."

Luc pressed his full lips on Meredith's. He crushed her to him, and then softened his embrace, spreading his fingers across the small of her back. His supple tongue tickled her lips open, but he delayed his entry into her mouth by first tracing her lips with his tongue. When he breathed into her mouth, he felt her shoulders relax and the intensity of her passion increase with her deepened breath. She curled the tips of her fingers into his back and thrust her tongue into his mouth.

Her mounting passion overwhelmed him, and he inadvertently nicked her tongue with his fang. She recoiled with a jerk, scraping her tongue along his fang, and displaying a line of fresh blood.

"Ouch." Meredith's hand went to her mouth.

Luc's eyes glowed red, and he quickly backed away from her. He closed his eyes and balled his fists at his side. "Just give me a minute," he said between clenched teeth.

"What's wrong?" Meredith slid her hand from her mouth to rest on her throat.

Luc opened his eyes slowly, burning them into Meredith's. "You can't imagine how amazing you taste. Your blood is like the sweetest honey." He squeezed his eyes shut, again. "It makes me hear music."

"What kind of music?" Meredith whispered.

"Ravel's Bolero. It's my favorite." Luc opened his eyes. He unballed his fists and tried to breathe more deeply. "Can I try something?"

"What?"

"Would you let me heal you?"

Meredith hesitated, and then said, "Yes."

Luc took Meredith's hand and placed it behind his head. He pressed his lips gently to hers and eased her mouth open with his tongue. Tracing the line of the scrape, he sealed the wound with his tongue, and then enticed her tongue back into his mouth.

"Feel better?" he asked as he finished the deep kiss.

"Completely," she said, though she stiffened as his lips

moved to her neck.

"Relax, Meredith. I'm under control. I promise I won't bite." Luc nibbled her ear playfully, and then he tucked her head under his chin and held her tight.

"When are you going home?" she murmured into his chest, wrapping her arms around him as tightly as he held her.

"Day after tomorrow." He kissed her gently on the head, and then gazed across the lawn to the lake, shimmering with the full moon's reflection.

"What about...us?" Meredith whispered.

"Ah, yes." Luc disengaged from their embrace and motioned for Meredith to sit. As she sat on the loveseat, he leaned against the gazebo and crossed his arms over his chest. "Can I level with you?"

"Please."

"I had a speech prepared about how you've changed my life, but it seems awfully trite now that I've tasted you." Luc chuckled. "I want you more than ever, but I'm struggling with bringing you into this crazy life of mine. I've never turned anyone. Never wanted to."

"Do you want to turn me?"

"Oh, yeah." His eyes glowed red as he fixed her with his seductive stare. "But I haven't thought through what happens next."

"Me, either."

"Your life would never be the same, Meredith. You know that."

"I think I'm ready for it." Meredith reached out and took Luc's hand.

Luc brought her hand to his lips and kissed her fingers. "I'm not sure I am."

CHAPTER TEN

Since Luc went home, some three weeks ago, Meredith has regaled me *ad infinitum* with the last conversation she had with him.

"Sweetie," I said, "I know he loves you. That's not the issue."

"Then why can't he commit?"

"After five hundred years of roaming the earth single, I guess he just can't imagine himself as a married man...er, vamp."

"John didn't seem to have a problem." Meredith paced back and forth in my living room. She'd always had an abundance of nervous energy, but even her revved-up nature was working overtime. "Why can't Luc see that I'm the best thing that ever happened to him?"

"He knows that. I think his bigger problem is that he's not sure you'd be happy as a vamp."

"But I would...I would...I know I would." Meredith was wringing her hands while Smokey and Penelope's little heads, propped together in Smokey's leopard skin dog bed, bobbed side-to-side in cadence with Meredith's pacing.

"Mere, give him time. I think he'll come around."

"What's time to him? I'll be thirty-one next month. He's locked in at thirty for eternity."

"This is an extraordinary step for him. Vamps don't divorce. You'd be looking at the same face, with the same foibles, until the end of time." I was getting dizzy from watching her pace. I blinked to clear my head. "Are you absolutely sure this is what you want?"

"One hundred percent." Meredith stopped her pacing and gripped the back of the sofa I was lounging on. "I've analyzed this every which way since he left. I don't want to live my life without him."

"Then I hope and pray you get what you want." I patted her white-knuckled hands.

* * *

The next few weeks flew by. John took the Florida bar exam in February, and he was so sure he'd done well that he rented office space just off Park Avenue and put up his shingle--The Law Offices of John A. Wright. He bought ads in the *Orlando Business Journal* and joined the Greater Orlando Chamber of Commerce. With a specialty in intellectual property and international business, he told me he didn't think he'd have people beating down his door, but if he could secure a couple of good clients, it would provide a cover for his vigilante work.

We were like your average professional couple during the day. John was energized by his work, and I was back to my usual routine. After work one afternoon early in March, I found him sipping a glass of B positive at the kitchen sink as I tossed my purse on the counter.

"You won't believe who retained me today," he said, leaning against the sink.

"I'm going to need a hint," I said, opening the

refrigerator to retrieve my own bottle of B positive and join him in a blood cocktail.

"You know how the police have been tailing the local Mob, trying to pick them up on something?"

"Yeah."

"The big kahuna strolled into my office today. Seems he's invented a new tool for clipping cigars, and he needs a copyright."

"I don't suppose that tool could also work on fingers?"

"In his line of work, probably." John refilled his glass. "Anyhow, this is a great in. Can't wait to tell the police chief."

"What's his name?" I sat at the bar and picked up *The Orlando Sentinel* on the counter.

"Rick Maroon. I'm meeting him for lunch at the Citrus Club on Friday. Which reminds me, I'll need to make sure Doreen can drive me."

"You know, darling, you should probably get a driver's license." I had been planning to wait until bed to tell John my news, but maybe this was as good a time as any.

"Doreen loves to drive the CTS, and she doesn't have that much to do, anyway."

"She's getting ready to be busier." I set my glass down and walked to John, who had moved from the sink to the kitchen island. I snuggled into his open arms.

"Really, doing what?" he asked.

"Babysitting."

REAL MEN HAVE FANGS

DCL Publications, LLC

CHAPTER ONE

"Mad? I'm furious!" Lauren huffed as only a vampire can, expelling a hint of purple-tinged haze into the front seat of John's Cadillac. "Can't you put the freaking Mafia off until the baby's born?"

If John's eyebrows arched any higher, they'd bump the roof. "I detect a trace of venom in your sweet breath, my love."

"A trace? It'll probably corrode the dashboard." Lauren angled her body to the door, where a subsequent puff fogged the window with violet iridescence. "And you're avoiding my question." She tapped her foot on the zebra-patterned floor mat. "You just passed the Florida Bar exam, for Pete's sake. Did your first client have to be the most dangerous man in Orlando?"

The air in the car was so thick with Lauren's disapproval; John had to fan the space between them to squint at her. "Honey, I've had far more dangerous adversaries in my 500 years. He's only human, after all."

"Are you kidding? He has an army of contacts—all over the globe." Lauren shook her head, rolled down the window and waved out some of the haze. "You think you're safe because he doesn't know you're a vampire, but what if he finds out?" She looked back at John. "He'll load his gun with silver bullets faster than you can say 'Dracula.'"

"Lauren, I'll be fine, and I would never put you and our baby in harm's way."
John reached over to touch Lauren's tummy, which had recently blossomed with roundness.

"I am *so* not happy about this." Lauren folded her arms over her bulge and chewed on her top lip. She continued to stew for a minute, building up her next head of steam. "What if he captures you and wraps you up in silver chains? Lots of help I'd be. I can't even morph to bat form in my present condition, and you still haven't taught me how to vaporize."

John ran a hand over Lauren's hair. "You have to trust me." He veered onto the entrance ramp for Interstate 4 and merged between two cars that were barely a Volkswagen length apart, let alone a Cadillac. Lauren gasped as both startled drivers laid on their horns, but John ignored them and continued to weave through the heavy traffic, creating spaces that humans couldn't fathom.

Lauren squeezed her eyes shut. "I know I encouraged you to get your driver's license, but reckless driving can get you a whopping fine and possible suspension."

John laughed and then touched Lauren's cheek. "Don't worry; the Orlando Police are in my debt. They won't ticket me." John exited Interstate 4 at the Altamonte ramp and deftly wound his way through residential neighborhoods. Careening around the final curve on Palmer Avenue, he slowed just before he reached their street, Bonita Place.

"Why don't you leave the car there?" She pointed to the circular driveway in front of their large Victorian home.

"Don't you think I can fit it in the garage?"

Lauren rolled her eyes. "Not without a crowbar. It's a

Goodwill warehouse in there. Until I get rid of the stuff from my house, there's no room."

John hit the button for the garage opener, and in a matter of seconds, wedged the big car between Lauren's floral sofa and her two overstuffed chairs. "Voila!"

Lauren blew her bangs out of her eyes. "That's the final driving lesson for you, Bubba. Next stop, NASCAR."

"That would be fun." John laughed. "Do you think I could drive the Viagra car?"

"Considering that's the last drug you'd need, it's a good cover. But I know my NASCAR, and Viagra isn't a sponsor this year. Maybe you could drive the Prilosec car." She couldn't help but smile.

"For heartburn? Don't think so." John reached over and unbuckled Lauren's seat belt. "The only heartburn I have is the pain of you being angry with me." He gave her that gorgeous lopsided smile, the one he'd held in abeyance for 500 years, until he met her.

She opened her car door and swung her legs to the garage floor. Turning to look at John across the black hood, she sighed. There he stood, the sexiest, most handsome man in the universe, looking back at her with those violet eyes. He ran his tongue across his top lip. *Oh, Lordy.* "Sometimes you make me crazy, but I'll love you forever, John."

He rounded the car at vampire speed to sweep her into his arms.

"Consider this a reprieve," Lauren said, "but only for as long as it takes me to have an orgasm." She batted her eyelashes playfully.

"In that case, I shall take my time." He pressed her against the door of the car and wedged his thigh between her legs.

"Squeeze," she commanded, taking his hand and placing it on her breast.

"Oh, I'll do better than that." He pulled up her tank top and drew her nipple into his mouth, sucking hungrily.

As desire gripped her core, she reached to free his penis from his jeans. "Now."

"No, I told you. I'm taking my bloody time." He gathered her into his arms and carried her to the house.

Crackling with electricity from head to toe, she squealed when he kicked the back door open. "If you're as anxious as I am, let's christen the kitchen," she said.

"Only if you promise not to dispel that purple haze, again. You'll kill the African violets."

"I promise," she said.

He plunked her down, albeit gently, on the kitchen counter. Spreading her legs under her handkerchief skirt, he played in her juices for a while, and then he took her chin in his hand as he plunged into her depths. "Nothing," he said, "nothing in the world comes close to this."

She moved against him hungrily, but he pulled back. "Not so fast," he said, withdrawing his penis. "Let's give each room its due."

Lauren's sexual frustration mounted as John teased her nipples through the butler's pantry, licked her feminine bud on the living room couch, and bent her over the foyer banister to enter her briefly from behind. By the time they reached their bedroom, she was frantic with pent up desire.

"Tonight, I say when." He carried her to the bed and then moved away from her to the Palladian window. He stood in profile, his erection prominent in the diffused light of the moon.

She swallowed hard, waiting. After a few agonizing moments, he turned to her.

"You have to trust me, Lauren. In everything." He moved slowly to the bed and eased his hand up the inside of her thigh. "When."

* * *

John stared at the heavy-set man sitting across the desk

from him. "Don't make this any more difficult than it already is." He drummed his fingers on his desk, hoping he conveyed a worried expression.

Rick Maroon, the Orlando Mafia don, guffawed. "Nothing difficult about it. I hired you. I expect you to make it work."

John stiffened for a moment as the don shifted his large posterior on the leather chair and reached into his coat pocket. He opened a pocketknife and began cleaning his fingernails. John relaxed and held back a grimace at Rick's uncouth behavior.

"Mr. Maroon, I'm an intellectual property attorney. You sought my services to patent your cigar cutters." John leaned back in his chair and folded his arms across his broad chest. "I don't do extortion."

"This ain't extortion. It's just a little song-and-dance. Should be easy for you." The don resumed his fingernail chore, and then his eyes moved to the walls of John's office, scanning the many-framed certificates, and pointing at one with the pocket knife. "Cambridge. That's one helluva law degree."

"My legal prowess doesn't mean I will skirt the law."

"No, but I bet it means you can stretch the interpretation. You in, or not?"

John sighed and leaned forward in his chair. "I'm in." *Nice bluff, John.* Though fooling humans was typically easy for vampires, Rick Maroon was shrewder than the average mortal. He played dumb, but John knew the guy was much smarter than he let on.

"Good." Rick Maroon snapped his knife shut, and John stood up, assuming the meeting was over. Rick walked around John's desk, took hold of his shoulders, and planted a kiss on both cheeks. "*Ciao.*" As he swaggered out of John's office, he turned. "One more thing, now that you're family, I'd like you and the wife to come to my house this Sunday for a barbecue. We start with drinks at five p.m. No way you'd miss it, right?"

"Lauren and I will be there." *But she's not going to like it.*

"Great. I'm on Via Tuscany in Winter Park. The Mediterranean villa where Via Capri intersects. Mickey'll let you in."

"Brilliant."

"Brilliant?" Rick laughed. "You Brits are too much. Brilliant. Sure." He chuckled his way out of John's office.

As soon as John heard the front door close, he turned off the recorder, made a mental note to pick up flowers for Lauren on the way home, and called the Orlando Police Department. "Don't swallow your toothpick," he said to Chief Compton, "but Rick Maroon just hired me."

The chief laughed. "That didn't take long."

John could picture Orlando's female police chief removing the ever-present toothpick from her mouth. It was her signature, first employed as a rookie when she wanted to look like one of the boys.

"I've already got a good case for extortion. He called the import company from my office and threatened them." John smiled as he glanced at his Cambridge law degree on the wall. He'd had to change the graduation date from 1525 to 2000, but with a bit of updating, what he'd learned almost 500 years ago had still enabled him to pass the Florida Bar.

"If we can't pin him on cocaine, we may have to fall back on the cigar cutters. It would allow us to haul him in," she said.

"We'll pin him, Chief. I taped the conversation in my office, and I should be able to get more information this weekend. Lauren and I are invited for dinner at his house."

"That should be interesting."

"And I can hear through walls."

The chief snickered. "You're our secret weapon, John. Just make sure he doesn't find out who you really are."

* * *

Lauren arranged the dozen red roses in a crystal vase and placed them in the center of the dining room table. She inhaled the rich scent of her favorite flowers. "I appreciate your attempt to butter me up," she said to John, who leaned against the arched doorway to the dining room, "but nothing's going to make me feel better about your new client."

"Honey, the police have been after this guy for years. This is a one-time opportunity."

"It's bad timing, John. Couldn't you at least put him off until the first of the year?"

"I would if I could, but his plan's already in motion."

Lauren crossed the room and snuggled into John's arms. "I feel like our lives finally have a semblance of order. And you've even gotten over your allergies."

"It was that musky coffin. Now that I sleep in a bed, I don't sneeze anymore."

"I feel very uneasy about this. What if it turns bad?"

"It won't." John kissed the top of her head.

She relaxed into John's embrace. "I've never been to a house on Via Tuscany."

"It's the most prestigious address in town." John pulled Lauren into the butler's pantry that separated the dining room from the kitchen. He grabbed a bottle of Pinot Grigio from the wine rack. "Think this'll do?"

"Yes, though he'd probably prefer a good red."

"How about some B positive?"

"Cute. Go with the Pinot Grigio. At least it's Italian." Lauren twirled around once in her peach-colored sundress. "Am I dressed appropriately for a Mafia barbecue?"

John held her at arms' length. "You look like a ripe apricot, and the cleavage display may get you invited back without me."

"I can't help it. Pregnancy has popped them out to monumental proportions."

John wrapped her in his arms. "Believe me, I'm not

complaining, but I don't want to set my wife up for a lewd reaction from this guy."

"Maybe my décolletage will distract him while you wander the house."

"Are you kidding? I'd never leave you alone with him."

"What's he like?"

"If he were any more over the top, he'd be under himself."

"That stereotypical, huh?" Lauren shivered. "Though he's probably charming, in a smarmy sort of way."

"Not in the slightest. Do me a favor and watch my eyes when he's around. They may glow red in spite of my self-control." John frowned and checked his watch. "Time to go."

Lauren picked up her polka dot purse and the bottle of wine. "Are you driving?"

"Uh-huh, unless you have an objection."

"No, I'll just wear a neck brace to guard against whiplash."

"Such a comedienne." John offered Lauren his arm.

***

The late afternoon sun beat down on the black car. "I hope we'll be inside for part of the evening," Lauren said. "This built-in thermostat of mine is registering 100 degrees, at least." Lauren adjusted the seat belt under her tummy bulge.

John took his eyes off the road and rested his hand on her thigh. "You are one hot mama."

"Literally. I know why women in Florida try to time their deliveries in the winter. The bigger you get, the hotter."

"December should be perfect. Not that we planned it that way."

Lauren chuckled. "True. We weren't thinking about my due date when we threw away the condoms, though vampire gestation is puzzling. From the research I've done, I figure I'm due somewhere between November 15 and December 31."

Lauren sensed John stiffen as he pulled into a bricked driveway with a wrought iron security gate. A huge man in a black suit and dark sunglasses stood by the gate. He approached the car.

"You must be Mickey," John said.

The man nodded.

"I'm John Wright. This is my wife, Lauren." John handed Mickey his driver's license.

Mickey glanced at the license, and then bent down to look in the window at John. "So, you're the new consigliari." He handed the license back to John, and this time, he looked at Lauren. "Drive through to the valet station. And welcome." Mickey smiled lewdly and adjusted his crotch.

As John drove past Mickey, he said to Lauren, "I believe that's the caliber of slime we can expect from Maroon's employees."

John stopped at a small blue tent, where an attendant hopped out of a lawn chair and raced to the passenger door. Opening the door for Lauren, the attendant helped her out and then bolted around the car as John tossed him the keys.

Lauren and John held hands as they walked up the circular drive to Maroon's palatial villa. Granite steps led to a portico flanked by two life-size statues of bare Roman beauties with Mona Lisa smiles on their marble lips. Wrought iron bars on all the windows had a decorative effect, while the armed guards that lurked at the home's corners served a more obvious purpose. The massive front door sported a gilded family crest.

John pushed a button that chimed loud enough to scare the birds out of nearby trees. "That tune's familiar."

Lauren cocked her head. "I believe it's the theme from 'The Godfather.'"

"Is that supposed to be funny?" John screwed up his nose.

Lauren squeezed John's hand as the door opened slowly to a grinning man in a silky, peach-colored shirt, unbuttoned to mid-chest. A thick gold chain glinted against curly dark chest hair. He glanced briefly at John, and then turned his attention to Lauren. It takes a lot for a vampire to blush: blood doesn't rise to the skin's surface as quickly as humans. But Lauren felt a blush creep up her neck to her face as his eyes grazed her wedged sandals, traveled up her calves, stopped briefly at her tummy bump, and then settled firmly on her cleavage. His eyes never made it to her face. "You must have gotten the memo," he said.

"Excuse me?" Lauren asked. Her skin crawled with prickles from his slimy stare.

"That's my favorite color, and we match." The man seemed proud of himself as he patted his comb-over.

Lauren laughed. "Mine too, Mr. Maroon...I assume." She handed him the bottle of Pinot Grigio. It was all she could do not to scrunch up her nose. The man reeked of Aramis and garlic.

"Thanks," he said, "And please, call me Rick." He kissed Lauren on both cheeks, and then turned to John. "You, get outta here." He guffawed and gave John a thumbs-to-the-road gesture. "Just kidding. Come in, come in."

He motioned for them to follow him through the house. "Annetta!" He bellowed as he moved into a two-story great room.

A large-breasted platinum blonde clip-clopped into the room on gold sling backs. Her white bikini looked more like a bra and thong underneath her see-through cover-up. "Coming, coming," she said, as she took her husband's arm. "I believe that's what I said this morning," she stage-whispered into his ear.

The don smiled broadly, revealing a huge gap between his front teeth. Lauren's trained eyes as a dentist honed in on the gaping space. "Bet you'd love to get hold of me, huh, doll?" He shook his finger at Lauren. "Nothin' doin'. This gap has brought me good luck." He clipped John on the shoulder. "Just lookin' at her, I'd have pegged her as a trophy wife. Who knew?" He chuckled.

"I don't recall mentioning that Lauren's a dentist," John said, and Lauren noticed the defensive set of his jaw.

The don winked at Lauren. "Just a little background check. Can't be too careful." He motioned to his wife, and Annetta pointed a French-manicured finger in the direction of the pool, visible through floor-to-ceiling windows in the expansive room.

"Follow me," she said. As Annetta jiggled through the room and out to the pool, her shapely bottom swayed to the beat of a steel drum band playing "Under the Sea." *Wasn't that exactly where many of the don's enemies were?*

Sunlight glinted against the shiny steel drums, and Lauren winced as the rays of light assaulted her eyes. She rummaged through her purse for her sunglasses, never far from reach.

"What, you don't like the sun?" the don asked.

"I love it, but it doesn't like me."

"Hmm, the way you ripped out those sunglasses, you'd think you were from Seattle." He laughed. "And you're so pale. You should be tan like Annetta." Rick slapped his wife on the bottom, which was still gyrating to the beat of the drums. "It ain't natural to be so white."

"My family has a history of skin cancer. I'm just very careful." Lauren hoped she'd adequately dismissed the issue.

"I guess it's your funeral." The don motioned to a grass-skirted bar. "Libation? I like Campari, myself. With soda." He nodded to the bartender.

"That's good for me," John said. "How 'bout you, honey?"

Lauren smoothed her hand over her tummy. "A cranberry juice would be nice."

As the bartender prepared their drinks, Rick eyed Lauren's bump. "Congratulations Pop." He slapped John on the back.

"Thank you," John said, wrapping an arm around

Lauren's waist. "We're pretty excited about it."

"Nothing like family," the don said. "Annetta gave me three sons." He held three fat fingers in front of John's nose. "They all work for me." He pointed to three tan, burly guys on lawn chairs, each sipping a tall drink. Their shapely female companions had identical highball glasses, except theirs were decorated with tiny umbrellas. "That's Carlo, Bernardo, and Anthony, and their significant others." Rick chuckled. "I believe they're significantly from the strip club."

The three men waved to their father.

"You have handsome sons," Lauren remarked. She also took note of the guns on their hips.

"You think so? The oldest thinks he knows it all, and the youngest thinks with his dick. The only one with any brains is Bernardo, my middle boy." Rick paused to look Lauren up and down. "Too bad you weren't around before this lout snatched you up." He poked John in the chest. "Jeeze, man, you're like a brick wall. How do you stay so fit?"

"I do crunches on an inversion machine," John lied.

"No shit? I have one of those old machines with a big belt that goes around your middle. All it does is jiggle my fat and make me horny." He slapped himself on the thigh. "Come on; let's prime our appetites with some shrimp while the ribs are on the grill."

The don put his sweaty arm around Lauren and led her to the hors d'oeuvres table where a melting ice sculpture of Neptune flanked the display of fruit, cheeses, and shrimp. Food held no appeal anyway, but the garlic smell that oozed from the don's pores almost made her gag.

"Next time, get Venus de Milo," Rick said to his wife as he pointed at the melting Neptune ice sculpture. "I'd rather see her boobs dripping on the food than this guy's wanger."

Annetta rolled her eyes. "Why don't I take Lauren out of this heat? I'm sure you fellas want to talk business, anyway."

Lauren blew John a kiss in parting and cocked one

eyebrow, hoping he took her cue that his eyes held angry specks of red. As she walked toward the house, she heard Rick say to John, "That's one gorgeous woman. You better keep an eye on her."

CHAPTER TWO

"Your home is beautiful," Lauren said as she and Annetta walked through an arched loggia into the house.

"Thanks.   I had lots of help pulling it together." Annetta took Lauren's elbow, guiding her up the stairs. "I'll show you the bedrooms first. They're all upstairs 'cause Rick thinks it's safer that way." Lauren caught Annetta's sideways glance.

"You can't be too careful."

Annetta shrugged. "Here's our room." She opened heavy double doors to an enormous bedroom, anchored by a heart-shaped bed located under a full-mirrored ceiling. Nodding at the ceiling, Annetta said, "Rick likes to be his own audience. "

Lauren started to enter the room, and then stopped herself. A mirror. No reflection. That would freak Annetta out. "Hope you don't mind if I just stand here in the hall," Lauren said. "I'm catching a breeze from up the stairs."

"Sure, honey, I've been there. Pregnancy can make you hotter than a volcano." Annetta pointed to the master bathroom, also with double doors. "Can you see the heart-shaped tub? We both have a place to rest our heads while we watch the weenie rise from under the bubbles."

Lauren laughed. "Who knew a heart shape could be so practical?"

"At least you didn't blush." Annetta smiled. "You're our kind of people. Come on, let's go back downstairs. I'll show you the library." Annetta took Lauren's arm and steered her toward a flight of stairs at the far end of the hall.

"What are the rest of the rooms up here?" Lauren pointed to other doors, where her extraordinary hearing was picking up muted sounds.

"Just guest bedrooms. I was going to show you, but with the doors closed, who knows what's going on." She rolled her eyes and hurried Lauren down the hall, rushing her down the stairs.

At the bottom of the stairs, Annetta opened a tall, elaborately carved door, depicting a scene of ancient scholars gathered around a large table. Opening the door revealed a very different scene—a threesome studying each other's anatomy—on a table much like the one featured on the door's relief. The blonde sandwich consisted of two of Annetta's sons with one of the women from the pool. To say they were in a compromising position would put it mildly.

Without missing a beat, Annetta shooed them away like they were stray cats. "Off the table, guys," she said. "Take your act upstairs. We got company here."

Lauren heard a mild "pop" as one appendage unplugged an orifice. Scrambling for clothes, the three exited through a recessed passage behind a bookcase, which slid back in place with none the wiser. *Clever.*

Annetta winked at Lauren. "Kids."

Kids? They're at least 30 years old.

"Mind if I take a bathroom break?" Lauren rubbed her tummy.

"Oh, sure, honey. The guest johns are off the foyer. We

have a separate one for girls because the guys smoke cigars in theirs." She pointed out the door to the left.

Lauren approached two doors off the expansive foyer, one with a replica of the Mona Lisa on the door and the other with her creator, Leonardo da Vinci. More like something you'd see in a restaurant than a private home. She entered the Mona Lisa room, closed the door behind her, and breathed in cigar smoke, which wafted from the adjoining bathroom. Not just cigar smoke; voices also seeped into the black and red bathroom.

"So, when's the drop?"

Lauren's ears perked up.

"October 30th. The shit'll be packed in the boxes with the cigar cutters. They shoot the powder into the bubble wrap. You can't even see it."

She didn't recognize either voice.

"Who's going to Jacksonville for the pickup?"

"Me and Mickey."

Lauren heard water running, and moments later, the sound of retreating footsteps. She waited a few moments before exiting the ladies' room.

When the two women returned to the patio, the sun had set and several of the revelers were playing water polo in the lighted pool. Lauren faked a big yawn.

"I believe my wife is fading," John said, curling an arm around Lauren.

"Hey, you just got here," Rick said, "but okay, I guess you got a good excuse." He leaned in to kiss Lauren on the cheek. "Gotta get your beauty sleep, right?" He laid a fat paw on Lauren's bulge.

Cringing, Lauren angled away from Rick's hand. "Yes, I'm pretty tired these days, and I'm still keeping a full schedule at the office." Lauren looked to Annetta. "Thanks so much for your hospitality."

"Sweetie, let me pack you up some food. I didn't see you eat a bite." Annetta scurried around the banquet table, loading a plate with ribs, cole slaw, and biscuits.

"Oh, thanks so much," Lauren said, "but I'm really more tired than hungry."

"That's okay. You can have it for breakfast."

Once out of the house, John and Lauren waited for the attendant to bring their car.

As they pulled out of the driveway, John said, "I'm going to have to keep myself from killing Maroon before the police arrest him. My skin crawled when he touched you."

"Yeah, mine too. I don't know how his wife stands it, though she's a piece of work herself. She's what you'd expect of a Mafia wife, but I can't help but like her."

"And for all that, I didn't learn a thing." John slapped the steering wheel with his open hand.

"You didn't need to. I got the mother lode."

On the way home, Lauren told John about her house tour with Annetta, from the secret passage in the library to the overheard conversation in the bathroom.

"That's just two months away," John said. "I'm going to need the Italian."

"Oh, no. No. No. No. No. No! You'd better not be thinking what I think you're thinking." Lauren stared at John.

"Honey, he's the only one who can help. He knows the Mafia inside out."

"Meredith cried for three solid months when Luc went back to Italy." Lauren's voice went up a few notches. "She's just beginning to recover."

"I thought she liked this new guy she's been dating."

"Yeah, she likes Dane, but she was head-over-heels in love with Luc. I don't think she's ready to see him again."

"So, we don't tell her."

"Right. She's my best friend. Good luck with that." Lauren stared out the window. "How soon do you need him?"

"With an October 30 drop date? Yesterday. I'm going to call him as soon as we get home."

"All right." Lauren breathed a resigned sigh. "I'll tell

Meredith tomorrow."

* * *

Lauren heard an intake of breath, and then complete silence on the phone line. "Meredith?"

"Yeah, I'm here—barely."

"I'm so sorry, sweetie. If John didn't need him..."

"Hey, I'm a big girl. I can handle this." The tremor in her voice told Lauren otherwise.

"I'll do my best to keep him away from you, and I'm sure he'll be sensitive to your feelings."

"Ya' think?" Meredith's quavering voice morphed to steady confidence. "He did love me. I know that. But without a commitment..."

"Six hundred years of playing Casanova dies hard." Lauren closed her eyes, wishing she had more soothing words for her best friend.

"So does immaturity." Meredith sighed. "At least Dane wants a relationship. He's already hinting at marriage."

"You're kidding. After a month?" Lauren paused. "How do you feel about that?"

"I'm not getting any younger. I don't have the same weak-in-the-knees feeling I had for Luc, but there's a lot to be said for sweet and reliable. Dane's everything you'd want in a husband."

"Sure you're not just trying to convince yourself?"

"Maybe Luc's visit is my test. If I can see him without my heart pounding out of my chest, I'll know I've cleared the hurdle."

"So rather than keep him away, you want me to arrange a chaperoned meeting?"

"No, I want to face him alone. He needs a piece of my mind." Meredith's voice held the angry conviction of a woman scorned.

CHAPTER THREE

Luc removed his eyeshades and stretched. Arriving at midnight at the Orlando International Airport was the perfect time for a vampire to feed, and he looked forward to joining John on a prearranged drug raid.

"Ready for a snack?" John asked when he met Luc at baggage claim.

"As soon as the pilot announced the preparation for landing, I got a hollow feeling in the pit of my stomach."

"You need to feed."

"I think it's more the feeling of being back here, and I'm not comfortable with—feelings."

"Speaking of which, Lauren's talked with Meredith. Get prepared for a serious tongue lashing, and not the good kind."

"I deserve to be drawn and quartered. I've never hurt anyone that deeply."

"How would you know? You don't hang around long enough to find out."

"Ouch." Luc's throat constricted with emptiness. Was

it from extreme thirst or the shallow quality of his life?

* * *

Luc always traveled in style, so renting a Lamborghini for his Florida stay was in character. Sunny yellow wouldn't have been his color choice, and with the convertible top down and his blonde hair blowing, he felt more like a ripe banana than Italy's sexiest bachelor. Actually, more than ripe—more like rotten. Six months earlier, he'd professed his love for Meredith, and then left her flat.

He whipped the car into a spot in front of Meredith's boutique, Bellisimo. Running his fingers through his windblown hair, he took off his sunglasses and stashed them in the glove compartment. He didn't bother putting the convertible top back up.

He was there at six, as Meredith had asked. She'd said they could walk to Park Plaza for a glass of wine, al fresco.

Luc felt the thud in his chest that only Meredith could cause as he looked into her shop window and saw her straightening a stack of sherbet-colored sweaters. Her long blond hair was pulled back in a simple ponytail.

The closed sign was already hung on the glass door, but Luc didn't need to knock. He knew she'd be able to feel his eyes on her, and sure enough, she looked up. He swallowed the lump in his throat as she glanced at him. She wore a lime green shirtdress belted in wide black patent. The high collar framed her beautiful face, and the flared skirt, ending just above the knee, flattered her to-die-for legs. *Diavolo*. Time hadn't diminished his longing. But she had a new love, according to Lauren. Someone who offered safety and security. Someone who didn't require a blood exchange with his lovemaking.

Luc watched Meredith take a deep breath and walk toward the door, unbolt it, and turn back into the shop, leaving Luc to open the door himself. Speaking over her shoulder, she said, "I'll just get my purse."

He noticed that her hand shook as she downed a half-full glass of something and reached for the strap of her bag, draped over the back of her Louis XV desk chair. She stopped for a moment, bracing her hands on her desk, and then said, "Let's go."

They walked briskly down Park Avenue, Meredith practically hugging the store windows along the way, presumably to keep her distance, and they didn't speak. Luc thought about the first time they'd met when he'd come to Orlando to assist John. Later, he and John flew to London to eradicate a dangerous gang of vampires, and when they returned to Orlando after their successful mission, Meredith was waiting for him at OIA. He recalled the thrill of seeing her at baggage claim. She was the first person in his long vampire existence who really cared, almost as though he were human again. Ah, well, water over the piazza.

Their two-block walk brought them to the busy Park Plaza, where patrons spilled out of the restaurant to the street's café dining.

"They have some of the best martinis in town," Meredith said as Luc pulled out a chair for her at a tiny table draped with a white tablecloth. A single pink rose in a bud vase provided a stand for the bar menu. *I should have brought her flowers.*

Meredith ordered a Grey Goose dirty martini, and Luc asked the waiter to bring him a Coppola Cabernet Sauvignon.

When the waiter turned back to the bar to get their libations, Luc said, "I deserve to be shot—with silver bullets."

"I was thinking more of a stake in the heart."

"More painful." Luc thumped his fist to his chest. "You could start by screaming at me."

"I'm not a screamer, and I'm cried out. If you'd come back during those first three months, I would have begged you to make love to me. Even if you wouldn't stay, I wanted you close to me. I thought if I had you inside me, just once, that memory would sustain me for the rest of my life."

"I'm so sorry, Meredith. I wish there was a way..."

"I'm not finished." She took a deep breath. "Then, in June, I met Dane. I was a mess. My eyes were red and swollen from the tears, and I wasn't into wearing makeup or caring about my appearance. He saw beyond my pain."

"Sounds like a great guy."

"Oh, he's better than great. And he just proposed to me last night."

Boyfriend was one thing. Husband was a whole new level. Luc's pulse quickened. "And your answer?"

"I'm seriously considering it." Meredith crossed her legs and began jiggling her foot. She seemed nervous, Luc thought. When the waiter brought their drinks, she gulped her martini down and ordered another in the time it took for the waiter to uncork Luc's wine.

"Slow down, *amore mio*, this isn't a marathon," Luc said when the waiter headed back to the bar.

"Don't tell me what to do, and I'm not your '*amore*.'" Her cheeks, which were already peachy, turned pomegranate red.

"Meredith, I'm not asking for forgiveness. What I did was unconscionable. I'm willing to be your punching bag if you think that would help."

"You mean slap you around?" Meredith dabbed at her eyes with a napkin. "And don't think I'm tearing up over you."

"I'm not worth crying over, but you're welcome to bloody my nose. I have a Gucci fashion show at Mall at Millenia coming up. You could alter my appearance for the runway."

"Don't be ridiculous." Meredith took a long draw on her second martini. "Even if I gave you two black eyes and broke your nose, you'd heal in a few hours." She paused to sniffle. "Think I don't know anything about vampires? I did a lot of research when I thought you and I were going to be together."

The waiter returned to pour Luc a second glass of wine, but when Meredith held up her hand to signal another martini, Luc said, "How about a club soda, instead?"

Meredith glared at Luc, and then said to the waiter, "I'll have another martini."

When the waiter left them, Luc said, "If you think I'd let you drive home with three martinis under your Diane von Furstenberg belt, you're crazy. You've already drunk about eight ounces of vodka, and I suspect this isn't the first alcohol you've had tonight."

"Oh, cut the chivalry. You're not my..." she covered her mouth in an attempt to hold back the hiccup, "knight in shining armor."

"No, but I am a hundred times stronger than you, and I will stop you from what would be certain suicide." Luc took Meredith's chin in his hand and directed his mesmerizing stare at her.

She slapped his hand away. "Don't try to glamour me, you big oaf. I'm not one of your girl-l-l-l toys," she slurred.

Luc held up his hand for the check and when the waiter returned with Meredith's martini, Luc took the glass and handed the waiter his American Express. He poured the martini into a potted palm next to their table.

"Pretty expensive fertilizer, don't 'ya think?" Meredith said, blinking. She swayed precariously in her café chair.

Luc couldn't help but laugh. He got out of his chair to assist her. "Had it been your plan to get drunk this evening or was it a spontaneous decision?"

"All part of a grand scheme," Meredith said to a woman at the adjacent table. "And the next thing I'm gonna do is j-j-j-jump his bones." Meredith's head moved up and down like a dashboard bobble head.

"Can't blame you there," the woman said as she looked at Luc.

Luc rolled his eyes and wrapped his arm around Meredith's waist. "There's nothing I'd rather do than make love to you," he whispered in her ear, "but I won't complicate your life."

She looked up at him and rested her head on his shoulder. "I hate you," she said.

"I know."

"And I love you."

"*Si, amore mio.*" He turned her to the sidewalk. *I love you, too.*

Luc braced Meredith and with her feet barely touching ground, walked her back to Bellisimo. Settling her in the desk chair, he asked, "Is Barnie's still open for coffee?"

"You want me w-w-w-wide-awake drunk?" She didn't raise her head from where it had plunked on the desk.

"No. On second thought, you need to sleep it off. I'm going to take you home and put you to bed."

"Oh, g-g-g-goody. You gonna take my clothes off?" Meredith looked up and squinted around the room until her eyes met Luc's.

"Come on, Loopy."

She pushed away from her desk and fell backward. Luc caught her descending dead weight and picked her up, chair and all. As she slumped forward, he swept her over his shoulder, grabbed her purse, and carried the tipsy maiden out to his car, depositing her in the front seat of the Lamborghini.

Bounding around to the driver's side, he leapt over the door and into the seat. Meredith's eyes were closed. Luc buckled her seat belt, kissed her briefly on the forehead, and then started the car.

Five minutes later, he pulled into Meredith's driveway. Glancing at her, with her mouth agape, he smiled and tilted her chin to close it. "Don't want you catching any fireflies."

She opened her eyes. "Hah," she said, "we don't have fireflies in Orlando. We have love bugs."

"You're kidding, right?"

She inclined her head his way. "Unlike you," she poked his hard bicep, "they d-d-d-don't bite. They just fly around conjoined, smashing into windshields."

"At least they die happy." Luc sprang out of the car. Just as he reached for Meredith, she hurled a mixture of vodka and masticated olives over the front seat of the Lamborghini.

"Oops," she said, "I only meant to burp." She scrunched up her nose. "Sorry 'bout that."

"I'd say you overplayed your intent—by a mile." He shook his head and then retrieved a handkerchief from his pocket to wipe her mouth. He scooped her up and carried her to the door as she swung her purse in the breeze.

Once inside the house, Luc spirited Meredith to her bedroom. Her dog, Penelope, a Boston Terrier mix who Luc knew was already fond of him, ran in circles to the bedroom, jumped up on the bed, and bounced around Meredith when Luc laid her down.

Luc scratched Penelope's head and then sat down on the edge of the bed. Releasing Meredith's hair from her ponytail, he brushed her hair with his fingers and propped her head on a pillow.

"That feels go-o-od," she murmured. "Don't stop."

Luc massaged her scalp and temples with his strong fingers. Meredith let loose a deep sigh, and then seemed to doze.

Moving his hands to her dress, he slowly unbuttoned it to the waist, undid the belt, and unbuttoned it the rest of the way...to the hem. Sweeping his hands under the hem and up her body, the dress fell open, revealing a lacy white camisole and matching bikinis. Luc clenched his fists and raised his eyes to the ceiling. *Merce*. The last time he'd been this close to Meredith, he'd accidentally nicked her tongue with his fang. The taste of her blood had tortured him for days, resonating like a symphony on his psyche (Ravel's Bolero, to be exact). He'd come so close to claiming her then. With one mating, she'd have his fang marks, nothing more. But once wouldn't be enough—not with Meredith. And three times would turn her. Could he be faithful for eternity? No, he couldn't be sure of that—not even with her.

He eased Meredith's arms out of her dress and folded it neatly across her boudoir chair.

Running his fingers down the length of her silky arm, he bent down to whisper in her ear, "Be happy." Then he left her.

* * *

"I'm an idiot."

"Don't be so hard on yourself, Meredith." Lauren leaned across the bistro table to pat her friend's hand, which gripped an untouched caramel frappucino.

"I was determined not to get emotional, and what did I do? One look at Luc and all reason flew out the window."

"So, you got drunk." Lauren nodded sympathetically.

"I had two glasses of wine before I saw him, just to keep the jitters at bay. But the martinis did me in." Meredith whined as she massaged her eyebrows. "I can't control myself around him sober, let alone plastered."

Lauren sighed, thinking about the first time she saw John. "Love can sure do a number on you."

"I don't want to be in love with him." Meredith straightened in her chair. "I want to marry Dane."

"Sure about that?" Lauren gave her friend a sideways glance.

"Yes." Meredith slapped the table, sending her frothy drink airborne. "And tonight, I'm going to say yes to his proposal."

* * *

Luc awoke in a cold sweat. Highly unusual for a vampire, but he knew the cause—Meredith. *Merda.* He huffed. He'd never regretted anything in his life— before he met her. Not the years carousing with Casanova or the sex games with the Medicis. Then she appeared, and the notion of true love, enduring love, had crawled into the chambers of his stone cold heart. What was it about her? Sure, she was beautiful, but her honesty and generosity were the clinchers. When she told him she chaired a non-profit organization for the homeless, he couldn't look at her as simply another conquest. This woman had true character and depth.

He threw off the sheets from the bed and moved to the window in his suite at the Grand Bohemian Hotel. Raising the blinds slowly to gauge the early morning sunlight, he saw Orlando City Hall and beyond that, the expanse of interstate leading to the Mall at Millenia, where today he'd meet with the general managers at Neiman Marcus, Gucci, and Tiffany. He stretched...and frowned, dreading the same old, same old. They'd all have heard of him. As president of the European Fashion League, he traveled the world predicting styles and colors years before the runway shows. He'd let them know today that eggplant would be the accessory color in another two years.

He splashed water on his face in the hotel bathroom, glad that the mirror wouldn't show him the scowl he knew was written on his handsome mug. He took his looks for granted, but without them, he wouldn't have risen so high in the fashion world. It was tedious, but it paid the bills and provided cover for his real work, nailing the Mafia for the Venice Police.

* * *

The day couldn't end soon enough. He'd dropped the car at the Octopus Car Wash that morning and took a taxi to the mall. When he picked up the car, the vodka vomit odor had been replaced with over-the-top pine. It was a small improvement. Rounding John and Lauren's driveway at 6:30, he knew his friends would be expecting him. Before he could ring the doorbell, Lauren opened it, offering a glass of B positive in an etched crystal goblet.

"Thanks," Luc said, taking the blood cocktail from Lauren and pecking her on the cheek. "You look radiant."

"Aw, you're just saying that. I feel like I'll never be svelte again, but I'm deliriously happy."

Luc held Lauren at arm's length. "It shows. Now where's that lucky husband of yours?"

"He's upstairs changing out of his suit." Lauren paused, and then said, "I met Meredith at Barnie's this morning."

Luc took a deep breath and raised his eyes to the chandelier that anchored the Wrights' foyer. When he exhaled and looked back at Lauren, he said, "What did she say?"

Lauren frowned. "She's going to accept Dane's marriage proposal."

"When?" Luc's heart stopped.

"Presumably tonight. Not to pressure you, but you've got about four hours to intercede. Dane's working until 11 in the ER, so he'll head to Meredith's once he's cleaned up." Lauren paused. "Though there's nothing more appealing than a man in scrubs."

Luc set his glass on the foyer table. He'd only taken a sip, but the tightness in his chest had overcome any thirst. "I hope he's worthy of her."

"I don't doubt he loves her."

"If you're going to tell me she loves him..."

"You know what, Luc?" Lauren crossed her arms. "That's not your concern. Your only concern is whether you love her—enough."

"You're right." He ran his hand through his hair. "She's not mine."

"Why don't you go up to the study? John will join you there shortly."

Luc shook his head, bringing himself back to the task at hand. "Aren't you involved in our strategy?"

"No, I'm still angry about John's involvement, and I'm not too happy with you, either."

"I'll have his back, Lauren."

"That's not why I have an issue with you." Lauren's arms were still crossed, and you wouldn't call her face friendly.

"Meredith."

Lauren rolled her eyes. "Duh."

"She's better off without me." Luc turned and bounded up the steps.

* * *

Lauren moved to the porch and her favorite chaise. She tried to get comfortable, but her expanding tummy and stewing thoughts weren't cooperating. She plumped the cushions on the chaise with more gusto than necessary, but the frustration wouldn't budge.

When she fell in love with John, she'd struggled with her decision to become a vampire. Since her transformation the previous December, she'd grown accustomed to his super strength and the intensity of his lovemaking. But underneath his supernatural abilities, he was still a stubborn man, and his friend was the same.

Needing a diversion, she picked up *All Together Dead* and read a few chapters before dozing off. She opened her eyes when her vampire senses pinged. There stood Luc, like a marble statue. "What are you thinking, Mr. Fashionista?"

"I was thinking about how lovely you look pregnant, and I was imagining Meredith heavy with my child."

"Well, what're you waiting for?" Lauren checked her watch. "It's 11:10."

"I believe I'll fly."

DCL Publications, LLC

CHAPTER FOUR

Meredith's heart was already beating out of her chest as she anticipated the doorbell. *Why am I so nervous? Marrying Dane is the right thing to do.*

She flinched when the doorbell chimed, cueing Penelope for a barking bonanza. "Hush, girl." Meredith patted Penelope's head. "It's not a burglar." She looked through the peephole. "Egad, it's worse."

Opening the door, she said, "You can't be here now." She looked out to the street. "Where's your car?"

"I flew." Luc smiled. "Aren't you going to invite me in?"

"No! I'm expecting Dane—any minute now." Meredith gnawed on her bottom lip and looked up and down the street.

"Good. I'd like to meet him."

"Are you crazy?" Meredith put her hands on Luc's marble chest and pushed...to no effect.

He took one step back, and Meredith sensed the heat rise in her cheeks as he regarded her from top to bottom. "You know, Meredith, for a woman getting ready to accept a marriage proposal, you could have worn something sexier. I mean, really, a t-shirt and jeans?" He grinned. "Of course, I think you look adorable."

Meredith reached down and picked up Penelope. "Bite him, girl. Just take a big hunk out of him. He won't miss it, but it'll make me feel better."

"Let her bite me. I'll be healed by the time your boyfriend arrives."

Meredith pointed Penelope's muzzle at Luc's muscled forearm, but all Penelope did was waggle her little body and lick.

"She likes me," Luc said.

"Oh, don't I know it." She rolled her eyes and set Penelope down. "Stay right there," she commanded. "I'm going to get my gun."

"You mean the water pistol you keep in your kitchen drawer? I'm not a witch, Meredith. I won't melt."

"Erg!" Meredith tried to close the door on the hulking man filling her stoop.

"Before you go all apoplectic on me..." Luc paused, "oh, wait, you're already apoplectic. Why don't you hear me out?" Luc crossed one foot over the other and leaned against the doorframe.

"Oh, for Pete's sake, I don't want to have to deal with you, especially right now!" Meredith clenched her fists as tears welled in her eyes. "Can't you just leave me alone?"

"Sorry, Meredith, but no, I can't."

"Look, if you're hungry, just take a bite of me and be on your way." Meredith held out her wrist to Luc's lips, and then she squinted at the glare of headlights coming down her street. "Oh, terrific. Here comes Dane." Again, she tried to push Luc, but she threw up her hands as her almost fiancé pulled into the driveway.

He slid out of his Hummer and walked up Meredith's brick path. He was still in his scrubs.

"You're guzzling some gas with that hog, aren't you?" Luc asked, nodding at Dane's car.

Meredith stood with her head in her hands. "Dane, Luc. Luc, Dane." She peeked through her fingers. The men eyed each other, but neither moved. Acknowledging defeat with a heavy shrug, she said, "Okay, come on in, both of you. I'll put on a pot of coffee."

"Thanks, Meredith," Luc said. "Coffee's my favorite beverage." He winked at her.

Meredith's eyes met his in a fiery confrontation. "I'd better not find Dane bloodless when I get back," she mouthed silently to Luc.

Dane frowned in a clueless sort of way. Meredith gave him the sunniest smile she could muster before she stormed into the kitchen and stared at the coffee pot like she'd never seen it before. Let's see, pour water in receptacle, and put filter in basket. Where did she keep the coffee? Oh, yeah, the refrigerator. She only did this every morning. Her hands were shaking as more water landed on the countertop than in the pot. Oh, who cares? One cup would be sufficient. She sure didn't need any, and Luc wouldn't drink it. She paced the floor while the drips began to fall into the pot. Then she did a full-body jerk. Why was she leaving those two alone? She grabbed the pot and dumped the contents into a cup.

She returned to the living room with a half-cup of coffee for Dane. Spilling a bit in transit, she set the cup on the coffee table. Could Luc hear her heart pounding?

The men were sitting at opposite ends of her tan leather sofa, legs crossed male style, ankle-to-knee.

"Well, aren't we just bookends?" Meredith said. She took a deep breath, and said, "Okay guys, I'm not orchestrating this little get-together."

Dane aimed a thumb at Luc. "Why is he here?"

"Good question." Meredith crossed her arms and tapped her ballet flat on the hardwood floor. "Why *are* you here, Luc?"

"I'm here to make sure you don't make a mistake you'll regret for the rest of your life." Luc went from cavalier to intense in a vampire second. He had that sexy-serious look that always made Meredith weak in the knees.

Meredith gulped. She opened her mouth, and then snapped it shut. *Don't do this to me, Luc.*

"If you're talking about Meredith marrying me, it wouldn't be a mistake," Dane said. "I love her."

"I've got you beat by a mile on that one," Luc said. "She holds my soul in the palm of her hand." Again, that intense look. *Oh, criminy.*

Dane pointed a finger at Luc. "You relinquished any claim on her when you dumped her." He gave a curt nod and tight-lipped smile.

Did he have to say 'dumped'? That word churned in Meredith's stomach like a hairball, reminding her of the hurt she'd suffered from Luc's rejection. Her legs were shaking as she backed herself into a chair. *Holy shiitake. I'm not going to let him get to me.* She took a deep breath and blew it out through puffed checks, willing herself to look Luc in the eye. "All right, I've had enough of this. You've jerked me around for the last time." She turned her head to Dane, though her eyes didn't immediately follow. "Dane, I will marry you."

"You can't," Luc said.

"Yes, she can," Dane interjected.

"Is that what you want, Meredith?" Luc's voice sounded distant.

She couldn't meet his eyes. "Yes," she squeaked.

"Then I wish you both a lifetime of happiness." Luc got up, walked out the front door, and disappeared into the night sky.

Meredith sat frozen, staring at the empty space where Luc had been. She managed a weak smile for Dane. *I'll be fine.*

* * *

Lauren's phone rang at 7 a.m. She stretched and

turned over sleepily to answer it. Seeing Meredith's number appear on her caller I.D., she asked, "Are congratulations in order?"

"Um, I guess so." Meredith sounded way too tentative.

"Uh, oh. Didn't Luc come over?"

"Yes, he popped in with some vague statements about his soul, and then I told Dane I'd marry him, and Luc left."

"What did Luc say about his soul?" Lauren squeezed her eyes shut and crossed her fingers.

"He said I held his soul in the palm of my hand, whatever that means."

Lauren whooped. "Mere, that's vampire-speak for a proposal."

"Of marriage?"

"Yes, there's no greater commitment a vampire can make than to pledge his soul. It goes beyond the heart because it's for eternity."

"He proposed? And I didn't even know it?"

Lauren had to hold the phone away from her ear while Meredith ranted. In fact, she probably could have heard Meredith without the phone. When she thought it was safe to put the receiver back to her ear, she said, "Poor Luc."

"What should I do?"

"Do you know what you want?"

"Absolutely. Dane's a nice guy, but like every other guy I've ever dated...except Luc...he treats me kind of like a trophy. When he introduced me to his parents, I had the feeling he was presenting me as the 'ideal doctor's wife.' Luc is the only man who's ever loved me for who I am inside."

"Well, go get him, girl."

"I intend to. Err, where is he?"

"He's got another day at the mall."

"Oh, criminy." Lauren heard something tapping through the phone. Meredith's nails on the receiver? "I'm going down there as soon as I can get someone to cover for me at the store."

"Mere, are you ready to become a vampire?"

"I'm more than ready." The line went silent for a moment. "What am I going to tell Dane?"

"Don't worry about that now. Just get to Luc. And Mere, don't be surprised if he isn't welcoming. I can't imagine how he's handling rejection."

* * *

Meredith parked at Neiman Marcus, dead center of the mall, and began her search from there. With at least 30 international designer shops, Luc could be almost anywhere at the Mall at Millenia. The only saving grace was that she could eliminate stores like Gap and Talbots. She cruised Neiman Marcus, and then hit Gucci, Burberry, and Louis Vuitton. She was heading to Tiffany's when she spotted Luc through the window at Brookstone. He was reclining in one of the store's vibrating chairs with a sea green gel mask over his eyes.

Meredith's heart did flip-flops as she entered the store in a sneaky heel-to-toe way and approached Luc. She reached out to touch his hand, and then thought better of it. "Hi, Luc. Taking a break?"

He didn't remove the gel mask, but Meredith knew he'd recognized her voice by the way his body stiffened. "I'm kind of busy here," he said. "You wanted something?"

"I guess I didn't get the drift of what you were saying last night?"

He lifted one side of the mask and peeked at her, then covered his eyes again. "I thought I made myself abundantly clear."

"Try incredibly murky. Women who are proposed to usually know it. They expect to hear something along the lines of, 'Will you marry me?'" *Please don't shut me out.*

"Well, I apologize for being obtuse, but it's a moot point since you made your choice." Still masked, he slapped a hand on the arm of the chair. "I can't believe I fell in love with you.

My life has been completely satisfactory for 600 years." He slapped his hand down again. "And then you come along with your trust and your ponytail flapping in the breeze, and I was willing to commit my eternity to you."

Other shoppers stopped to stare at the hunk in the chair.

"Can't a girl change her mind?" Meredith nodded to the onlookers for support.

He appeared to consider her question for a long moment, and then he removed the mask and turned off the vibrating mechanism of the chair. He stood up slowly to his full height and stared at her—head-on. "Yes, you can change your mind—once."

"I'm yours, Luc."

Several of the shoppers clapped, and one said, "You go, girl!"

Luc steered Meredith toward a quiet corner in the back of Brookstone. "Say that again, Meredith."

She grinned. "I'm yours. Forever." She took his hand. "I know there's a process to becoming a vampire, and I'm ready to start."

"Are you absolutely sure?" Bringing her hand to his lips, he added, "There will be blood."

"I'm counting on it."

He squeezed her hand. "John didn't turn Lauren in one night, but I won't let you out of my arms until the transformation is complete. I've never turned anyone, and I want to be there for you. The process is painful."

"I know. Lauren told me all about it."

"Did she say anything about vampires' tongues?"

Meredith's eyes bulged. "No."

"Good. I'll let that be a pleasant surprise—tonight." Luc beamed at her.

She flung her arms around his neck in a sudden gesture that would have knocked any ordinary man sideways, but Luc was not ordinary. He spun her round and round. When her feet finally touched down, their lips met for the first time since that fateful kiss six months ago. She opened her mouth, encouraging him to kiss her deeply. Pressing herself closer, she curled her fingers into his hair and gave the kiss all the emotion she'd suppressed for months. When they parted, they'd attracted quite a crowd, both inside the store and through the window.

Meredith beamed when Luc bowed and said, "Thank you all. You've been a lovely audience, but my fiancée and I are ready for some privacy." She put her hand in his and they walked out of the store, grinning like the lovers they'd soon be.

After saying goodbye to Luc at her car, she checked her reflection briefly in the visor mirror. After tonight, she wouldn't have a reflection. Whoa. *Goodbye, Meredith, human.* She gave herself a close-mouthed grin.

Her head was such a jumble of happiness and anticipation that she almost missed her interstate exit on the drive home. In just a few hours, Luc would be hers. Forever. When she pulled into her driveway, she checked her reflection again, only this time when she smiled, she showed teeth. *Hello, Meredith, vampire.*

As she walked up the path to her house, she thought about what she'd need to do that afternoon. First, she'd talk with Dane. *Lord, help me let him down easily.* And second, she'd get ready for Luc. *Yippee!*

* * *

Luc arrived at Meredith's door at dusk. In his long existence, he'd felt primal lust for countless women, but he'd never had this kind of joyful excitement and—fear. He had his hands behind his back when she opened the door.

"What're you hiding there?" she asked.

"Pick a hand."

Meredith touched his right arm, and Luc brought forth a dozen red roses. He kept his left arm behind him.

"What's in the other hand?"

He presented her with a blue Tiffany box, tied with a white ribbon. "I hope you like emerald cut. If not, we can exchange it."

She pulled the end of the ribbon bow and peeked inside. "You didn't have to buy the biggest ring in the store. I'd have married you with something from a Cracker Jack box."

"Nothing doing." Luc took the two-and-a-half carat, platinum set diamond out of the box and slipped it on her finger. "See? Perfect."

Tears spilled down Meredith's cheeks. "Somebody pinch me."

He swept her into his arms and across the threshold. When he set her down in the living room, he asked, "Do you want a big wedding? It doesn't matter to me, but if *you* want the works, I'll get Vera Wang on the phone."

"Luc, I just want to marry you, and the sooner, the better." Meredith gave him a sideways glance. "Were you thinking you wouldn't turn me until we were married?"

"No, I want to turn you tonight." Luc took her hand and kissed her palm. "I'm asking you one final time...are you ready to share eternity with me?"

"I'd give my last breath for you, Luc."

"Meredith, you *are* giving your last breath. Doesn't that frighten you?"

"No."

"Then dance with me." Luc pulled Meredith to her CD player and started flipping through a stack of disks.

"I have 'Take My Breath Away' by Berlin," Meredith said, wrapping her arms around Luc's waist from behind and pressing her cheek against his back.

"That's a bit *too* prophetic. How about 'Every Breath You Take' by the Police?" Luc popped the CD into the player. He turned and guided Meredith to the center of the room. As he put his arm around her waist he asked, "Where's your little barker?"

"She's spending the night at John and Lauren's. I thought we needed the privacy." Her supple body molded to his as they swayed to the music.

"I bet this isn't how you danced 600 years ago," she said, looking up at him.

"No, we used to lift women in the air—like this." Luc placed one hand on Meredith's waist, and he cupped her crotch with his other hand, lifting her effortlessly. Setting her down, he said, "I can feel your wetness through the fabric." His eyes glowed red.

"Luc, all you have to do is cross my mind, and I'm wet."

"Good information. I hope I won't have to remind you of that in a few hundred years." He spun her around the floor, ending in a dip. "You showed me how to love, Meredith," he whispered in her hair.

"I feel completely safe with you, Luc." She looked up at him.

"I may be more frightened than you are." He kissed her forehead when the song ended. *Enough talk.* He needed to be strong for both of them. "Let's make love."

They walked together to Meredith's bedroom, where Luc swept off his black polo and stepped out of his jeans, revealing black bikini briefs. He closed the two steps that separated them and peeled her lilac silk tank top up from the bottom and over her head. He tossed it on a nearby chair. Sinking to his knees, he pulled the drawstring of her soft linen pants and let them fall around her feet. "My God, you're beautiful." Inching up her legs with his fingers, he stopped at her tiny lace thong and eased his fingers around the edge to her downy mound. Her breath caught as he rubbed her feminine bud, which engorged under his touch. He didn't want to scare her, so he suppressed the growl that he could feel rumbling in his gut. "Why don't you use the bathroom?"

"I don't really need to use the bathroom."

"Yes, you do, Meredith. I'm going to find your G spot,

and though I wouldn't object to your wetting the bed, you might."

"What makes you think I don't know where my G spot is?

"You don't. Now, get going." He swatted her behind and turned her to the bathroom. "Hurry." He wasn't a man who prayed regularly, but he took this opportunity to ask God for Meredith's protection—that the pain would not be too intense. He envisioned her under him, reminding himself to be gentle. Once they'd made love the first time, the second and third mating would have to come quickly. And they'd be more intense.

When she returned to the bedroom, Luc stood naked—and erect.

"Holy cannoli." She froze. "You're sure in proportion."

"You were expecting 'The Little Engine That Could?'" He cocked an eyebrow.

"No, not exactly."

"Are you displeased?"

"Are you kidding?"

Luc smiled. "To bed, *amore mio.*" He picked her up and laid her gently on the pillows. Positioning himself between her legs, he pressed his lips to the inside of her knee. Nibbling there for a moment, he slowly traveled up to her groin, where he sucked briefly at the top of her thigh. He spread her feminine lips with his fingers, licking her bud playfully while plunging two fingers into her, rubbing a spot about one-third of the way in. "There it is," he said as she moaned. And then he replaced his fingers with his rolled tongue. It lapped at her insides, touching every inch of her and teasing her womb. She moaned and twitched under him, and then her fingers entwined in his hair, pressing him deeper inside her. When she arched her back, he knew she was coming, and as the first waves of her orgasm caressed his tongue, he spread her thighs wide with his fingers and found the pulsing vein. While she continued to caress his hair, he withdrew his tongue from her sheath and sunk his fangs effortlessly into her femoral. He wanted to time her orgasm so that the puncture would prolong her pleasure, and he hit it just right. Her nails dug into his shoulders. She groaned and convulsed under him as he lapped at the double puncture wounds, sealing them shut.

He joined her on the pillow and cradled her tightly against him. "You are mine." Though she wrapped her arms around him, he could sense a diminishing of her strength. "Now you need my blood," he whispered. "Look at me." He opened his mouth and ran his tongue across a fang, creating a line of blood. "Kiss me." He waited for her to raise her mouth to his, and when their lips met and simultaneously parted, he felt her velvet tongue against his. Closing his eyes, he willed his blood into her mouth, revitalizing her. He let her drink from him as his hands began to wander to her small breasts, still encased in filmy lace. He pushed the bra straps off her shoulders and circled her nipple with his fingers, catching it between his thumb and forefinger and squeezing gently. Her chest rose and fell rhythmically, and he knew her passion was mounting.

He reached for his jeans to get a condom, opened the package, and slid it down his erection. He gathered her long hair into a twist and laid her head back on the pillow, touching her neck. "Here," he said, running his finger down the length of her vein. "Are you ready for me?"

"Oh, yes."

Without further prompting, he entered her.

She gasped and stiffened. "It's too big."

He pulled back slightly. "Take a deep breath and open yourself to me. I will fill you completely, but I won't hurt you." Outlining her face with his fingers, he looked into her eyes. "Forever, Meredith."

She melted underneath him, and though he continued to move, he saved his deepest thrusts until she wrapped her legs around him and seemed to urge him with her pelvis. As he sensed her climax beginning, he turned her neck and touched her pulsing vein. Like dual hypodermics, his fangs punctured her skin at the exact moment his own ecstasy began. And when he tasted her blood, the symphony in his head built his climax to a crescendo. Ravel's Bolero had never sounded so powerful and so poignant. He trembled from the passion of her sweet elixir, now streaming through his veins. Holding her close, he rolled over so that she was on top of him.

"That was exquisite, Meredith." He stroked her hair. "How do you feel? Any pain?"

"No pain. Just a little light-headed."

"Once more, my love."

"I don't think I can. I feel pretty weak." Her cheeks flushed a deep pink. "Besides, how can you get it up again—that fast."

"I'll be right back." Luc flashed to the bathroom, where he dispensed of the condom and cleaned up. When he returned to the bedroom, he said, "Why don't you take me in your mouth, and we'll see how fast I can recover?" He stood at the side of the bed, smiling as Meredith did a sexy slink toward him and closed her full lips around his semi-erect tossle. Caressed by her mouth, Luc closed his eyes as Meredith rolled his balls with her fingers. He drew in a big breath and letting it out, said, "I have to be the most fortunate man on earth."

He gently pushed her head away from his body. "I need to finish your transformation before the pain hits, and then I can comfort you." He rolled her onto her stomach, propping her hips up with a pillow. He put on a new condom, and kneeling between her legs, he teased his manhood over her buttocks and slipped two fingers into her sheath. Using her wetness, he massaged her feminine bud in circles until she moaned and arched her back. "Will you take me again?"

"Yes," she said, breathlessly.

"You need my blood. Here." He showed her the vein in

his wrist where he would make the puncture wounds. "When I feel your climax mount, and it will be more intense this time, I will offer my wrist."

He eased himself into her, and this time she didn't protest that it was too deep. It seemed that her sheath was pulling him in, undulating more intensely than the first time. Their lovemaking was more in sync, more primal. As Luc's release began, he pierced his vein and offered his forearm. He didn't need to urge her. With her warm fingers encircling his wrist, she drank his 600-year-old blood. It was beyond anything he'd ever experienced. Staying inside her until his erection subsided, he whispered, "Welcome to my world, *amore mio*."

She made a gurgling noise.

"Meredith?"

No response.

He turned her over. Her eyes were wide, but she wasn't awake.

"Meredith! Wake up!" Luc shook her, but she was completely limp. *Dear God, NO! What have I done?* A trickle of blood ran down her chin onto the pale valley of her neck. "Don't leave me, Meredith! Stay with me!" He closed her eyelids, picked her up, and carried her to the bathroom. Her body felt like burning coals from the chemistry of their mingled blood. Had he expected too much from her fragile humanity? He soaked a washcloth with cold water and put it on her forehead, but he knew he'd need more than a washcloth to cool her down. She was burning up. Propping her in the tub, he ran to the kitchen and filled a pitcher with ice from the refrigerator. Grabbing her phone from the kitchen counter, he punched in John's number. "You need to come to Meredith's house now!" Luc yelled into the phone when John answered. "I don't have time to explain. Just get over here, and bring Lauren."

When he returned to the bathroom, he could see the veins pulsing under Meredith's skin. Veins that would normally appear blue now glowed red as fire. Had his venom been too strong? Did she take too much of his blood, too soon? He put the stopper in the tub and turned on the cold tap. Laying her head on a kidney-shaped bath pillow, he dumped the ice into the tub as it filled up with cold water, and he made a compress from an ice-filled washcloth and placed it on her forehead. She was still hot to the touch. What more could he do? Aspirin? Maybe he could crush it up and get it down her somehow. His eyes scanned the bathroom for something, anything that could help.

When he heard John and Lauren come in the front door just moments later, he yelled, "In here." Yanking a towel off the rack, he secured it around his waist. He strategically placed three washcloths on Meredith's naked body.

"My God, what happened?" Lauren asked as she and John entered the bathroom and she saw her best friend, unconscious.

"I wanted to minimize her pain, and I thought I could complete her transformation in one night." He'd been so focused on the trauma; he hadn't allowed worry to invade his heart. Now, as he tried to cool her body, the prospect of losing her clamped his chest in a vice.

Luc felt John's hand on his arm. "If she's still human, it may be too late to save her, but if she's crossed over..."

"She has to cross over," Luc rasped. "I can't lose her." He studied her face, serene in unconsciousness. Guilt washed over him in waves. He'd taken too much of a risk. In his haste, he'd jeopardized everything. He ran an ice cube up and down her arm—and prayed.

Feeling a tap on his shoulder, Luc moved over for Lauren to sit on the edge of the tub. She took Meredith's hand. "Sweetie," she said, "you need to come back. Luc loves you, and John and I love you, and we need you here with us."

Luc squeezed the bridge of his nose, trying to keep the tears at bay. He couldn't go on without her. In his long existence, she was the only truth he'd ever known. He glanced out the little bathroom window to the night sky, illuminated by a crescent moon. When he looked back at Meredith, her eyes flickered open, and they were red.

"Am I missing the party?" she asked.

Emotions broke through the surface like an earthquake cracking cement as Luc gathered her in his arms and rocked her. "Oh, my love, my love."

In joy and relief, Lauren hugged John tightly and sent up a grateful "thank you" to the heavens.

CHAPTER FIVE

Rick Maroon grinned. All the details for the drop were coming together like clockwork, and his new consigliari hadn't missed a beat. He took a Cuban cigar from his bedside humidor and padded downstairs in his slippers and plush terry robe. Picking up the latest issue of *Playboy* from his stack of mail on the kitchen counter, he headed for the pool. He adjusted the lounge chair to semi-recline, lit his cigar, and flipped the magazine to the centerfold. As he scrutinized the knockers on the Playmate of the Month, the phone in his robe pocket began to vibrate.

Annoyed, he answered, "Yeah?"

"Ricardo, where have you been?"

Rick immediately recognized the gravelly voice of his Italian connection, Emilio Nova. "Emilio, what's up, and I don't mean your dick, *Amico*." He guffawed at his own wit.

The Venetian don did not laugh. "I am in no mood for jokes. Didn't you take my warning seriously?"

"What the hell are you talking about?" Rick adjusted

the lounge chair to sit straight up and braced himself.

"I called earlier this year. Talked with your son. I've been trying to get you for several months. Took me forever to track you down."

"Which son?" Rick smashed his cigar in the Hilton Hotel ashtray next to his chair.

"I believe it was the youngest."

Rick threw up his hands, and then returned the phone to his ear. "He was supposed to alert our important contacts when we had to change our phone numbers. The police had everything bugged." Rick squeezed his eyes shut. "Look, Emilio. What was the message?"

"We had a big drug deal *interrupted* earlier this year by a couple of guys and a woman. They killed my consigliari and bodyguards, as well as the people we were negotiating with. One of the bodyguards got away and called me before he was tracked down and killed."

"So?"

"He had the woman's business card. That's the information I gave your asshole son to check out. She's from Winter Park, Florida."

"Motherfucker! I'll kill him."

"And that's not all. These people aren't people."

"What the fuck does that mean?"

"Our guys had fang marks on their necks and they were drained of blood. Get it? The perps weren't human." There was a pause on the line. "This could break up our operations— worldwide. And he didn't think it was important enough to pass along to you? If he weren't your son, I'd whack him myself. I may do it anyway if you don't make this right..." The connection went dead.

Rick hurled the ashtray at the stone wall surrounding the pool. It shattered into glass prisms that glittered in the morning sunlight. His hand shook as he punched in Carlo's speed dial.

"Pop, jeeze, awful early isn't it?" Carlo yawned audibly.

"Get your sorry, cocksucking ass over here *now*!" Rick heard shuffling and a thump. "Did you fall out of bed, you lousy piece of shit?"

"Yeah, but I'll be there in a few minutes. Got anything for breakfast?"

"Sure. I'll be serving finger sausages...*yours*!" Rick hung up.

* * *

Rick was squeezing the stuffing out of a tennis ball when his son approached. "Stick your finger in the cigar cutter," he said.

"Come on, Pop. You gotta be kidding me." Carlo tittered nervously.

"Which one is the least useful? Your pinkie?" Rick pointed to the device he'd had Mickey bring poolside.

Rick was confident his son wouldn't disobey him. He might do a ton of shit behind his father's back, but he wouldn't defy him face-to-face.

Carlo kneeled next to the table, his face white, and put his pinkie in the slot.

Rick saw beads of sweat on his son's upper lip. "Stick it up to the first joint. That'll make a nice clean cut," Rick said as his eyes narrowed. He eased the lever of the cigar cutter down to where the blade pierced Carlo's skin.

"Ouch!" Carlo said. "That's enough." His eyes bulged.

Rick folded his arms across his chest. "I'll leave it there for a while before I go deeper. And in the meantime, why don't you tell me about the phone call you got from the Italian boss."

Carlo's forehead puckered as sweat dripped into his eyes. "I don't remember no phone call."

"Come on, genius. Think." Rick tapped a finger to Carlo's temple, and then pressed lightly on the cutter. "I believe it was something about an ambush and a woman's business card?"

"Nope." Carlo gasped. "Oh, wait a minute. He might have called sometime in the winter about that." He stared at the cutter, wide-eyed. "Yeah, I think we were having a little party that night."

"And you were drunk, I assume."

Carlo let out a nervous chuckle. "Uh, yeah."

"Did you tell your brothers?" He might have to cut off a few more fingers.

"Nah. I meant to tell them, but I guess I forgot."

"All right, Carlo." Rick said with a distinct edge. "See if you can get that gray matter between your ears to work for once."

Carlo squeezed his eyes shut. "Okay, okay, I'm thinkin'," he paused, "I believe Emilio said the dame was a doctor. No, a dentist. Yeah, that's it—a dentist. Her first name began with—'L'?"

Rick grabbed his son by the neck of his Metallica t-shirt. Carlo yelped as the cigar cutter went airborne, taking the end of his finger with it. The cutter crashed on the pool tile, breaking into pieces.

"Motherfucker! I should have known that new consigliari was too good to be true." Rick snarled. He ignored his son's attempt to find the end of his finger. "It's all coming together now." He began to pace. "Emilio said the two guys and dame who attacked his people weren't human."

"Yeah, I figured he was smoking something," Carlo winced and wrapped a napkin around his bleeding finger.

Rick sneered at him. "The next time someone tells you corpses had fang marks and were drained of blood, you might want to pay more attention." Rick's face slowly transformed into a gargoyle grin. "John Wright isn't who he appears to be." He conked himself with his palm. "In fact, we may have identified Orlando's Vampire Vigilante."

"I don't get it," Carlo said.

"Our consigliari, you idiot." Rick rolled his eyes. "Get

your brothers over here. Now."

* * *

Bernardo and Anthony arrived in record time. When Rick told his older sons the story, Bernardo slapped the back of Carlo's head with the palm of his hand. "Real smart, asshole. If Emilio hadn't called, we'd all be dead meat."

"All right, what's done is done," Rick said. "We have to concentrate on whackin' these monsters, and it won't be easy." He looked at each of his sons in turn, spitting into a potted plant when his eyes landed on Carlo. "And you, you *testa di merda*, keep your prick clean."

Rick looked from Carlo to Bernardo. "Find out their weaknesses."

"Silver is deadly to vampires, Pop," Bernardo offered. "And bat transformation is a myth. We don't have to worry about rabid rodents."

"*Eccellente.*" Rick put his hand on Anthony's shoulder. "You're in charge of supplies. We'll need silver chains, manacles, and silver bullets. Oh, and rig up some sort of guillotine. I've heard you have to cut their heads off to make sure they're dead." Patting his girth, he said, "I'm going to make some calls." He headed to the house.

"What does *testa di merda* mean?" Carlo yelled after his father.

"It means shithead, Shithead," Rick said over his shoulder.

DCL Publications, LLC

CHAPTER SIX

Lauren's head was in a tizzy. The past month had flown by in a blur. Her work schedule was slammed, and Meredith and Luc's wedding was in less than two weeks. John and Luc had been sequestered for days preparing for the Mafia's drug drop on October 30, upping her anxiety level to the boiling point, and her pregnancy had thrown her hormones into overdrive.

Sitting at her desk, head in hands, Lauren jumped when John touched her shoulder. "I can't believe you didn't hear me," he said, kneading her shoulders with his strong fingers.

"I was deep in thought." She rubbed her eyes and then nodded at the stack of wedding RSVPs. "I'm helping Meredith. We're up to around 70 guests."

"Did you include the Maroons?"

"No, do we need to?" Lauren scrunched up her nose.

"Sorry, I should have mentioned it earlier. I've already introduced Rick to Luc. I thought Rick would regard us more like family if we had a first-generation Italian as a friend."

"I suppose it's important to gain their confidence." She sighed. "I've finally accepted that you're going ahead with this, but I'm still nervous about it."

"Thank you, my love. It's a noble cause." John bent down and nibbled on Lauren's ear.

Lauren's juices began to flow, but she tamped down the heat to make her point. "I never questioned the nobility of it. I just don't want you risking your neck with the mob."

"Not to worry. They have no idea who they're dealing with."

* * *

Annetta clopped into the kitchen in her ostrich feather high-heeled slippers.

"Fuck, Annetta, those shoes are as loud as a pistol pop. Can't you ease into the day?" Sitting at the kitchen table, Rick glanced up from his newspaper as his wife handed him an envelope.

"We just got invited to the wedding of the year, and I'm going shopping." She clapped her hands and gave her husband a Cheshire cat grin.

"Like you need an excuse. So, whose wedding?"

"That gorgeous Italian friend of your consigliari. That man is a hunk on wheels."

Rick choked on a gulp of coffee. When the coughing subsided, he said, "Oh, yeah, I think John said something about that. What's the date?"

"It's Saturday, October 23, and the bride included a little hand-written note that says to please include Carlo, Bernardo, and Anthony. Isn't that nice?"

Rick got up from the table, sauntered over to Annetta and kissed her, dipping her back so far her feet left the ground. Still leaning over her, he purred, "Oh, it's better than nice." His smile was sinister. "It's a goddamn opportunity." Her stood her back up and straightened out her disheveled robe.

"What the fuck does that mean?"

"Nothin'. Just call the boys and get them over here—
rapido."

* * *

Rick corralled his sons in the library. "Okay, here's how
it's going down." He looked at each of his boys, slapping
Carlo's cheek to make sure he was awake. "Pay attention.
We're gonna kidnap the dentist at her friend's wedding.
Should be the perfect occasion. Everybody will be buzzing
around." He rubbed the stubble on his chin. "I'll get Annetta
to distract her."

"You gettin' Mom into the act? That's a first." Bernardo
said.

"I'm just gonna give her a little job to do."

"She'll blow it. She can't keep a secret about nothing,"
Bernardo said.

"I won't tell her what we're up to. She likes that dame,
and she doesn't need to know about the vampire business.
That'd freak her out." Rick rubbed his hands together. "It's all
gelling now, boys, but we don't have much time." He looked at
Anthony. "How you doing on the guillotine?"

"Great. It's under construction. We modeled it after
your cigar cutter—only a much bigger version."

Rick laughed. "Perfect. I knew I could count on you,
Anthony."

"What can I do, Pop?" Carlo asked.

"You can drive the car that night. Think you're up to
it?"

"Come on, Pop. How long you gonna punish me?"

"Until you show me you're not as dumb as you act."

CHAPTER SEVEN

Lauren met Meredith at Collection Bridal on Park Avenue for the final fitting of her Vera Wang gown. In keeping with Meredith's elegant, understated style, the gown was unadorned.   Just strapless, fitted satin with a wide cummerbund that accented Meredith's tiny waist. Flaring at the bottom, it swung around her graceful legs to end just at the ankle. No train.

"It's gorgeous, Meredith," Lauren said as Meredith twirled in front of her.

"I'd always thought I wanted candlelight white for my wedding gown, but now that my skin is so pale, I think bright white is better, don't you?" Meredith cocked her head. She lowered her voice and whispered to Lauren, "Since I can't see myself in the mirror, I'll take your word for the color and fit."

"Has that been difficult for you...not seeing your reflection?" Lauren wished there was a way Meredith could see how beautiful she looked.

"Kind of. I have to be careful in my shop not to walk behind customers at the big three-way outside the dressing rooms, and there's no more checking to make sure my slip's not showing."

"True, but if you ever want someone's fashion opinion, nobody beats your new roomie."

Meredith smiled dreamily and then floated back into the dressing room while Lauren checked the store's jewelry display. She was fingering a pearl choker when she heard a high-pitched, "Well, look who the cat dragged in."

Arms full of packages, Annetta walked toward her. "Are you getting your matron-of-honor dress?" She dropped her packages on the floor to give Lauren a hug.

"All taken care of. I'm here with the bride for her final fitting." Lauren looked up as Meredith emerged from the dressing room in a khaki skirt and a white-collared blouse. "Meredith, I'd like you to meet Annetta Maroon."

Meredith extended her hand to Annetta. "Pleased to meet you. I'm so glad you'll be attending the wedding."

"Wouldn't miss it," Annetta said. "I've met that gorgeous fiancé of yours. If he were mine, I'd have to wear an ice pack on my hootchie. I'd be so sore from keeping him busy, I wouldn't be able to walk." Annetta winked.

Lauren stole a "see what I mean" look at Meredith, but she'd forgotten her friend's talent for gauging the crowd. "Tell me about it," Meredith said. "I couldn't wear my favorite jeans today."

Annetta laughed heartily. "Well, onward and upward. Hey, maybe you can help me. I took a pair of silk pumps to the shoe repair place to have them match my hot pink dress, and they said they don't do that anymore."

"You should be able to find some cute shoes at Jacobson's. Just down the street," Meredith said.

Annetta's eyes brightened. "Thanks, I'm as good as there. See you Saturday." She gathered up her bags and left the shop.

When Annetta was safely out of sight, Lauren said, "She'll add some color to the ceremony."

"I'd call that an understatement." Meredith laughed.

* * *

Grand Central Station had nothing on the Wrights' residence. Florists and caterers scurried in and out, balancing their wares while avoiding collisions with musicians lugging instruments to the patio. Lauren orchestrated the comings and goings, checking off the list Meredith had provided.

She escaped to the kitchen for a quick sip of blood. Less than a year earlier, she'd married John here at their house, under the gazebo, and today her best friend would take her eternal vows with the second most gorgeous guy on earth. As she looked out the kitchen window to where the florists were assembling an arbor of pink roses, she let loose a happy sigh. Sure, she was still anxious about John's Mafia caper, but the promise of their baby kept her focused. She bent down to pet Smokey, who would serve as the ring bearer. Penelope would be the flower dog.

"Shouldn't you be getting dressed?" John walked into the kitchen in his black tux and pointed at his bow tie, which was askew.

"I needed a pick-me-up. And bless Luc for dropping off a few extra bags of blood. This baby has upped my consumption dramatically." Lauren reached up to straighten John's tie and make sure it was smooth under his collar. "You look good enough to eat."

"Later." He winked. "In the meantime, are we ready for this eclectic crowd?"

"We'd better be. The ceremony's at seven and it's already—uh-oh, I'd better get moving."

* * *

Lauren waved to the Maroons, four pinstripe-suited men in black and one female in a scalding shade of hot pink.

They looked like they were responding to a casting call for "The Sopranos." Watching them pat Luc on the back and take their seats among the draped white chairs on the groom's side, Lauren did a double-take at the lump in Rick's breast pocket. Was that a gun?

When the string quartet began playing Pachelbel's "Canon in D," she smoothed a hand over the bulging front of her turquoise matron-of-honor dress. Carrying a tiny bouquet of pink and white roses, she walked to the arbor, where Luc in his white tuxedo was flanked by John in black. She signaled to John's assistant, Doreen, to release the dogs, and Penelope and Smokey bounded down the center aisle. She issued a quick "sit," and the dogs obeyed her command, ears pricked expectantly.

The music changed to Mendelssohn's "Wedding March," and Meredith, on the arm of her father, walked gracefully down the aisle to take her place next to Luc. The couple turned in unison to Pastor Longchamps of Trinity Episcopal Church, and the brief ceremony ensued without a hitch, other than a brief snarl from Smokey when the pastor tried to untie the ring that was attached to the Chihuahua's collar.

Luc beamed when Pastor Longchamps pronounced them man and wife, and Luc and Meredith walked from the arbor amidst ear-to-ear smiles from the guests. When the bride and groom disappeared for wedding photos, Lauren announced the opening of the bar, and the string quartet exited to make way for an eight-member band and a lead singer who could have been Adam Sandler on a good day.

Though she'd managed to hold back tears during the ceremony, she let them flow when Luc took Meredith in his arms for the first dance, "This I Promise You." The wedding singer rose to the occasion, and Lauren swayed to the melody, sure her friends would be together, "'til our lives are through."

* * *

Lauren was conversing with Meredith's parents at the bar when someone tugged on her arm.

"Lauren, got a minute?" Annetta asked.

"Sure, Annetta. What can I do for you?"

"I brought something for the baby. It's in the car, and it was too big to bring into the wedding. Carlo can put it in your garage, if you just come with me. Won't take but a few minutes."

"Oh, that's so sweet of you. Just let me tell John what I'm doing." Lauren looked over the guests, trying to spot her husband, who would ordinarily tower over a crowd.

"I think I saw him go into the house," Annetta said. "Really, we'll be back in a flash."

"Uh, okay." She turned to Meredith's parents. "Will you excuse me? If you see John, please tell him I'll be right back."

Lauren followed Annetta around the house and down the street one block to a side street where Annetta pointed to a car. "There it is, the black Mercedes. Carlo should be in it, but the windows are so tinted you can't see inside. I'll just pop the trunk, and we'll let him get the package out."

As the women approached the car, the hydraulic trunk lifted slowly. Lauren peered inside, while her peripheral vision caught two men approaching from opposite sides of the car, presumably to carry the package. Before she could react, her feet left the brick street as large hands lifted her and pushed her into the trunk. The men covered her with something metal and meshy, like a coat of mail, and then slammed the trunk shut. As panic welled within her and jump started her vampire strength, she made a fist to bash the trunk, but her initial shot of v-drenalin was followed by an engulfing weakness that smothered her like a bad dream. She tried to scream, but the sounds got stuck in her throat. And then it hit her. The meshy covering was made of silver. She was being kidnapped.

CHAPTER EIGHT

"What the fuck?" Annetta screamed, and Carlo fastened a hand over her mouth. She bit him.

"Ouch! Mom!" He released his hand, shook it quickly, and then picked her up under the arms. "What is it with my parents and fingers?" With Bernardo's help, Carlo shoved her into the backseat of the car.

Rick clamped his arms around her. "Shut the fuck up, Annetta. I'll explain on the way home. Get going Carlo. *Rapido!*" Anthony slid into the backseat on the other side of his mother, Bernardo jumped in front, and Carlo peeled out and gunned the car down the narrow street.

Annetta roared, "No more *pompinos* for you, you bastard. How could you do that to a pregnant woman?"

"She's not a woman, Annetta."

"Right, and I'm Sponge Bob Square Pants."

"She's a vampire."

"What?" Annetta wriggled so hard, the pins holding her up-do sprouted like weeds from her scalp. "You gotta be kidding me."

"Scout's honor." Rick made a cross mark on his heart.

"Like you were ever a scout. Puh-leez."

"Honest, Annetta. Her husband's the Vampire Vigilante, and the guy who got married today is undercover for the Venetian Police. That's Venice, Italy, not Florida."

Annetta stopped wriggling, and Rick released his grip on her. "No shit? So, what're you gonna do with her?"

"I'm gonna make a deal with her husband to change places. Don't worry about the dame. I'm not gonna whack her."

"Promise? Cause even though she's a vampire, she's still pregnant."

"Sure, babe. I promise. Now, you weren't serious about no more blow jobs, were ya?"

* * *

Lauren thudded to the back of the trunk when the car stopped. She was paralyzed under the silver, and all she could do was squint through the mesh when the trunk opened. Lauren rolled like a sack of potatoes in the hands of the men, who wrapped the silver blanket securely around her before lifting her out of the trunk. She couldn't even muster a muted scream. "You'll never get away with this," she said weakly.

"Oh yeah we will, because that husband of yours will play right into our hands, and when he does, your days of do-gooding in Orlando will be *finito*." Rick looked from Lauren to Annetta. "Go inside, Annetta. We'll take good care of her, and don't worry, the boys got more sense than to try to have sex with a pregnant vampire." He shot what Lauren interpreted as a warning look to his sons. *Oh, great.*

The lump in Lauren's throat wouldn't let her swallow. What about her baby? She'd do anything to protect her child. Would these goons supply her with blood? Doubtful. In her advanced pregnancy, her baby needed lots of blood. She thought back to a friend of hers in high school who'd become a paraplegic following a water skiing accident—incapacitated. *Think, think, think.* They knew she was a vampire. Bad. They'd probably try to ransom her. Bad. They'd want to keep her weak, so they wouldn't feed her. Very bad.

Two men carried her, one with his arms under her armpits and the other holding her feet. They lugged her through the house, into the library, and through the passageway she'd seen when Annetta took her for a tour. The passageway led to a small room. As Rick flipped on the lights, his sons cuffed her wrists and ankles in silver manacles, which were attached to the wall with chains, and then they removed the silver blanket. They'd left enough slack in the chains to allow a little movement, but not enough for her to wrap the chains around their necks.

"How did you find out we were vampires?" she asked.

"Seems you did a little job in Venice earlier this year and left your calling card," Rick said.

Lauren mulled that over. Luc had chased down and killed the bodyguard who had Lauren's card. They'd assumed they were in the clear, but he must have already relayed the information to his boss.

"You comfy?" Rick asked. "Not that I care, but I figured Annetta would want you to have a place to lie down." Rick pointed to a tiny cot that she'd just barely be able to maneuver into. "I'm gonna turn off the lights now. I figure you don't mind the dark." Rick laughed and his sons guffawed in turn.

Just before the men left and the room went black, Lauren noticed something that Rick hadn't pointed out. It looked like a large version of the prototype cigar cutter John had shown her. But this contraption wasn't designed to cut off the tips of cigars. No, it looked more like something from the French Revolution. Egad. Lauren's heart froze. A manacled wrist went to her neck while her other hand cradled her belly. A little kick nudged her hand, and then a tear trickled down her cheek. *Don't you worry, sweetie.* She massaged the little appendage, probably a foot, which was pushing against her. *Your daddy will get us out of here.*

* * *

John didn't start to worry until he realized the whole Maroon family had disappeared. When Meredith's parents said that Lauren had gone with a woman friend to get something out of a car, he didn't think much of it. But when she didn't return immediately, and he figured out that Annetta was the "woman friend," he immediately began looking for the rest of the Maroon clan.

He found Luc on the terrace, feeding a piece of wedding cake to his bride. After the photographer snapped the shot, he watched Meredith spit the cake into a napkin. Not that vampires couldn't eat if they had to, but cake would be particularly cloying.

He grabbed Luc's arm. "I need to talk to you. It's urgent."

"What's up?" Luc put his arm around Meredith.

"Have you seen the Maroons?"

"Not lately, but I haven't been looking. Why?"

"Because I can't find Lauren, and the Maroons have vanished."

John's cell phone rang, and he registered Rick Maroon's number on his caller I.D. before he answered. "Yes?"

"I figure by now you must be missing your wife." The voice was deep and sinister.

"Yes, I am. Is she with you?"

"Matter of fact, she is."

"Let me speak with her." John spoke through clenched teeth. His anger welled up like a bubbling volcano.

"Well, now, that won't be possible this evening. I just wanted you to know that she's safe, and I'll be talking with you tomorrow about what you'll need to do to get her back. Don't try anything, Mr. Vampire Vigilante, or she and your baby will die. I know how to deal with you...people."

John stared at the reveling guests on the lawn. "Is Lauren at your house?"

"Think I'm stupid? I'll call you tomorrow." The phone clicked off.

John picked up a champagne stem and crushed the glass in his hand. He looked at Luc and Meredith. "Those assholes have Lauren."

"Oh my God," Meredith said as she grabbed the terrace railing. "I feel sick. Where is she?"

"I don't know." John tossed the pulverized glass into a waste bin and dusted the shards off his hand.

"They'll have an arsenal of weapons," Luc said. "And John, believe me, if Maroon tries to bribe you with a trade, he won't honor it. These guys *never* let anyone go."

"Well, I'm not waiting until morning to find out where Lauren is." John rushed back into the house and raced up the stairs to their bedroom, morphing to bat form and disappearing out a second-story window.

* * *

When John returned to his empty house, he scanned the debris from the wedding, thinking about how Lauren would have scurried around to clean it up. He'd have helped her bag the garbage, and then he'd have carried her upstairs and held her close in their bed.

He picked up a few errant beer cans and tossed them in the bin. The fact that he found out Lauren was at Maroon's house was a small start to his plan. He'd entered the house through the air conditioning vents and gotten close enough to catch her scent. She was somewhere off the library, probably through the passageway she'd told him about. *Oh, my darling. I'm so sorry.* This was his fault. He'd insisted she trust him, and look what happened. But he'd fix it. If it meant losing his life, he'd gladly give it up. He'd risk anything to get her back.

* * *

Lauren awakened on the little cot, momentarily forgetting where she was. She reached out to touch John, but the manacles restrained her, and she gasped, remembering. She closed her eyes again, wondering how long she'd slept and what time it was. Her throat was dry as sand in an hourglass. She and her baby needed blood.

The door opened, and Lauren shielded her eyes from the ray of light. There stood Annetta.

"I wanted to sneak down before the guys got up," Annetta said. "I don't get this whole thing, and I'm not here to rescue you, but I can't let you starve, either. Want some bagels and coffee?"

Lauren grimaced. "Thanks, Annetta, but that's not what I eat."

Annetta clipped herself on the head with her hand. "Oh, duh...and yuk! Sorry, but I don't know how to help you there." She backed away until she was plastered against the wall.

"Don't worry, Annetta. I don't feed on nice people." Lauren managed a weak smile. "But if there was a way you could track down some bagged blood, I'd take any type you could find." She smoothed her hand over her belly.

"Well, I can't let that baby starve, so I'll try." She pursed her lips. "My sister's a lab tech at Florida Blood Centers. She owes me about a million favors."

"I'd be grateful, Annetta. And if I ever get out of here, I'll make sure you're not harmed."

Annetta's shoulders sagged. "I know my husband and sons are into bad shit. I try to act like I don't know, but I hear things. A lot of people have gone missing, and I think my guys were responsible, but that don't mean I don't still love them."

Lauren nodded in sympathy. "Love's a funny thing. If you'd told me a little more than a year ago that I'd be married to a vampire, I'd have called you crazy."

"Yeah, well...I'll see what I can do." Annetta put her hand on the doorknob, and then turned back to Lauren. "Try not to get upset. It'll bother the baby."

DCL Publications, LLC

CHAPTER NINE

"I'll bet that's the fastest you've ever answered your phone, Mr. Hot Shot Lawyer."

"Don't fuck with me."   John's voice was deep and ominous. "What are your terms?"

"I don't really *want* to kill your pretty lady, so if you'd like to see her in one piece, all you have to do is change places with her."

"When?"

"I'm kinda busy today..."

"She needs to eat."

"You mean blood-suck? I don't think so. Besides, she's kinda cute all fragile. If she gets too weak, maybe me or the boys will have a chance to poke her."

"Listen to me carefully, you son of a bitch. If you touch her, and I mean even brush against her, I'll gag you with your own cock."

"I don't think you're in a position to threaten me, Batman. But let's say day after tomorrow at midnight. Come to my house."

"I'll be there."

"Just you. No police and no accomplices. Otherwise, you'll be taking your wife's head home in a box." Rick chuckled. "Oh, and I guess I forgot to tell you. We have our very own guillotine. We made a big version of the cigar cutter, and it works like a charm. We tried it on a ripe watermelon. Nice clean cut."

John slammed the phone down on the kitchen counter and walked out the back door, heading to the gazebo. Inhaling the sweet fragrance of Lauren's favorite rose bush, he ran his thumb down a thorny stem and purposefully pierced his finger. He didn't wince as his blood dripped on the leaves.

* * *

On day two of her capture, Lauren jumped when Rick and his sons entered the room. They flipped on the lights, which created an eerie, artificial aura in the windowless space. Lauren blinked through black spots as her eyes adjusted.

"Aw, you and your little blood-sucker must be hungry," Rick said. "Sorry about that, but I can't risk you having the strength to get out of your restraints."

Carlo brandished a gun, and though Lauren had little knowledge about firearms, she knew this one had a silencer attached.

"I wonder who would die first, the broad or her baby?" Carlo pressed the gun against Lauren's swollen belly.

Though she was fortified by the blood Annetta had provided that morning, she leaned against the wall to appear frail to her assailants.

"I'll bet she's almost weak enough to screw," Carlo said. He looked at his brothers. "If you guys hold her down, I'll have a go."

Rick grabbed the gun from Carlo's hand. "Get serious, you moron. We need to deliver her in one piece to her husband. He's the one we want."

"You've talked with John?" Lauren's heart raced.

"Yeah, we're workin' out a deal, but in the meantime, how about telling us what you and your friends were up to." Rick placed a knife against Lauren's belly and sliced across the fabric, nicking her skin and drawing a thin line of blood.

Lauren gasped, but she knew they wouldn't do their bargaining chip any serious harm. "I have no idea. I'm just the wife, and I'm quite busy with my dental practice. I'm not involved in John's business."

"Don't play coy with me." Rick walked back and forth in front of her. "We might not put any noticeable bruises on you, but we could hurt you in places that don't show." He leered at her.

"Try it," she said, reddening her eyes. "I'd squeeze your dicks so hard, they'd look like pencils." She'd learned something about intimidation in her ten months of being a vampire. She saw a line of sweat appear on Carlo's upper lip. *Good.*

"Now, now, we're not here to hurt you...much," Rick said. "I'm sure you want to go home and take care of that baby. Gosh, I hope he's all right." He waggled his eyebrows at his sons. "You don't think he's already shriveled up and died, do you?" He put his pinky to the side of his mouth in a Dr. Evil gesture.

"I'm sure my child will live to see the day you all get yours." Lauren directed a stare at Rick.

He laughed. "We shall see. We shall see." He motioned for his sons to exit, and they flipped the lights off and walked out the door, leaving Lauren in total darkness again. She followed their conversation as they walked down the passageway. Though they'd obviously done some homework on vampires, they seemed to be unaware of the undead's acute hearing.

"If she gets too ornery, we can blind her with acid," said Carlo. "Or, what I'd really like to do is strap her under the guillotine. That blade right above her neck would be a turn-on."

"Sometimes I think you're too dumb to live," said his father. "We need to keep her in one piece until we get the husband. Then we can whack 'em both to kingdom come."

"Ah, come on, Pop. Let me have my fun."

Lauren held her breath.

"All right. If you and your brothers want to see how she fits under that guillotine, have at it. Just make sure the safety latch is on."

Lauren let out a sob and cradled her tummy with her manacled hands, rocking back and forth. *Please, John, please save us.* She'd had so much to look forward to, and now...

* * *

Lauren woke with a start to Carlo jangling keys in front of her nose.

"Time for some role play." He leered at her. "Me and my brothers are bored. We want to see a vampire squirm."

Bernardo pushed Carlo to the side and addressed Lauren. "Look," he said, "Anthony and me are humoring Carlo here. You won't get hurt as long as you cooperate."

Lauren gritted her teeth. Her best line of defense was to remain calm and pliable. They wouldn't *intentionally* kill her. She just hoped they'd have enough sense not to bungle their fun.

Anthony grabbed the keys from Carlo and used one to unlock the chain from the wall. While he fiddled with that, Bernardo clamped manacles on Lauren's ankles. The weight of the silver was like an anvil on Lauren's legs, rendering her helpless. Between the manacles on her ankles and the ones on her wrists, she was a limp rag—with fangs.

The three men lifted her from the cot and laid her on her back on the platform, nudging her up until her neck was positioned below the blade. They used leather straps to secure her position. Lauren looked up at the shiny blade, glinting in the cold fluorescent light of the sterile room. She squeezed her eyes shut.

"D'you put the safety on, airhead?" Bernardo asked Carlo.

"Nah, I thought I'd let her sweat a bit."

"Well, do it. Pop'll have a shit fit if she's headless," Anthony said.

This isn't really happening. Lauren willed herself to a happier time and place. She thought about the gazebo and the sweet scent of climbing roses. John's arms wrapped securely around her. *Rescue us.*

* * *

John fed like a hungry Grizzly on a salmon run the evening before his appointment with Maroon. By the time he finished off a pedophile and a heroin dealer, he was well fortified to tackle whatever the Mafia had in store. He stood at the kitchen window in the early morning light, gripping the window frame so tightly the wood began to splinter. *She didn't want me to take this job, and now I may have lost her forever.* If she couldn't feed, the baby would be in jeopardy. He pushed away from the window. He had to get her home.

The doorbell rang at 7 a.m.

"Put me to work," Luc said when John opened the door. He wore black sweats and Reeboks.

"I need you to fly to Maroon's house and find out exactly where Lauren is. There's a passageway off the library, downstairs, and she's there somewhere."

"When I find her, should I leave a message?"

"I doubt you'll be able to. I'm sure she's heavily guarded." John ran his hand through his hair. "Just make sure you can pop out the air vent in that room."

"Sounds like you have a plan."

"She's going to have to morph to bat form. It's the *only*

way we can escape."

"Can she do that, as pregnant as she is?"

"God knows, but she has to."

* * *

Lauren woke to Annetta poking her in the shoulder. "Wake up," Annetta said, "and down this nasty stuff before the guys get back. I made them a big breakfast, but they eat fast as pigs. I've got about two minutes."

Lauren gratefully accepted the bag of blood Annetta offered, popping the plastic with her fang and guzzling the rich liquid. "Thanks so much. An adult vampire can go days without blood, but the baby," she patted her belly, "needs regular feeding."

Annetta bit her lip. "I shouldn't tell you this, and you're going to have to act dumb when Rick comes in, but your husband will be here at midnight. You'll be trading places with him. Rick will let you and your baby go." She picked up the empty bag of blood with two fingers and a creeped-out look on her face.

"Thank you, Annetta." *But I don't believe for one minute that he'll let us go.*

"Just try to get some rest," Annetta said as she left the room.

Lauren's heart sped as she thought of seeing John, perhaps for the last time. An ache of longing gripped her, and she let the tears flow.

* * *

At 11:30, John paced the living room floor, waiting for Meredith to pick him up. The plan was as air-tight as it could be, given he'd had less than two days to put it together. Meredith's role was easy, but crucial. While the men were inside the house, she'd wait in the car outside the Maroon's gate until she saw Luc fly out of the garage, where the central unit of the air duct system was housed. She'd signal the police to make their move, and then she'd high tail it out of there before the bullets started flying. Sounded good—in theory.

John was out the door as soon as he saw the headlights on Meredith's little BMW. He moved so quickly that she gasped when he opened the door. "Will I ever be able to move as fast as you and Luc?" she asked.

"We've got a few years on you." John settled in the seat. *I just hope Lauren will be able to do what I'm going to ask her to do.*

As though she'd read his mind, Meredith said, "Lauren won't want to morph to bat form if she thinks she might lose the baby."

"It's our only chance for getting out of there." John stared out the window. "She may miscarry, but dammit, we have no other choice."

When they reached Maroon's house, John pointed to a spot outside the gate for Meredith to park. Without another word, he touched her shoulder briefly and exited the car. As he approached the gate, he counted ten guards in plain view, and he was sure there were at least that many more behind the dense vegetation on Maroon's property. All this security for a lone vampire?

Mickey and three other goons walked toward him. "Hold out your arms," Mickey said, frisking John from top to bottom. "You're hard as marble, man." Mickey leered as he ran a hand up the inside of John's black jeans. When he reached John's crotch, he investigated more thoroughly.

John kept his mounting anger in check, steeling himself for the task ahead.

Mickey turned to his colleagues. "He's clean. Packed tight as a drum, but clean." He looked at John. "Put your hands behind your back."

"I never put my hands behind my back." John stared straight-on at Mickey, vampire-glamouring him. It worked.

"All right. Put them in front of you then, but we're not taking you into the house without cuffs."

One of Mickey's cohorts approached John cautiously and with trembling hands, slipped the silver cuffs on John's wrists. John gritted his teeth, but he had to keep his cool.

"Let's go," Mickey said.

John followed two of the men, while the other two fell in step behind him. Four guards at the front entrance opened the door to the house, and John and his goony entourage stepped inside. Four additional men in the foyer motioned for them to follow. The troop, growing exponentially, surrounded John like flies and moved as one to the library, through the recessed passageway and down the hall.

"I can't fit you all in here," Rick said as he opened the door at the end of the hall. "Who's carryin'?" To the last man, they all raised their hands. "All right, all right. Mickey, you and your three stay. The rest of you go back to your posts." John watched Rick count the eight men left in the room, which included his three sons but not John, of course. "We'll be fine. He can't avoid silver bullets from eight guns."

John's eyes found Lauren, who was huddled on the cot. She looked tired and tattered. Her turquoise dress had been slit across the front, and it was all John could do not to wrap his cuffed wrists around Rick's neck. Maroon would be dead in an instant, but then so would Lauren and the baby. Fists clenched, he held his mounting temper.

Rick looked at John and then at Mickey. "Why's he hand-cuffed in front?"

Mickey had a confused look on his face. "I don't know, boss."

Rick backhanded Mickey across the face. "I told you not to look him in the eye."

"Sorry." The scolded Mickey looked like a 300-pound gorilla, but not as smart.

"Okay, Mr. Ex-consigilari, here's how it's goin' down. We'll have six guns pointed at your head while two of the guys trade manacles from your wife to you. One false move and you'll both get blasted to hell. We'll escort your wife out of the room. Then you and I will have a talk."

"Sounds reasonable," John said, "but I want a moment with my wife."

"No way I'm lettin' you alone with her," Rick said. "You have 30 seconds, but I'm standin' right here."

John approached Lauren and took her manacled hands in his. With her vampire hearing, he knew he could speak to her without anyone in the room hearing.

"Darling, are you strong?" he asked.

She nodded.

"Don't look up, but there's a vent at the top of the wall behind you. When I count to three, expel a big huff of purple haze, and morph to bat form. Fly straight up to the vent. Luc's on the other side, and he'll pop it open."

Lauren's eyes got wide. "The baby."

"I don't know, my love, but if you don't morph, we'll all perish."

Tears welled in Lauren's eyes.

"I'm so sorry, Lauren, but it's the only way. I love you— both. On the count of three..." John squeezed her hands. "One...two...three." He let her hands go. For an agonizing moment, nothing happened. He'd used the 30 seconds Maroon granted him, and he expected Rick's fat, clammy paw to clamp down on his shoulder any second. He wouldn't morph if Lauren couldn't. But then a cloud of purple haze emanated from her mouth and nostrils, and in a bat's blink, she flew straight up. John morphed immediately after she did, heading straight for Rick's face. He thought the distraction of his attack would provide the time Lauren needed to reach the vent. He scratched Rick across the cheek, and then flew in a zigzag pattern toward the vent. Shots rang out, and John jerked from the impact of a bullet just as he made it to the vent.

The three bats flew, bounced, and skittered through the

ventilation system. Led by Luc, Lauren followed and John brought up the rear, dripping blood along the ductwork. The blood was fairly gushing from his shoulder. Had he severed a major artery?

Through sonar, John issued a sharp *Hurry!*

They swooped into the main air handler, where Luc had slashed the central tubing for their exit, and they flew out the small garage window above the back door. Luc made a quick pass by Meredith's car, and then joined his friends at the top of a large oak tree.

As soon as they saw Meredith leave, a squad of police cars surrounded the Maroon compound and officers emerged with firearms to rival those of their adversaries.

Maroon, his sons, and their guards ran out of the house with guns blazing indiscriminately into the sky. When the order to "cease and desist" came through a deputy's bullhorn, Carlo pointed his gun in the direction of the sound. He got off a round before he was shot several times and collapsed on the front lawn. Rick immediately dropped his weapon, and his entourage followed suit. The officers closed in, handcuffed Rick, Bernardo, and Anthony, and began rounding up the rest of the goons.

John stole a look at Lauren, who was clinging to a branch and breathing heavily. He couldn't tell whether her stomach was distended, but he knew she was winded and would probably need a few more minutes to recuperate before heading home. He waited for her nod, and when she gave it, the three bats launched into the late October sky, passing over houses in full Halloween regalia, with bats, skeletons, witches, and zombies draped on front steps and in trees; and, of course, an occasional Dracula.

CHAPTER TEN

The threesome flew to the kitchen door, where John morphed back to human form, accessed the stowed house key under the potted geranium, and opened the door. Luc also immediately morphed, but Lauren stayed in bat form, skittering across the threshold and settling on the braided kitchen rug. She looked up at the two men who'd saved her life. She wanted to be grateful. She *was* grateful, but she was also deeply afraid that when she morphed back to human form, she'd miscarry. *Please, God, don't let me lose this baby.*

John clutched his shoulder, and Lauren focused her attention on her wounded husband. She watched as Luc inspected the wound. "It went straight through, so that's good," he said. "Silver can corrode a vampire's tissue quickly, but you didn't have much contact with it. The bigger issue is your loss of blood."

"I'm fine," John said. "Nothing a pint or two won't heal." He crouched down in front of Lauren. "Sweetheart," he said softly, "you're going to need to change."

Lauren heard a car door slam, and soon after, Meredith raced into the kitchen. She hugged her husband, touched John's uninjured shoulder, and then saw Lauren on the rug. "Oh, honey, God love you. What a horrible scare you had." She knelt in front of Lauren and stroked her little head.

A tiny tear trickled down Lauren's bat nose. She whispered a prayer and took a deep breath to center herself. Commanding her body to be gentle in the process of restoring her to human form, she filled her lungs with air and bore down. Woof. She stood before John, her tattered matron-of-honor dress much the worse for wear.

"I can't look down," she said to John. "Tell me."

John closed the two steps between them and placed his hands on Lauren's belly. "You both made it." He folded his arms around her, and she collapsed in his embrace. "Let's get you off your feet." He picked her up like she weighed no more than a few ounces and carried her upstairs to their king-size bed.

* * *

Lauren slept for two days, waking only when John roused her to feed. Several times during her brief convalescence, he insisted she feed off him.

"Nothing's more healing than my blood, Lauren. It's 500-year-old elixir."

"You need the healing, too," she said, but she couldn't help but extend her fangs when he offered her his wrist.

"I'm fine. I'll have a tiny scar from the silver, but it hasn't affected my range of motion one iota." He started to roll up the sleeve on his white dress shirt.

"Speaking of range of motion..." Lauren licked her lips. "Want to know what I'm *really* hungry for?"

"Are you strong enough?"

"Absolutely." Lauren reached for the buttons on John's shirt.

"If you're sure…"

She pulled John's shirt out of his pants, and then proceeded to his belt. By the time his pants dropped to his ankles, he was already erect.

He gave her that gorgeous lopsided grin. "Welcome home."

MISTLETOE FANGS

CHAPTER ONE

"Even for a vampire, you're lookin' pale, boss." Doreen pushed a glass of blood across the kitchen counter to John Wright, Orlando's Vampire Vigilante.

"I'm worried about Lauren." John rested a muscled forearm on the counter and picked up the glass of blood.

"She'll be fine. I'd say pregnancy agrees with her."

"She's never looked more beautiful," John smiled briefly, "but she's on edge. Constantly looking over her shoulder. Jittery in crowds."

"You can't expect someone to get kidnapped without after-effects. Give her time." Doreen cleaned a few drops of blood off the kitchen counter with a paper towel.

"Vampires don't obsess like humans do. Her fear is...unusual."

"Think about it—she'd been a vampire for less than a year when the Mafia grabbed her. If those guys had held me for three days while they erected a guillotine to cut off my head, I'd have gone insane. Cut her some human slack."

"True, it's been half a millennium since I was human. I've forgotten how it feels to be afraid." John downed the last of his blood and picked up his car keys. "I'm doing everything in my power to make her happy, and in the meantime, you're in charge of Christmas."

"Not to fret, boss. I'm on it."

Doreen had honed her holiday to-do list to a mere 30 items, and to emphasize the Wright's black and silver Christmas theme, a black-flocked tree was on the list, number 28 to be exact. Number one was the nursery for John and Lauren's baby, and though Doreen was grandmother to five, preparing for the arrival of a *vampire* baby required more than a stop at "Babies R' Us." To start, what kind of pacifier do you get for a kid with fangs? Would the baby be born with fangs intact or would they start coming in at six months? Better to knock off the easy items on her list, and then proceed to the challenges.

She bid her boss goodbye, finished straightening up the kitchen, and picked up her purple motorcycle helmet and matching leather gloves from the mud room. Walking outside, she breathed in the crisp, dry air that made December the best month in Orlando.

Five minutes later, she swerved up to Greenery Jungle, and then hoisted the motorcycle onto its kickstand with her combat boot. Removing her helmet, she ran her fingers through her spiky, silver hair. Earlier that morning, she'd taken out her pierced tongue ball after rolling it over her husband's manhood. Following a string of satisfied moans that ended in a full-body shudder, Bill had advised her that enunciating "black-flocked" with that thing in her mouth could come out wrong.

Doreen headed into Greenery Jungle and spied an aproned clerk, who was sweeping pine needles from the showroom floor. "Hi! I'm about to hit you with the most unusual request you've had in awhile."

"Don't count on it." He stopped to rest on his broom. "I

just dressed eight wooden reindeer in bikinis for Mrs. Grady's front yard."

Doreen took a deep breath and crossed her fingers. "I'm looking for a black-flocked Christmas tree."

"That's a new one." The clerk, whose name tag read Norman, scratched his chin. "But I've got black spray paint, so it's doable. Give me a few days. How big a tree do you want?"

"Huge. The room we're puttin' it in has a cathedral ceiling, so the tree could be 12 feet or so."

"Not a problem. I should be able to deliver it on Friday."

"Great. One seventy-five Bonita Place."

"The big white Victorian?"

"Yep, that's the one. And can you spray a sprig of mistletoe while you're at it? And throw in a couple of black wreaths and four dozen silver balls."

"Sounds gothic," Norman said over his shoulder as he moved to his desk.

"You have no idea."

Doreen thanked Norman profusely, left a credit card number for the charge, and marked a big check on her list by number 28. She scanned the remaining items and settled on "presents for Rosetta's kids." Lauren's dental hygienist had six children, so that should take the rest of the day.

Mounting her Harley, she'd stop by the bank first to deposit her generous Christmas bonus. Doreen was well-rewarded for being a personal assistant to vampires whose professional lives included dentistry and the law, but more importantly, she loved John and Lauren Wright like family. She revved the 1,250 cc engine of her Night Rod Special and sped off.

* * *

Around 7 p.m., Lauren heard the deafening "potato-potato" of Doreen's bike coming down their brick street. She opened the front door as Doreen careened into the circular drive. Packages were piled on the back of her bike, secured with a bungee cord.

"You should have taken the Cadillac," Lauren said. "I don't like you out on that bike after dark."

"I may not be a spring chicken, but I'm a whiz on this bike." Doreen dismounted, and then executed a karate chop to her bike seat, presumably demonstrating her toughness.

Lauren chuckled. "For a human, you've got good reflexes, I'll give you that." She waddled down the steps to help Doreen with the packages.

"There's nothing too heavy here," Doreen said, "but let me take the big ones."

"Doreen, even pregnant, I can lift the rear end of a car with one hand." Lauren rolled her eyes. "And at this point, I'm looking for ways to start my labor. I was due on November 15."

"And today's December first." Doreen handed Lauren two of the smaller packages.

Lauren shivered. "Hard to believe I've been home a month."

Doreen put her arm around Lauren's shoulder. "That's all behind you now, honey."

"That's what John keeps saying, but I can't shake this feeling of impending doom."

"You just worry about getting this baby born. John will keep an eye on the bad guys." Doreen went back to her unloading. "Didn't you work today?"

"Yeah, I did a root canal this morning and two more fillings for a 12-year-old I see on a regular basis. I swear, if he doesn't stop drinking Mountain Dew, his mouth will be more amalgam than enamel."

"All that sugar. I keep telling my grandkids—"

"Actually, it's not the sugar. It's the acid." Again, Lauren shivered to dispel the memory. The Mafia had threatened to use acid to blind her. "I guess vampires aren't immune to post traumatic stress disorder. Weird how just one word can bring back a flood of memories."

Doreen took Lauren's chin in her hand. "Honey, you need to talk to a professional about this."

"You're right. I'll call Meredith. She's been working on a *Vampire Services Directory*."

* * *

The following morning, Lauren woke to John's hands on her pregnant belly. She tousled his wavy black hair, and said, "Are you going to sleep with a basketball once this baby makes his appearance?"

"I'll admit I'm much attached to your ripeness, but once our *daughter* arrives, I'll be quite busy holding her little body." John stretched his long arms over his head, and then returned to caressing Lauren's belly. "In fact, I may never set *her* down."

Lauren traced her fingers over John's full lips. "You're going to be a great father. That's how I knew I was ready to be a vampire, you know, seeing you with Rosetta's kids."

"I've waited five hundred years for this, but now that you're two weeks late, I'm running out of patience." John slipped his hand from Lauren's belly and urged her legs apart with his fingers.

"Are you going to talk to our *son* in utero?"

"No, my darling, I'm going to see if I can hurry our *daughter* along." She turned her chin up to him, and he blew his intoxicating vampire breath across her eyes before covering her mouth with his. While blending their tongues, he separated her feminine folds and slid his fingers inside her warm, wet sheath. "I love how hot you are."

He turned her gently to her right side and plumped the pillow underneath her head. Positioning himself behind her, he bent her left leg at the knee and pulled it back to his hip. Continuing a rhythmic circling of her feminine bud with his fingers, he entered her from behind and felt her welcome his manhood and grip him there before beginning his slow, deep thrusts.

Lauren pinched her swollen breasts, and then reached between her legs to caress the base of his penis. She closed her eyes and arched her back, encouraging his deeper penetration.

He gathered her long hair in his hand and whispered in her ear, "What do you want, Lauren?"

Her chest vibrated with a deep growl. "I want...I want you to get bigger."

"Just for you," John said as his manhood swelled to her command.

Lauren threw her head back and reached behind to circle her arm around John's neck. "Now...now." She shuddered in his arms as her climax undulated in waves of intense pleasure, gripping John and sending him into spasms with her.

They lay, spooned and spent, catching their breath, for several minutes before John spoke. "If that didn't speed things up, I've overestimated my powers."

Lauren chuckled. "This is not yours to control. Nor mine." Lauren took John's hand and put it on her belly to feel a tiny appendage pushing against it.

"*She's* stretching after that workout," John said.

"Or *he's* getting ready for round two." Lauren fluttered her eyelashes at John.

"*She'll* have to wait for that one, because I've got to take a deposition at the courthouse at nine, and it's already eight-fifteen." John kissed Lauren on the forehead and gracefully slid out of bed.

"Will I ever be as lithe as you?" Lauren asked as John headed for their walk-in closet.

"You've made remarkable strides, darling, in your one year of vamphood. I've had a bit more practice." John held a baby blue Prada shirt out the closet door. Lauren nodded her approval.

"Which suit today?" he asked. "Should I go conservative or intimidating?"

"Just don't wear the pinstripe." Lauren shuddered, recalling her recent kidnapping and the pinstripe suits the Mafiosos wore. "I think we should burn that one."

"Or donate it to the Mafia thrift shop?"

Lauren grimaced. "The wound's still too fresh."

"I'm sorry, my love." John returned to the bed and sat on the edge. "They can't hurt you anymore."

"Just because the local don's out of the picture doesn't mean they won't send somebody down from New Jersey or wherever to take over."

"I don't want you worrying about that." He brushed Lauren's bangs out of her eyes. "You are everything to me, Lauren, and I will never let anything harm you."

"I can't seem to shake this fear. Doreen suggested I talk with someone who can help me cope."

"Do whatever you need to do, my love. If you're worried, you'll have our *daughter* fretting, and then she'll never want to come out."

"Enough with the gender preference."

"Hey, you're the one who didn't want to know. I'm just going with my gut."

Lauren eased out of bed and retrieved a towel that was draped on the back of her vanity chair. She popped John's behind with it.

"Ouch!" He grabbed the towel from her.

"As accurate as your gut usually is, this time you're wrong." Lauren shook her finger at him and then waddled into the bathroom, where John joined her for a shower. When they emerged, she in her maternity dental uniform and he in his lawyer's attire, she kissed him quickly before he exited the bedroom, and then she picked up her cell phone from the nightstand and punched in Meredith's number.

Meredith answered with a breathy, "Don't you know better than to phone newlyweds before nine a.m.?" Lauren heard Luc moan in the background.

"Sorry, we working stiffs are already into our day."

"And if I know you, you started it off with a bang...literally."

"If this baby doesn't come soon, I'm going to have to replace John's wanger with a stick of dynamite." Lauren couldn't begin to see past her stomach, so she slipped into her white clogs by feel.

Meredith laughed. "That baby must weigh ten pounds by now."

"At least."

"Your obstetrician's not a vamp, is she?"

"No, and she has no idea I'm one."

"Maybe that's part of the problem. Do we really know how long vampire gestation is?"

"From the research I've done, it's close to humans."

"Yeah, but you may not be as overdue as you think you are."

"You've seen me. I'm the Goodyear blimp."

"If I'd had my *Vampire Services Directory* done nine months ago, you could have started with a vampire doctor. Geeze, Lauren, what if you need a blood transfusion? You don't have a blood type."

"I've already considered that. I have a card that says I'm AB positive, which is the universal recipient."

"All right, I can see you've thought about this, but I still wish you had a vamp doctor."

Lauren listened to Meredith's account of her progress on the *Vampire Services Directory* as she walked down the stairway to the kitchen, where John had already set out a glass of blood on the granite countertop. She smiled at his thoughtfulness, and then said, "Mere, do you have any psychologists on that list?"

"A couple, why?"

"I can't shake the kidnapping," Lauren began. "At first, I was relieved to be safe and back in John's arms. I thought I was all right, but now I'm having flashbacks."

"Oh, sweetie, I'm so sorry. You *do* need some help."
Lauren could hear Meredith shuffling papers over the phone.
"There's a guy up in Cassadaga who sounds great. I've got his
contact information here."

"I thought Cassadaga was a community of psychics.
I'm looking for a legitimate psychologist."

"This guy has a doctorate in psychiatry, and he's also an
M.D. Both degrees from the University of Oxford. He comes
highly recommended. Got a pen?"

"Yep, right here. Go ahead."

"Dr. Erasmus Gephart, 728-1420, and he has evening
hours, of course."

* * *

Lauren's first session with Dr. Gephart was on
Thursday evening. Cassadaga was 30 miles north on
Interstate 4, an easy drive though John didn't like her
traveling alone at night in her advanced state of pregnancy.

"Sometimes you forget I'm no longer human," she
teased.

"I'm fully aware of your capabilities, my love, but I
don't want you going into labor that far from home. You're
too pregnant to resort to bat form, and if you could, I'm not
sure you'd get off the ground. Sure I can't drive you?"

"No, not for this first session. I need to face my
demons alone." She touched his cheek. "Don't worry. Doreen
says I'll start nesting behavior when labor is imminent, and
that hasn't happened."

"What does that mean?"

"You know, rushing around, straightening things up,
plumping pillows... that kind of stuff."

"That would be a departure. Harkens me back to our
first date when you had your house cleaned to impress me."

"You could say that clutter is my strong suit."

"So, if I see you scurrying around, tidying things up, I should call the hospital?"

"Yes, immediately. In the meantime, it's safe to let me out of your sight."

"All right, but I still don't like it." John flashed the intense look that always got Lauren's heart going.

"Aren't you hunting tonight?" She put on her pink hoodie and picked up her purse.

"Yes, I'm trailing a pedophile for the Orlando Police."

"I'll be home long before you are." Lauren kissed John, inhaling his intoxicating breath that never failed to make her dizzy. "I can't live without you, John."

"Nor I, you." He opened the front door for her. "And remember, this is the last time I'm letting you travel such a distance—alone."

* * *

Pulling out of her driveway that evening, a whistle through the palm trees caught her attention, and a large barn owl swooped in front of her car and seemed to eye her knowingly. She took the owl's appearance as a friendly greeting between creatures of the night. As she headed to another creature of the night, she thought about the brief conversation she'd had with Dr. Gephart when she called for the appointment. He'd told her he knew her husband was the famous Vampire Vigilante, and she smiled at the notion that her husband was a legend among their kind.

The drive up Interstate 4 took thirty-five minutes, with the Cassadaga exit just minutes from the heart of the little community, yet Cassadaga seemed light years away from the busy metropolis of Orlando. Majestic oaks, heavy with Spanish moss, lined the main street into town, where the architecture was 1920's vintage. In what she guessed was the center of town, a single string of Christmas lights were suspended across the intersection. She found Dr. Gephart's office/house just off the main thoroughfare. A lantern at the curb flickered next to a shingle, where Erasmus D. Gephart, M.D., PhD, was displayed in Olde English script.

Lauren parked in front. There were no other cars on the quiet street. As she approached the house, careful of the irregular sidewalk buckled from the roots of hundred-year-old trees, a shiver of foreboding ran up her spine. The house looked like a grande dame in partial ruin, clutching the remnants of her former glory. Lanterns on either side of the front door revealed peeling white paint and massive columns reminiscent of Tara after the Civil War, while an audio background of creaking planks strained under Lauren's feet. A swing swayed eerily on the expansive front porch.

Before she reached for the gargoyle knocker, the door opened with a pop, like it had been sealed shut. She peered into the musky foyer. A deep voice issued from the darkness, "Good evening. Please come in." Lauren inched across the threshold. She didn't need to close the door behind her. It creaked shut on its own.

A large, looming figure stepped out of the shadows. "Light?" The figure walked to a table in the foyer, struck a match and lit three candles in a candelabra. "There. That is better."

Lauren suppressed a gasp as the figure turned to her. There stood a reasonable facsimile of Rasputin. He flashed a dazzling smile, and the dentist in Lauren took over. She was a professional. She could handle this.

"So nice to meet you." She held out her hand.

"And you," he said, caressing her hand with long, cold fingers. "Would you like me to turn up the heat? It is a touch chilly this evening."

"No, I've got a built-in oven here." Lauren rubbed her pregnant belly.

"I am Erasmus Gephart," the man said, eyeing her round tummy, "though I am sure you surmised that already." His incisor glistened in the candlelight as he smiled.

She'd hoped he'd been the butler. Best not put too much stock in first impressions. "You come highly recommended."

He dismissed her compliment with a wave of his hand. "My credentials are impressive, but what is more important is whether I can assist *you*." For the first time, he gazed into her eyes with a penetrating stare. No doubt the same hypnotic gaze Rasputin used on Queen Alexandra.

Dr. Gephart curled his index finger in a hokey "come hither" gesture, and Lauren followed him through an arched doorway hung with mistletoe into a dimly-lit Victorian parlor.

"I see you've decorated for Christmas." Lauren nodded to the mistletoe.

"That has been up for years," Dr. Gephart said. "I have not yet put it to use."

Lauren shivered at the thought of Dr. Gephart's lips, which would surely be ice cold. She took in his eclectic decor, replete with red velvet upholstery on the ornately carved furniture and an assortment of Cuckoo clocks on the walls. He indicated a small loveseat for Lauren with a footstool at its base. She settled in, propping up her high-top pink sneakers.

Sitting in a throne-like chair across from her, Lauren thought that Dr. Gephart had a freakish sort of magnetism. Maybe it was his long black hair, streaked with silver, or the intensity of his dark blue eyes. She could understand how an unsuspecting human female could be seduced by him. He picked up a small notepad and pen from the chair-side table. "Before we begin, would you like some refreshment? I am partial to B positive, myself, but my cabinet is well-stocked. I even have a bit of AB negative for special occasions." His chuckle rattled in his chest. "Though I think of O positive as humans' cheap wine."

"A little B Positive would be nice," Lauren said. "I'm ravenous these days."

Dr. Gephart licked dry, colorless lips and pulled on a chord suspended from the ceiling. A small female in a black tutu materialized with two crystal goblets of blood. She was the size of an average first-grader. "Teensy is half human and half fairy," Dr. Gephart said, nodding to the figure who swirled in and out of the room in a matter of seconds. "It is an efficient genetic mix. She has the physical prowess of a fairy but with human cunning and intelligence." Dr. Gephart twittered his fingers, waiting for Lauren to sip her blood. "Take a few sips, my dear."

"Thank you," she said. "My husband and I have human employees, but they're really more like family." Lauren took a swig of her blood cocktail.

"Yes, Teensy is like family to me. I have no relations in this country, and I never married, you see." Dr. Gephart winked.

Lauren gulped her blood a bit too quickly, choking on the last swallow. "Your speech has the cadence of a bygone era, and your accent is...interesting. Some words sound British, but there's an element of what... Russian?"

He reared back his head and laughed. The large vase of withering red roses on the table vibrated with his guffaw. "I was forty when I was turned in Victorian England, but I have lived all over the world. And yes, I lived in Russia at the turn of the last century. "

"You've chosen an interesting community to call home. Cassadaga does seem to be in a time warp, though I have to say that my husband didn't fully enter this century until we met."

Dr. Gephart's lips curled in an insipid grin. "Ah, the love of a good woman can surely change a man."

"Well, that goes both ways."

He cocked one bushy eyebrow. "Did your famous husband turn you?"

"Yes, but not by force. It was my decision."

Dr. Gephart closed his eyes and sucked in an audible breath. What he said next had Lauren shaking in her sneakers. "There is nothing more seductive than the thrill of co-mingled blood, and I am long overdue."

Lauren gulped. "I guess the clock is ticking. Can we get started?"

"Of course." Dr. Gephart picked up his notepad and pen. "You briefly described your incident over the telephone. Tell me more." He leaned forward in his chair, and the air around him seemed to swirl.

Lauren took a deep breath. "I was kidnapped by the Orlando Mafia a month ago. They held me for several days until my husband and his friend rescued me." She closed her eyes. "It was horrifying." For more than an hour, Lauren recanted the harrowing details, gripping an arm of the loveseat. When she was finished, she reached for a tissue to dab her teary eyes.

Dr. Gephart paused. "You are having flashbacks?"

"Yes! One word can set me off, and it all comes back like I'm experiencing it for the first time." Tears ran down her cheeks. "I don't want to live like this!" She clasped her hands together, plaintively seeking a solution.

"When you have a thought about the kidnapping, do you try to suppress it?" Dr. Gephart touched his index finger to his lips and left it there.

"Sure. I do whatever I can to get it out of my mind." *Duh!*

"Do not suppress it. Let it flow through you. Recognize it for what it is—something in the past that can no longer touch you. Cry if you need to. Scream if it helps. But do not push it aside."

"I'll be a basket case."

"No, you will come to accept it, and you will realize that your past has no hold over you." Dr. Gephart wrote something on his pad. "Do you feel hyper vigilant about your surroundings?"

"Hyper vigilant for a vampire?"

Dr. Gephart chuckled. "True, we do see things humans do not, but do you find yourself constantly looking for the perpetrators?"

"Sometimes, when I'm in a crowd." Lauren rubbed her arms.

"Ordinarily, I would prescribe medication, but given your pregnancy, that would not be advisable. Besides, I do not believe you are clinically depressed, and I think we can work through this if you commit to diligence in your therapy."

"I'll do anything, Dr. Gephart."

"Call me 'Ras.'" The corners of his mouth turned up. "As you allow yourself to feel and accept your trauma, you may need to contact me. Put my number in your phone, and please know that you may ring me anytime."

"Thank you." Lauren looked at her watch. "Oh my, I need to get home." She jumped up. "Whoa." Her head spun with dizziness, and she felt strong arms around her before everything went black.

* * *

Dr. Gephart cradled Lauren in his arms and settled her into his lap on the loveseat. His heart raced and a surge of lust elongated his incisors to piercing length, but as he considered her full breasts pressed against him and her scent of lavender and spice, he took a few deep breaths and willed his teeth back to human size. Looking at her angelic face, with her full eyelashes brushing her cheeks and her red lips slightly parted, his better self took hold. To stab her with his manhood and sink his teeth in her neck would satisfy his lust, but to possess her completely would be divine.

Teensy materialized with smelling salts.

"That sixth sense of yours is working overtime," Ras said, taking the smelling salts from Teensy. He hesitated before passing them under Lauren's nose. "I do not want this to end too soon."

"Don't even think about it, boss. Her husband would flatten you."

"I am fully aware of the Vampire Vigilante, but that does not make his wife less desirable."

"You wouldn't have a tinker's chance in hell with her." Teensy closed her eyes and pursed her lips.

"What is stirring in that conniving mind of yours?" Ras squinted at his assistant.

"Hmm. I'm thinkin'. Your life mate's supposed to be a virgin."

"True, but I gave up on that notion long ago. She is also supposed to be a born vampire, not made."

"So, if you could arrange for the mother to go into labor, we could disappear with her child. What's time to you? The baby'd grow up soon enough. You'd have a virgin bride *and* a born vampire."

Ras tapped an index finger to his lips. "Brilliant idea—so glad I thought of it."

Teensy rolled her black eyes. "I'll get to work. Let's see, what prescriptions will we need? Pitocin to start her labor and morphine to knock her out? Of course, all this hinges on the child being a girl."

"I'll write the prescription for the meds." Before Ras passed the smelling salts under Lauren's nose, he eased his hand under her pink sweatshirt and placed his palm on her round belly. The baby pushed against his hand, and he closed his eyes, envisioning the tiny bundle in her mother's womb. Ras smiled broadly. "She has violet eyes."

CHAPTER TWO

Recovered from her fainting spell but still tentative, Lauren observed the speed limit on her way home. She never drove as fast as John, but she had been known to gun it on occasion. She thought about how Dr. Gephart had flirted with her. Well, she'd seen that before. Since she'd become a vampire, men were falling over themselves to get her attention. Mostly, she ignored the seductive glances, and though Dr. Gephart was behaving unprofessionally, the more important issue was whether he could help her. She'd heard about the patient/therapist relationship and knew it wasn't unusual for a romantic link to develop, but she'd put him in his place if it came to that. She'd be fine.

An illuminated billboard advertising maternity services at Florida Hospital caught her eye on Interstate 4, and she patted her belly, only to shudder with the thought that her baby might never have been born. Rather than push the thought aside, she tried Dr. Gephart's advice and acknowledged the painful memory of her kidnapping. The Mafia had used silver cuffs around her ankles and wrists to chain her to a bed where she'd lain for three days. Every moment that ticked by had left her less hopeful of rescue.

Lauren took several deep breaths. *The Mafia can't hurt me anymore. That horrible experience is in the past. I'm safe now.* As tears streamed down her face, a surprising wave of calm washed over her.

By the time John arrived home from his evening hunt, she was in bed. She roused when he kissed her forehead, fluttering her sleepy eyes open.

"How'd it go at the doctor's?" he asked.

"He's a bit creepy, but he knows his stuff."

"I'm going with you next time."

Lauren touched John's cheek. "How was your hunt?"

"I probably sucked four pints out of the fat pedophile before the police arrived. I'm feeling grubby." He tucked the sheets around Lauren's shoulders. "Go back to sleep, my love. I'm going to take a shower."

* * *

The phone rang at nine the following morning, and Lauren noted Meredith's number on the caller i.d. before answering. "A bit early for you, isn't it?"

"Luc joined a Friday morning running group. It's part of his human masquerade. Rather than zero to 60 in three seconds, he's trying to slow down to a 5-minute mile."

"Like Dr. Gephart said, 'the love of a good woman can change a man.'"

"If you're already quoting him, you must have been impressed."

"I'm impressed with his knowledge, but he's weird. His first name is Erasmus, and I swear, he looks like Rasputin. He said I could call him 'Ras.'"

"He didn't come on to you, did he?"

"Kind of, but I can handle him. Besides, I look like a whale, and I went there in sweats and sneakers. Hardly your sex goddess."

"Seriously, Lauren, you'd be gorgeous in a gunny sack, and anyway, some men are extremely attracted to pregnant women. Look at John."

"He does love my roundness, but he has a vested interest."

When they hung up, Lauren thought about Dr. Gephart's intentions. Yes, she had to admit, he found her attractive. She just wouldn't give him an opening.

The phone rang again as Lauren was downing a juice glass full of blood in the kitchen. It was her dental hygienist, Rosetta.

"Hi, doc. How you feelin'?"

"I'm still here, fat as ever." Anticipating that she'd be on maternity leave by now, Lauren had cut her patient load to those who'd understand that they might be canceled. "No patients today, right?"

"You didn't have anyone on the schedule, but Mrs. Bates is sitting here with her maxillary first molar in a glass of milk."

"How the heck did that happen?"

"She's not talkin'. I'm guessin' she bit down on a crowbar during sex with that 80-year-old husband of hers."

"Sounds logical." Lauren chuckled. "But don't knock senior sex."

"True, she doesn't have to worry about getting pregnant."

"Don't tell me you're..."

"Geeze, no, six is enough."

"Phew. All right, back to Mrs. Bates. Tell her to sit tight, and I'll be there as soon as I can. Is she in pain?"

"No. She took a Percocet left over from her last root canal, so she's kind of loopy. Maybe I can get the story out of her before you get here."

Lauren opened the Bahama shutters on her kitchen windows. Bright sunlight streamed in, and she shielded her eyes and closed the shutters. This was going to be a day she'd rather spend inside, but at least her dark sunglasses and the tinted windows on her new Mercedes would keep her comfortable until she got to her office. No windows there. Of all the modifications she'd had to make when she became a vampire, adapting to the Florida sunshine she'd once worshipped had been the most difficult. Her remarkable new vision allowed her to see things she'd never noticed before, like the delicate veining in a butterfly's wings, but the sun could be a handicap. Besides the glare, her skin burned more easily now. Thank goodness for SPF 75. She went back upstairs to dress in her dentist scrubs and slather some sunscreen on her bare arms and across the bridge of her nose. Before leaving the house, she filled a thermos with blood from the refrigerator.

She was singing along to the soundtrack from "Mamma Mia" on her five-minute drive to the office when she saw a man in a pin-striped suit walking down the street. Immediately, her mind jumped back to the kidnapping. She took a deep breath and let the memory wash over her. *Loaded with silver bullets, the gun pressed hard against her extended belly. A sinister voice said, "I wonder who'll die first, the dame or the baby?"* Lauren pulled her car into the closest on-street parking space, turned off the engine, and let the tears run down her cheeks. *They can't hurt me anymore. What's past is past.* She sat for a few minutes, allowing her tears to subside. *That wasn't so bad.* By the time she reached her office parking lot and the space reserved for "Dr. Lauren Marsh Wright," she was ready to put Mrs. Bates' tooth back in its socket.

* * *

At the Wrights' house, Doreen was tugging on her nose ring. Aggravated with having to wait for the Christmas tree delivery when there were other items to knock off her list, she peered out the stained glass front door. "Hurry up," she said to the street. "I'm a busy woman."

Her biorhythms must have been in tune with the universe because her utterance to the street produced results. The funky Greenery Jungle truck, with gorillas, zebras, and giraffes painted on the doors, pulled into the Wrights' circular driveway.

"If they think it's a jungle out there," Doreen mused, "wait 'til they get inside."

She walked out the front door to greet the two men, who had exited the truck and were lifting the heavy rear door. One man held a clipboard. "Just confirming. This the Wright residence?"

"Yep." Doreen peered into the back of the truck.

"I've got a 12-foot, black-flocked Christmas tree, some black-flocked mistletoe, two black wreaths, and four boxes of silver balls. Is that the whole order?"

"Yep, and can you string the lights on the tree?"

"Not for free, lady."

Doreen batted purple eyelashes. "I didn't expect it to be free."

"All right then, but it'll take about two hours at twenty-five dollars an hour. We don't just wrap the lights around the tree. We run them up and down each branch." The man entered the truck bed and tugged at the tree, which was wrapped in netting. He reached into the tree for a good hold on the trunk and passed it out the back of the truck to his partner.

"This here's Sam, and I'm Jake." Jake handed a stepladder to Sam.

"O.K., guys. I'm Doreen." She motioned for the two men to follow her up the front steps.

"Beautiful house," Sam said. "What do your employers do?"

"One's a lawyer, and one's a dentist."

"Always knew I shoulda stayed in school." Jake shook

his head.

"Like my momma used to say, 'just be professional in whatever you do,'" Doreen advised as she led the men through the house and into the huge family room. "There's the spot." She pointed to the Palladian window at the far end of the cathedral-ceilinged room. "You should have plenty of head room to put the star on top."

"Yes, ma'am. Should be fine," Sam said.

"I'll leave you guys to your work. The boxes of lights are there on the floor, and I put two brooms by the window for clean-up." Doreen turned to the stairway that led from the family room to the second floor. "I'll be up in my office. Yell if you need me."

Doreen straightened up her bosses' bedroom first. She smiled to herself as she pulled the lilac satin sheets taut around the corners of the mattress, remembering when she'd bought those sheets for John. Before he fell in love with Lauren, his bed had been a coffin. Today, the sheets were tousled as usual, with traces of activity. *Those two'll be banging on the way to the maternity ward.*

She settled at her desk to pay a few bills, working for about an hour when she was interrupted by a commotion from downstairs. It sounded like something was flying around down there. She jumped up from her desk chair and ran down the hall. She screamed when she hit the landing between the first and second flight of stairs. "Stop!"

Sam and Jake were swinging the brooms at a bat that seemed to be trying its darndest to get out of their way.

"I'm gonna kill that varmint." Jake swung hard at the tiny bat. He motioned for Doreen to stay on the stairs.

"No, that's..." she stopped. *Who is that?* She hit the bottom step and ran into the room. The bat swooped by her face. Doreen detected pink lipstick on the little rodent before it flapped to the chandelier and attached itself to the chain. She looked back at the men. "Don't you know that bats eat mosquitoes?"

The two guys stopped their swinging momentarily.

"Lady, are you crazy? Those things carry rabies." Sam moved his ladder from next to the tree to underneath the chandelier.

"Don't swing at the chandelier, for Pete's sake." Doreen grabbed the broom from Sam. "You guys go into the kitchen and relax. I'm experienced with this." She pointed in the direction of the kitchen and waited until the men were out of sight. They didn't seem reluctant to leave the work to Doreen.

"You can come down now." Doreen climbed the stepladder and reached up to the bat. The shaking creature fluttered into her hand. When she set it down on the floor, it morphed into beautiful, statuesque Meredith.

"Next time, I'll call first." Meredith smoothed out the creases in her hot pink, Juicy Couture sweatpants and jiggled her arms. "I just learned to do the bat thing, and I thought I'd show Lauren my new skill."

"I'm sure she'd be proud, but she's not here. Rosetta called this morning with an emergency at the office."

One of the men yelled from the kitchen. "Lady, what's this red stuff in the refrigerator?"

The two women exchanged wide-eyed glances and bolted to the kitchen. They were met by Sam, who held up an unmarked glass bottle of blood.

"That's pomegranate juice, but it's loaded with prenatal vitamins for my boss. You won't like it." Doreen snatched the bottle from Sam and put it back in the empty refrigerator. "How about a coke?" Doreen opened the pantry to her stash of soft drinks.

"I'm already jittery from that bat," Sam said. "Don't think I need any caffeine."

"Ginger ale?" Doreen offered.

"Yes, ma'am. That'd be good." Sam plunked himself down on a stool at the kitchen counter.

"Me, too, please." Jake joined Sam at the counter.

Doreen got two big glasses, loaded them with ice, and

set the sparkling ginger ales in front of the two men. She handed them paper towels to mop their foreheads. "Here, guys. Relax for a few minutes. I think you've put a big enough dent in the tree that I can take it from here. How much do I owe you?"

"We'd be happy to finish the job," Sam said.

"No, you've had your excitement for the day. I'll pay you for the full two hours."

Doreen watched Sam and Jake eyeing Meredith from top to bottom, lingering on the bottom. They probably wondered where she came from, but they weren't asking. Besides, Doreen thought, the eye candy took their minds off their ordeal. Little did they know, their object of lust was the bat.

After several minutes of slurping and ogling, Jake said, "Well, I guess we'd better head to our next job." He thanked Doreen, tipped his baseball cap to both women, jabbed Sam in the shoulder, and the men left via the front door.

Doreen turned to Meredith. "All right, Batty, want to help me hang the mistletoe?"

* * *

Sunday night, Lauren woke screaming from a nightmare flashback in which Rick Maroon, the Mafia don, showed her the guillotine he'd rigged in his basement to cut off her head. John jumped at the sound of Lauren's scream, and then wrapped his arms around her and rocked her through a crying jag that left her limp as a rag doll.

"What can I do for you, love?" John handed Lauren a tissue from the bedside table. "A cold washcloth?"

"Yes, please." Lauren propped herself against the headboard and took a few deep breaths. When John returned, he sat on the edge of the bed

"Are you sure this doctor knows what he's doing?" He pressed the washcloth to Lauren's eyes.

"I know I seem even more emotional, but I do feel better. It's like I'm chipping away at the hurt."

"You are the most caring person I've ever known, and you deserve to be happy. If this therapy is working for you, then I'm 100 percent behind it."

"Thank you."   Lauren gave John a sheepish grin. "Know what I want now?"

"Happy to oblige." John bent to trace Lauren's mouth and ease his tongue into her parted lips.

"Mmm, that was nice," Lauren said as the kiss ended, "but I have a special request tonight." She ran her hand down John's rippled stomach muscles. "I want you to bite me."

"That isn't necessary, my love. You are already marked as mine."

"I know, but the baby needs it." Lauren rubbed her tummy. "I want her protected by the strength of your venom."

"Did you say *her*?"

"Oops, that was a slip."

John chuckled. "This will heighten your pleasure, you know."

"Uh-huh, I'm aware of that."

"Think you can take it?" John flashed a teasing smile.

"Humor the pregnant lady." Lauren lifted her heavy curls and pointed to a spot at the back of her neck. "Right here, where I can cover it with my hair."

"Wait a minute, let's have some fun with this." John touched the tiny scars on Lauren's neck where he'd claimed her for eternity, and then ran his hand down to her breast. "I could nip you here," he said, touching a spot just above her right nipple, "or here." He traced his thumb across the top of her thigh. "How about here?" He circled her belly button with his tongue.

"The baby might punch your nose if you do it there." Lauren ruffled her husband's hair.

"I'm willing to take that chance."

"Nope, you've more than sufficiently turned me on, but

we're doing this my way." Lauren eased herself to a kneeling position, propped on her elbows and knees. Her swollen tummy rested gently on the bed. "I want you inside me when I feel your teeth hit my skin."

John knelt behind her, and Lauren reached between her legs to caress his erection. He leaned over her, gently bracing one hand on her back as he brushed the hair off her neck. A low growl rumbled through his chest as he claimed her with his penis, and then he whispered in her ear, "You are mine, and I will always protect you."

The ease with which his razor-sharp incisors punctured her skin caused Lauren to gasp as the warmth of his venom coursed through her. She could feel it traveling in her veins to the core of her womanhood, where liquid velvet spread through her sheath and the baby seemed to reach for the source of the heat. With John's teeth locked in her neck and the steady rhythm of his thrusts inside her, Lauren melted into her ecstasy. Just before the first wave of pleasure rocked her, her mind clasped the intensity of the moment and tears welled up in her eyes. She allowed her body to take her to a safe place, where there was no Lauren separate from John or her baby, where nothing could harm her.

* * *

Monday morning, Lauren rolled over lazily. *I can't believe those shenanigans last night didn't send me into labor.* She nudged John, who glanced at the bedside clock, and then leapt out of bed.

"I thought I set the alarm," John said.

"You were distracted." Lauren smiled to herself and watched him disappear into the bathroom. "What's your rush today?"

"I've got jury selection and a tough judge on the bench. I pity the potential jurors. This could be a long one."

"You'll be out-of-pocket if I need you?"

"Just for today." John popped his head out of the bathroom. "Do you think today's the day?"

"No, don't worry, I don't feel any different." Lauren smiled. "I take that back. I've never felt more satisfied." She stretched her arms over her head and then patted her belly.

"No labor twinges?"

"Nope." Lauren sat up in bed and looked out the large window in their bedroom. "Looks like a nice, overcast day, and no patients on the schedule. Think I'll drop in on Meredith."

John emerged from the shower, a towel wrapped around his middle, and headed for the closet. After a few minutes, he stepped out in a navy, double-breasted suit, sky blue shirt and a burgundy-striped tie. "Intimidating enough?"

"Perfect. Is this the teenager's murder?"

"Yeah. Remind me again why I gave up a lucrative practice to become a prosecutor?"

"First, you're dedicated to public service. And second, intellectual property brought you some unsavory clients." Lauren shivered, remembering the Mafia connection that led to her kidnapping.

"I saw that shiver." John walked to the bed and took Lauren's chin in his hand. "When's your next appointment with Dr. Gephart?"

"Thursday."

"Remember, I'm going with you."

Lauren smiled up at John, and he kissed her forehead.

"See you tonight." He walked out of their bedroom, and Lauren closed her eyes and stretched languidly on the 800-thread-count sheets, savoring the memory of their lovemaking. John was her universe. How could she live without him? Then, as quickly as the fond memory had come, it dissolved into a flashback from her kidnapping. She clenched her teeth at the memory of being strapped to a plank, her head positioned under a guillotine. Bile rose to her throat, and she swallowed it back and shook her head. Tears spilled over her cheeks.

She rolled over and with a shaking hand, picked up her cell phone from the bedside table, punching in Dr. Gephart's phone number. He answered on the second ring.

"Erasmus Gephart here."

"It's Lauren Wright." She paused. "I'm getting tired of these flashbacks."

"How are you handling them?"

"Like you said, I'm riding with them, not trying to suppress them. I actually feel less frightened, but I'm emotionally exhausted."

He murmured a sympathetic sound. "It might be time for some cognitive work. I use a therapy called EFT, emotional freedom technique. I believe it will benefit you greatly."

"I'll try anything."

"Instead of waiting for your appointment on Thursday evening, can you come up today?"

Lauren looked out the window to the overcast sky. "Sure, it's a good day for a vampire to be outside."

"Excellent. I will be waiting."

Lauren dressed in black maternity tights and a pink cashmere sweater. She slipped on flip-flops, gathered her hair in a ponytail and tied it with a hot pink scarf before heading downstairs to the kitchen.

Sipping on a large glass of B positive, she phoned Meredith to see if her friend could go with her to Dr. Gephart's.

"Wish I could, Lauren, but I'm in pre-Christmas retail madness at the shop, and the college student who was supposed to help me today is sick. Can't Doreen go with you?"

Lauren sighed. "She's already got a long to-do list. Besides, I'm fine. No labor twinges, not a one. I just know that John wouldn't like me going alone, and he's tied up in court today."

"Tell you what, if you have any trouble, any at all, call

me, and I'll close the store. Promise me you'll do that, even if it's just a little heartburn."

"Mere, for future reference, vampires don't get heartburn, even when we're pregnant."

Meredith laughed. "You're letting John know, right?"

"Of course. I'll text him when he's in court."

"So, you're waiting until he's in court 'cause you don't want him to talk you out of it, right?"

"He can be a bit over-protective."

"He adores you, Lauren."

"I know, but I'll be fine. I'll be back before he has a chance to worry."

CHAPTER THREE

Ras smiled to himself. This might be easier than he thought.

"Teensy!"

"What's up, boss?" His assistant appeared out of thin air. Literally.

"You will never guess. Did you get the pitocin and morphine?"

"Yeah, but she's not coming until Thursday, right?"

"Wrong. She's on her way."

"Goody." Teensy rubbed her little hands together. "I'll prepare the syringes of morphine. You're putting the pitocin in a cocktail, correct-a-mundo?"

"Yes. I have given this much thought." His lips curled in an evil grin. "I realize I cannot have her. Her child, on the other hand, will be pliable."

"And you're 100 percent sure it's a *girl* child."

"Absolutely. I have danced with her in my dreams. We waltzed at St. Albert's Hall, and she gazed up at me...adoringly. She has flowing, dark brown hair, and is even

295

more beautiful than her mother."

"I don't care what she grows up to look like. I just want a child to play with." Teensy reached in the pocket of her black hoodie and pulled out a tiny suede bag. She knelt on the hardwood floor, made a circle with a length of yarn that floated to her through the air, and dumped the bag of marbles on the floor. She pulled her stringy hair back in a ponytail and secured it with a scrunchy before picking up her black shooter and aiming it at a bubblegum pink cat's eye.

"Play with her you shall, Teensy." Ras chuckled. "And then, when she is eighteen, I shall marry her."

"It's a brilliant plan, boss... assuming the pitocin brings on her labor."

"I've doubled the human dosage, so I am sure it will." Ras squinted out the dirty parlor window to the street. "She should be here soon." He tapped his finger to his lips.

"You havin' second thoughts?" Teensy knocked an emerald green marble out of the circle with her shooter.

Ras nodded. "I have walked this earth for several hundred years without committing a crime."

"It's not too late to call it off."

Ras slapped his hand on the arm of his wing chair. "No, this child is my destiny. We were meant to be together."

"All righty then." Teensy placed her hand on Ras's arm. "Have you had your morning cocktail? You're going to need your strength for the get-away."

"Yes, I am fortified. It looks like you have had your donuts."

Teensy licked the vestiges of powdered sugar from her lips. "Fresh out of the oven from Dunkin' Donuts, and I filled up the car in DeLand."

"Excellent." Ras's hands met in a resounding clap. "Now, go pack some bags of blood in the big cooler for our trip."

"Such an adventure. We haven't had this much fun since spring break moved from Ft. Lauderdale to Daytona

Beach." Teensy giggled.

Ras gave Teensy a stern stare. "This is serious business, my pet. I need you to be on your best behavior." He crinkled his aquiline nose. "And how long has it been since you showered? The air around you smells particularly ripe."

Teensy sniffed the tuft of curly black hair in her armpit. "Whew, you're right. I guess hygiene hasn't been a priority."

"Well, clean up your act."

"Yes sir."

A knock at the front door brought them both to attention.

* * *

Lauren fidgeted at the door, anxious to get some relief and return home as quickly as possible. When the door opened and both Ras and Teensy stood there, she was taken aback.

"I wasn't expecting a welcoming party." Lauren looked from Ras to Teensy.

"I was just dusting the foyer." Teensy brandished a feather duster.

"Haven't felt the urge to dust," Lauren responded. "I keep waiting for the nesting instinct, but it hasn't kicked in yet."

"Who knows? Today might be the day." Ras motioned for Lauren to enter the parlor. Teensy smiled, curtsied, and then disappeared down the hall.

When Lauren settled into the loveseat, Ras asked, "Are you comfortable?"

Lauren nodded.

"Good." He picked up his notepad and a pencil. "Now, close your eyes for a moment and think about the essence of your distress. For some, it is forgiveness. For some, unrequited love. For you, I suspect it is fear."

Lauren shivered. "Yes, that's exactly what it is." She

closed her eyes.

"I want you to think of a phrase that dispels that fear. For instance, you could say something like, 'my fear has no hold on me,' or 'I have no reason to fear,' but it needs to be a phrase that is specifically linked to your distress."

Teensy entered the room and set a tray with two glasses of blood on the round table in the center of the room. "Thank you, Teensy. Could you please bring us napkins, too?" Ras asked.

Lauren opened her eyes and reached for her glass, but Ras interrupted her. "Do not drink yet. Tell me your phrase first."

Lauren took a deep breath. "I suppose it would be, 'the Mafia cannot harm me. I am safe.' How's that?"

"Excellent. Now, here is what you do. Any time you have a painful memory of the kidnapping, take your first two fingers and tap seven points on your body seven times, like this." Ras tapped his fingers to his forehead, temple, between his nose and top lip, chin, throat, collarbone, and just above his heart. "Each time you tap, say your mantra to yourself. It is a re-training and re-conditioning of your thought process."

"Does it work?"

"Absolutely. It is called Emotional Freedom Technique. It has been highly effective in treating post-traumatic stress disorder. It was first used to help post-war soldiers."

"Does this mean that when I have a thought about the kidnapping, I should use this technique rather than what I've been doing this past week, which has resulted in a lot of crying?"

"I no longer see grief in your face, but this technique will get you past your fear." Ras smiled. "Now, have a sip of your blood."

Lauren took a sip, and then another. "Wow, this is delicious."

"Special occasion, it is AB negative."

"What's the occasion?"

Ras smiled. "Oh, you will know soon enough. Why not try your Emotional Freedom Technique?"

Lauren tapped her fingers to her forehead, and said, "The Mafia cannot harm me. I am safe." She continued to tap each meridian seven times as she said her chant, and then she took a deep breath. "You're right. A feeling of well-being and peace has washed over me."

"Any other physical manifestations?" Ras raised his eyebrows.

"No, just—," Lauren gasped. "Oh, wait a minute. I think--," she clutched her stomach. "I think my water just broke."

Ras jumped out of his chair and Teensy, napkins in hand, was at his side in a flash. Ras helped Lauren stand. "Let us get you to a bed." He nodded at Teensy, who disappeared down the hall.

"Can you make it up the stairs, my dear?" Ras took Lauren's elbow.

"I need to get to the hospital." Lauren stared wide-eyed at Ras.

"Teensy will call an ambulance, and if you give me your cell phone, we can alert your husband. Is there anyone else we should call?"

"Yes, call my friend, Meredith deSalvo." Lauren winced and supported her swollen belly with one hand as Ras led her slowly up a staircase.

"Where are we going?" Lauren asked.

"I have a guest room at the top of the stairs. I think you should lie down until the ambulance arrives."

The quilt on the queen-sized bed had already been turned down, and Teensy stood at the ready, with one hand on an I.V. stand. The bottle swinging upside down on the stand's hook was filled with clear liquid.

"Wait a minute here. This is all going too fast." Lauren winced, again. "What's in that bottle?"

"Normal saline, my dear. It will keep you hydrated."

"Why is this room all set up? It's like you were anticipating this." Lauren looked at Teensy, who smiled broadly.

"Our motto is 'Be Prepared,'" Teensy said. She gave the Boy Scout salute, and then twirled around the bed in her Hello Kitty t-shirt, matching shorts, and black sneakers.

Ras shot a stern look at Teensy. "Calm down, my pet."

"How soon do you think the ambulance will arrive? Does it have to come from DeLand?" Lauren stiffened as a contraction rocked her womb.

"Not to fret, my dear. I am sure it will be here momentarily." Ras took the plastic sheath off the I.V. needle and turned Lauren's right arm to access her vein. "Why don't you practice your breathing?" He slid the needle into Lauren's vein.

Lauren began the Lamaze breathing she'd been practicing for the past six weeks. Though the contractions were closer together, the searing pain was becoming less intense.

"You said that's just normal saline, right?" Lauren's eyes were getting heavy.

"Yes, my dear. Relax. Teensy is going to help remove your clothing, now." Ras nodded to Teensy, who removed Lauren's flip-flops and eased off her leggings and underwear while Lauren moaned dreamily. Teensy propped pillows behind Lauren's back.

A woozy Lauren tried to lift her left arm, but it was too heavy. "Wait, pleeeeez," she slurred.

"Hush now, my dear. I will deliver your child."

It was the last thing Lauren heard.

* * *

At the first 10-minute jury selection break, John read the text message from Lauren. "Quick scoot to Dr. G. Home before you are." John scowled. He called her, but her phone was off. He tapped his foot impatiently on the granite floor of the courthouse hall, and then he called Meredith.

"Hi, John."

"Did you know she was going to see that doctor today?"

"Yes, and I wanted to go with her, but I'm swamped at the store. I told her to call me immediately if she went into labor, and I haven't heard from her, so I'm sure she's fine."

"Well I just tried to call her, and her phone's off." John pinched the bridge of his nose between his fingers.

"She's probably in the middle of her session with the doctor.   I'm sure she'll let you know when it's over." Meredith's voice was calming, and John did his best to believe her. "But call me as soon as you hear from her."

* * *

Teensy swaddled the baby girl and cooed to her as Ras pulled the old Lincoln Town Car out of the garage and motioned for Teensy to get in. "Hurry, my pet."

The drive to Lake Beresford took only fifteen minutes, but Ras was anxious to get out on the water where his scent, and the baby's, would not be easily detected. The massive yacht was in its slip, heavy in the still water, as Ras and Teensy, with the baby, hurried on board.

Ras unhooked the ropes that moored the boat to its slip, started the big Evinrude engine, and backed the huge boat out into the open water.

"Where you gonna anchor, boss?" Teensy bounced her bundle gently.

"There is a small channel about a mile south of here that should disguise us well. The cypress trees there are particularly dense."

Teensy looked down at her little charge, whose eyes had closed. "Darn, the hum of the big engine put her to sleep. I wanted to give her a bottle before she conked out." Teensy touched the baby's cheek.

Ras smiled. "She really is a beauty, is she not?" He patted the baby's plump foot. "I was conflicted about doing this, but just one look at her, and I was in love."

Teensy kissed the baby on her forehead. "What'll we call her?"

Ras raised his chin to the cool breeze. He steered the boat into the main channel and set his course. "She is Victoria."

"After your queen, I suppose?"

"Yes, but she will not be fat and dumpy like the queen. She will be lithe and elegant like a panther."

"Nice that you've got a vision, boss, but have you thought about where we're gonna live?"

"Yes, yes, that is all worked out. We shall hide out on the water for a week, and then I have hired a private helicopter to rendezvous with us up the river."

"We'll never be able to go back to Cassadaga." Teensy's lips curled into a pout.

"No, my pet. We shall head to the Amazon to hide out for a few years with a coven of witches there. Beyond that, I am not sure."

"I'm glad we're not going anywhere cold."

The large yacht cut through the lake like it was soft butter. Ras inhaled the scent of brackish water stirred by the boat's wake. He'd never liked the smell of salt water mixed with fresh, but tonight the musky smell represented hope. A belted kingfisher flew alongside the boat, probably looking for a handout. Ras accelerated the yacht to full throttle, and the pattern of the wake intensified, creating deep ripples in the frothy water. Looking up at the full moon, he set his course for a new beginning, and at long last...love.

* * *

When the judge adjourned court at five-thirty, John still hadn't heard from Lauren. He'd left her two more messages, and as he drove home, weaving through rush-hour traffic on vampire autopilot, his fears escalated when Lauren's car wasn't in the garage. *Dammit!* Tires screeched as he backed the car out of the driveway. He punched in Meredith's number on his phone.

"I'm going up there. Get Luc and meet me there as soon as you can."

John drove like the bat out of hell he was to reach Cassadaga in record time. Lauren's car in front of Dr. Gephart's house provided little relief for his racing pulse. As dusk darkened the December sky, John ran up the sidewalk. He rapped on the door with the gargoyle knocker, but his patience ran thin, and in only a few moments, he kicked the door in. "Lauren!" No response.

He ran through the house, first downstairs and then four steps at a time up the broad staircase. He sniffed the air, which reeked of drugs. In a frenzy, John flung open the first door on his left. Lauren lay senseless on a bed with an I.V. drip in her arm, pale as the new moon, and definitely not pregnant. A quilt was tucked neatly under her arms, and her hair had been brushed out and spread across plumped pillows. She wore a pink negligee with antique lace circling the collar.

He rushed to her side, gathering her in his arms and pressing his lips to her pulsing temple. He rocked her limp body for a few moments and then laid her gently back on the bed. Lifting one of her eyelids, her black pupil was so dilated it obscured the green of her eye. Voices downstairs jarred him. "Up here," he yelled.

Meredith gasped as she and Luc entered the bedroom. "Oh, no."

"What happened?" Luc asked.

Without taking his eyes off Lauren, John said in a voice like frozen fury, "I believe Dr. Gephart has knocked Lauren out and taken our child."

Meredith's voice rose an octave. "She'll go crazy if she wakes up to find her baby's gone."

"I know." John caressed Lauren's fingers. "My first impulse was to take the I.V. out of her arm, but its better that she's drugged." John looked from Meredith to Luc. "We need to find the baby before Lauren wakes up. There should be enough of the doctor's scent to track him."

"I'll scour the house for clues." Luc raced out of the bedroom.

John sat on the edge of the bed, reluctant to sever his physical connection with Lauren. He looked at the fluid in the I.V., which was about half gone. "The doctor obviously knows how to knock a vampire out. With the drugs left in that bag, she should be unconscious for awhile."

"The drugs can't kill her, can they?" Meredith asked.

"I forget how new you are, Meredith. No amount of drugs can kill a vampire. If the doctor wanted to kill Lauren, he could have driven a stake through her heart or cut off her head while she was drugged." John shivered and ran his hand through his hair.

After a few minutes, Luc rushed back into the room with papers in his hand. "I broke the safe in his basement, and this," he shook a document at John, "is the title to a yacht he keeps at the Lake Beresford Yacht Club. My guess is he's holed up over water where he thinks we can't pick up his scent."

"How far is that from here?" John looked to Meredith, a Central Florida native.

"It's about fifteen minutes or so."

"Stay here with Lauren." John nodded to Meredith. "Luc and I will take my car to the yacht club."

"Why don't you just fly?" Meredith asked.

"Because we'll be returning with a baby."

CHAPTER FOUR

With lightning speed and instincts that required no map, John and Luc arrived at the Lake Beresford Yacht Club in ten minutes. John parked his Cadillac on the approach road to the club, and he and Luc morphed to bat form to search the two rows of yachts moored at the lake's marina.

"The boat's called 'The Doctor's Folly.'" Luc flew up one row as John took the other. It wasn't there.

"They're already out on the water." John scanned the moonlit lake. "I'll head south, you head north." In bat form, they could communicate over a distance through sonar, but the ultrasound waves couldn't extend more than a few hundred yards, so their communication had its limits. "We should be able to cover the lake quickly. Double-back here as soon as you can."

Five minutes later, the two bats reconvened. "Follow me," John said.

John led Luc south to a well-concealed channel. "I'd have missed it, but my sonar bounced off an alligator on the shore, and that led me to the channel."

They flew low over the murky water to the dark yacht. Landing soundlessly on the deck, they immediately changed back to vampire form.

John stretched his arms overhead to ease the constriction of his webbed wings. He motioned for Luc to check the windows in the yacht's cabin, and then looked around the deck for something he could use as a weapon. Nothing. He'd have to use his bare hands to wrench the doctor's neck and then find a kitchen knife to decapitate him.

Luc circled back to John, touched his finger to his lips and pointed to a small round window. He whispered, "The doctor's in the living area, sitting at a desk, and the fairy's got the baby in the bedroom."

John's heart thudded with love for the child he had not yet seen. He balled his fists, planted a foot on the cabin door and pushed. The flimsy lock broke easily, and he and Luc stood facing the ashen doctor, who jumped out of his chair.

"Sit down," John hissed. He pushed the doctor, who fell heavily back in his chair. "Did you actually think you could get away with this?"

"I...I...I...," Ras stuttered.

"Tell me, doctor, have you ever killed a vampire?"

"I...I...no."

"I'm an expert. Would you like to know how it's done?"

"Not really."

"Good, because it's a messy business. Give me my child, and I won't kill you. And believe me, I'm angry enough to rip you limb from limb." John directed a deadly stare at the doctor's haunted eyes. "Did you attend to my wife after the birth?"

"What do you mean?"

"You know exactly what I mean. Did you heal her?"

Ras shrank in his captain's chair and buried his face in his hands. "No. I bathed her and made sure she was comfortable. Teensy dressed her in a gown of my mother's."

He looked back up at John. "I am not a bad man."

"But you thought you could take my child?" John clenched his fists at his side. John nodded to Luc to check the bedroom. "How could you do this to my wife after all she's been through?"

"She is strong. She will recover and have other children."

John shook his head. "You're wrong. Of all people, you should know what the kidnapping did to her. If she doesn't get our baby back..."

Ras put his head down on the desk and moaned. "Take her."

Luc rushed back into the cabin. "They're gone!"

"What?" John ran to the bedroom, and then yelled to Ras, "Can the fairy fly?"

Ras raised his head from the desk. "Yes."

"Dammit! Don't move." John held his hand up as Ras squirmed in his chair. "Are there any fairy rings close by?"

"I would not know. Teensy has been estranged from the fairy world for many years."

John didn't need to ask Luc to morph back to bat form as the two vampires flew out a porthole in the cabin. He didn't know where to begin the search, but since fairies were known to bury themselves, he figured the immediate area was a good start. Teensy couldn't have gone far since she'd only escaped minutes ago.

They began to search the dense brush, but after two futile hours of scouring the cypress swamp surrounding the lake, John called off the search. "I have to get back to Lauren. She might have woken up by now, and I need to be with her."

"Yes, go. I'll continue to look for a while, and then I'll go back to the boat to keep watch over the doctor. The fairy could have headed back there."

"You're right." John scanned the horizon. "Call me immediately if you find her."

The ten minutes it took for John to drive back to Dr.

Gephart's house felt like ten hours as he played through the scenario of what he'd say to Lauren. He parked at the curb in front of the house and clutched the steering wheel until his hands ached. Finally letting go, he exited the car and made his way up the walk and steps to the front door. He let himself in and eyed the stairs expectantly before he ascended.

Thinking of all the times he'd faced difficult situations in his 500 years, the one that would greet him at the top of the stairs was the most heart-wrenching. Abandoning his usual speed, he reached slowly for the doorknob of the room where his wife lay, sure to be awake by now. How could he tell her their child was missing? How could he comfort her? He turned the knob and inched the door open. Looking down at the hardwood floor, he raised his head to take in the four-poster bed where he'd left Lauren just a few hours ago.

"It's about time," she said. "Our daughter's most anxious to meet her daddy."

John's heart sped as his eyes scanned the tranquil scene of his wife and newborn daughter. He reached forward to greet them, and the baby inclined her head and smiled a toothless grin.

"No fangs yet," Lauren said. "I wondered about that."

John kissed Lauren on the forehead, and then picked up his new daughter and cradled her to his broad chest.

The bed was flanked by two figures that he now acknowledged. He looked quickly to his left, where Meredith raised her hands in prayer, and then to his right where Teensy mouthed, "Sorry."

"Give Luc a call," John said to Meredith, who immediately left the room.

John looked back at his firstborn, who stared back at him with the same violet eyes as his own.

"She's beautiful." John took Lauren's hand and squeezed it.

Teensy, who began hopping from foot to foot like she had to pee, said, "I think she's probably hungry. I'll go get her a bottle." She crept toward the door.

John handed the baby back to Lauren. "I'll go with you. You can show me how to prepare a bottle."

John followed Teensy out of the room, grabbing her arm as she headed down the hall.

"Ow! Let me go." She tried to shake off John's grip, but he was too strong. He pinned her shoulders to the wall in the hallway.

"You'd better talk fast." He spoke through gritted teeth.

"I'll explain everything," she pointed down the back stairs, "in the kitchen."

John let her go and followed her down the stairs. When they reached the kitchen, he said, "Out with it."

"First, I'm really, really sorry." Teensy motioned for John to sit at the kitchen table.

"I'll stand. Go on."

Teensy took a deep breath and closed her eyes for a moment. Opening them, she said, "As soon as you landed on the boat, the baby got restless. She started squirming in my arms and whimpering."

John couldn't help but smile. "Of course, she would know my scent." He thought back to the night he'd bitten Lauren.

"I could barely hold her. Her little arms were straining toward your voice." Teensy turned to the refrigerator. "And then I heard you threaten the doctor, and I didn't know what would happen next. I thought that if I took the baby, you couldn't blame Ras." She put a plastic bag of blood on the counter and opened a backpack to retrieve a baby bottle. Filling the bottle with blood, she continued. "I didn't know where I was going when I flew out the window with her. I just had to get off the boat."

"I'd have found you, eventually."

"Yeah, I knew that, and I also knew that it had been a really stupid idea to kidnap her in the first place. But that's not why I brought her to your wife."

"No?"

"Nope. I could tell you that I had a big attack of conscience, and that did have something to do with it, but the biggest reason is that I realized that what I really wanted was to be with Ras myself. I want to be his wife, and I don't need a gorgeous little vampire around as competition."

John chuckled. "At least you're honest."

Teensy giggled. "Yeah, who knew? Anyway, I'm gonna give it my best shot." She handed the full baby bottle to John. "I'm heading back to the boat. I'm hoping Ras will be so glad to see me, he'll propose on the spot."

"Good luck. Sounds like you deserve each other."

Teensy screwed up her little nose. "Thanks—I think." She picked up her car keys and then laid them back on the counter. "One more thing—you don't have to worry about us giving you anymore trouble."

John nodded. "Truce."

* * *

Teensy suspected that Ras hadn't moved from the chair in the boat's living quarters since she left with the baby, so she wasn't surprised to find him with his head in his hands, still captive under Luc's watch. She thought he'd heard her return, but he didn't look up.

"You can go now," she said to Luc. She strode toward Ras and knelt in front of him, placing her hands on his knees. "Really, everything's peachy." She turned her head to Luc. "The baby's back with her parents. Call your wife if you don't believe me."

"Meredith already called. I was just waiting for your return to make sure you didn't have anything else up your sleeve."

"Like I told the Vampire Vigilante, you don't have to worry about us anymore."

Luc morphed to bat form and flew out the window.

Ras looked at Teensy through bleary eyes. "That was not the most intelligent thing we have ever done."

Teensy touched Ras's cheek. "Hey, everybody's entitled to a brain fart, now and then." She winked at him. "Looks like we're back to where we started."

"You mean—alone."

"Not exactly. We have each other." She leaned forward on her knees, exposing a hint of cleavage from her black tank top. Following Ras's eyes, which were zeroed in on her breasts, she said, "Didn't know I had boobies, didya?"

Ras shook his head. "I cannot say that I did." Ras sniffed the air. "Your fragrance is...appealing."

"It's that Chanel No. 5 you bought me ages ago. After I put the baby in her mother's arms, I took a shower and washed my hair. I scrubbed my fingernails, too." Teensy held out her hands to Ras. "And check this out." Teensy raised her arms to reveal clean-shaven armpits.

Ras licked his lips. "Your cheeks and lips are pink."

"Yeah, samples from the Avon lady. They've been in a bag under the bathroom sink." Teensy pulled down her tank top to reveal her small, perky breasts. "I've behaved like a child, but I'm not a child. In fairy years, I'm almost middle-aged. And my human side is well past jail bait." She slid her hands up Ras's thighs to his crotch. "I may not be a vampire, but I meet one of your criteria—I'm a virgin. Have you ever considered...?" She fluttered her eyelashes.

"No, Teensy, I have not."

As Teensy began to massage the length of Ras's penis through his pants, she said, "Seems like you might be considering now?"

One side of Ras's mouth turned up in a half-smile. "I do not know if you can accommodate me."

Teensy plopped herself in Ras's lap and ground her bottom into the growing bulge in his pants. "There's only one way to find out. And if push comes to shove, pardon the pun, fairy dust has been known to alter the size of things."

"I assume that means making you larger, not me smaller."

Teensy rolled her eyes. "Men."

Ras scooped her into his arms and carried her to the bedroom.

* * *

When John returned to Lauren with the bottle for the baby, Meredith picked up her purse. "I just spoke with Luc, again. He's on his way home, so I'm heading there. Love you both, and you, too, little one." She blew a kiss to the baby.

"I'll walk you to your car." John followed Meredith out of the bedroom. When they exited the house, John said, "Lauren doesn't seem to have any idea the baby was kidnapped."

"No, absolutely none. In fact, she was raving about how great the doctor and Teensy were and how skillfully they handled the delivery. And get this— she said this last session with him did wonders for her anxiety about her own kidnapping."

"I was ready to kill the guy, but in a weird way, I owe him a debt of gratitude."

"No one's all bad, or all good. I think Ras and the fairy just got a bit sideways."

"Sideways? I expect by now they're perpendicular."

* * *

Lauren smiled when John returned to the bedroom. "Don't be surprised if Mere and Luc start a family soon."

"Like tonight?"

"If they can wait that long."

John sat on the edge of the bed. "How are you feeling, my love?"

"I'm still a bit groggy—and sore. But very, very happy."

"I have the cure for your soreness, you know." John gave Lauren his best under-the-eyelashes look.

"What do you mean?"

"Vampire men have been doing this for their life mates since the beginning of time." John rolled the quilt up from the bottom of the bed to Lauren's feet, and then swept it off the bed. He slipped his hand under the soft, silky fabric of her negligee, inching it up Lauren's thigh. "Relax, love." He kneeled between her legs and kissed the inside of her knees, working his way up her legs. "Are you torn?"

"Just a little."

John touched her there, tenderly, and then lowered his head to the small tear. Placing his tongue against it, the torn flesh responded to the gentle pressure of his tongue.

Lauren clutched the sheets and gasped.

"Does it hurt?" John looked up at her.

"No, it's—soothing."

"I'm just getting started." John pressed his lips to her tear, letting his venom spread like a salve over her flesh.

"Humans don't know what they're missing," Lauren whispered to her baby.

"They'd probably be mortified by this practice." John inspected the tear, which now looked like a tiny white scar, and then he eased himself up next to Lauren, propping on an elbow and offering his daughter his pinky finger to hold.

"She's like a six-month-old," Lauren said. "So strong and alert."

"Vampires mature much quicker than humans. We'll have to start watching for boys at about age 10."

"Hear that, little one?" Lauren pursed her lips. "Hmm, which brings me to her name. We can't call her 'little one' forever."

"I like all the names we were considering. Holly, Gabriella or Noelle all work for our little Christmas elf."

"There's a name that *means* Christmas elf—Avery."

"Avery Marsh Wright. I like it." John looked down at

their daughter. "What do you think?"

She beamed a broad, toothless grin.

* * *

Back home under the mistletoe in their foyer, John lifted his daughter to touch the black-sprayed berries above her head.

"Don't let her pull them down," Lauren said, entering the room and snuggling into John's chest. She placed her hand over John's, which was firmly planted on Avery's behind.

"Dibs on the first kiss." Lauren nodded at the mistletoe and turned her chin up to John.

With one arm holding their baby and one around Lauren, he pressed his lips to the woman he would love until the end of time. And then Avery stretched up and yanked down the mistletoe.

Susan Blexrud was born in Cincinnati, Ohio, but has lived most of her life in Orlando, Florida. She currently divides her time between Orlando and Asheville, North Carolina, with her husband of 23 years, John. She has two children, Christopher and Allison, a feisty Chihuahua, and a noisy Cockatiel. Susan holds a bachelor's degree in Journalism from the University of Central Florida, and a master's degree in media studies from Webster University, St. Louis. She is the former director of communications for the City of Orlando.

LaVergne, TN USA
05 August 2010
192229LV00004B/306/P